PRAISE FOR

QUEENS OF GEEK

FROM THE SWOON READS COMMUNITY AND BEYOND

"*Queens of Geek* is an emotional, lively story full of characters
that leap off the page and slip their hands into yours, inviting you
into a world where the geeks and nerds are royalty and fandom
is court. Richly realized and defiantly affirming, *Queens of Geek*
reminds us that adventures and romances aren't limited to
archetypes but are, in fact, for all of us."

—*Katherine Locke,*

AUTHOR OF *SECOND POSITION*, MODERATOR OF #GAYYABOOKCLUB

"This book, in my opinion, is just so empowering!"

—*brio*

"This is the first book I've ever read that I've seen myself in. I felt
like Taylor was me. . . . I wish I could have had this book 20 years
ago. One of the best things I've read in years."

—*Mandy.Valentine*

"There is a certain magic to fandom conventions.
Our intrepid, adorable heroes harness it to find love
and find themselves at SupaCon."

—*LeKesha Lewis*, BETA READER

"I love the idea of the book taking place
at a convention. It's a lot of fun!"

—*stacy*

"I loved how real the characters felt, especially Taylor. I absolutely adored all of them, and I couldn't stop reading once I started."

—*Lucy Mawson*

"[*Queens of Geek*] was an incredibly compelling read, just because it contained a storyline I ABSORBED, and characters so diverse they were a pleasure to read! . . . Mix that with the romance, self-discovery of self-worth, and all the geeky references, this made for a perfect read! I honestly couldn't put it down, reading late into the night to see what happened next!"

—*Zoie K*

"SO CUTE."

—*Nadia J. Nitol*

"I love everyone in this book, and it deserves a space on my Swoon shelf right next to where I'll place *All the Feels*."

—*Catherine Tinker*

"I love how interesting the story was and how the author addressed the characters' diversity without glossing over it or making it all about that. . . . It reminded me a little of *Fangirl*."

—*Lizzie*

"I really liked the characters, and especially that they weren't afraid to be themselves and express their geekiness."

—*Mike*

QUEENS
OF GEEK

JEN WILDE

SWOON READS • NEW YORK

A SWOON READS BOOK

An imprint of Feiwel and Friends and Macmillan Publishing Group, LLC

QUEENS OF GEEK. Copyright © 2017 by Jen Wilde. Excerpt from *Meg & Linus* copyright © 2017 by Hanna Nowinski. All rights reserved. Printed in the United States of America by LSC Communications US, LLC (Lakeside Classic), Harrisonburg, Virginia. For information, address Swoon Reads, 175 Fifth Avenue, New York, N.Y. 10010.

Our books may be purchased in bulk for promotional, educational, or business use. Please contact your local bookseller or the Macmillan Corporate and Premium Sales Department at (800) 221-7945 ext. 5442 or by e-mail at MacmillanSpecialMarkets@macmillan.com.

Library of Congress Cataloging-in-Publication Data
Names: Wilde, Jen, author.
Title: Queens of geek / Jen Wilde.
Description: First edition. | New York : Swoon Reads, 2017. | Summary: "Three
    friends go to a convention and find love—and themselves"—Provided by publisher.
Identifiers: LCCN 2016022454 (print) | LCCN 2016043437 (ebook) |
    ISBN 9781250111395 (trade paperback) | ISBN 9781250111388 (ebook)
Subjects: | CYAC: Friendship—Fiction. | Love—Fiction. | Self-realization—Fiction.
Classification: LCC PZ7.1.W533 Qu 2017 (print) | LCC PZ7.1.W533 (ebook) |
    DDC [Fic]—dc23
LC record available at https://lccn.loc.gov/2016022454

Book design by Liz Dresner

First Edition—2017

10   9   8   7   6   5   4   3   2   1

swoonreads.com

TO THE WEIRDOS, THE GEEKS, AND THE FANDOM QUEENS.
TO THE OUTCASTS, THE MISFITS, AND EVERYTHING IN BETWEEN.
THE DAYS OF PLAYING THE SIDEKICK ARE OVER.
YOU ARE THE SUPERHEROES NOW.
YOU ARE MY PEOPLE, AND THIS IS FOR YOU.

CHAPTER 1

TAYLOR

"THIS IS IT, YOU GUYS," I SAY AS WE APPROACH. **"EVERYTHING** we've always dreamed about. This is our Holy Grail."

Charlie, Jamie, and I stand before it side by side, tears in our eyes as we admire its indescribable beauty.

"Our Disneyland," Charlie adds, her pink hair blowing slightly in the warm breeze.

Jamie nods as a wide smile spreads across his face. "Our Graceland. I can't believe we're actually here."

We each take in a deep breath.

"Are we truly worthy of so much awesome?" I ask.

Charlie takes a brave step forward. "Yes. We are."

When we say it, it's a whisper, like the name itself is to be cherished: "SupaCon."

We take the final steps toward the building.

Crowds of cosplayers line the entrances.

I smile at those who look my way.

We pass Batman posing for a photo with Groot, Jessica Jones walking hand in hand with Michonne, and Goku lining up behind Darth Vader to buy coffee. A little girl dressed as Captain Malcolm Reynolds runs toward a group of Marty McFly cosplayers and asks for a closer look at their hoverboards.

My geeky kindred spirits.

"For years," I say as we get closer, "we've stalked the SupaCon posts of strangers on the other side of the world. And now here we are."

"Charlie!" A woman with curly blond hair is speed-walking toward us, waving and smiling.

"Oh, hi!" Charlie lights up with excitement and hugs her. She gestures to us. "These are the friends I told you about: Taylor and Jamie. Guys, this is my new manager, Mandy."

"Hey," Jamie says with his stellar grin.

I nod. "Hi."

"Hey, welcome to SupaCon! How was your flight?"

"Long," Charlie replies. "When did you get here?"

"Yesterday. Had to get a few things organized." She starts rummaging through her handbag. "I've got three passes for you all, but I'm afraid I could only get one VIP pass for you. Your friends will have to stay on the public floors while you do your publicity rounds."

Charlie's smile fades, and she glances at Jamie and me apologetically. "Mandy, isn't there anything you can do? Maybe you could call the studio and tell them these two are my entourage. I need them."

Mandy shakes her head slowly. "Sorry, all the VIP passes were snapped up months ago. I don't have the pull to get any more. I can get you guys inside now without lining up, but if you want to attend any panels or signings, you'll have to line up like everyone else."

My shoulders tense, and my palms start to get clammy. The thought of spending the next three days in lines with hundreds of people makes me break into a nervous sweat. Jumping the lines was supposed to be one of the perks of tagging along with Charlie.

Sensing my quiet panic, Jamie flashes me a reassuring smile. "It's all good, Tay." He leans in, his brown eyes looking at me from behind dark lashes. "At least this way, we don't have to worry about Charlie's fangirls swarming all over us everywhere we go."

I push up my black, thick-rimmed glasses and look away, choosing to focus on his Converse sneakers instead. "Okay."

Mandy watches me curiously, her eyes darting between me and Jamie, then landing back on me. "I love your cosplay! Queen Firestone, right?"

"Yep!" I grin, smoothing out my coat.

I've never cosplayed before, but I couldn't resist the chance to dress as my literary hero for SupaCon. I look down at my outfit, quietly congratulating myself. I nailed it. Black trench coat over a tank top and gray jeans tucked into Doc Marten boots, I *am* Queen Firestone. I'm also shaking with nerves, but now that I'm here, it's so worth it. It's even worth getting changed in the air-plane bathroom so we could dump our suitcases at the hotel before check-in and come straight to SupaCon.

Charlie smiles proudly and puts a hand on my back. "She even sewed the crown sigil on the back! Spin around, TayTay!"

I drop my backpack to the ground and do an awkward spin, showing off my handiwork.

"That's epic!" Mandy says. "I love those movies. I haven't read the books, though."

My eyes widen. "You gotta! They're the best books ever writ-ten! They changed my life. I mean, the movies are life-changingly awesome, too, but the books are where the true magic happens."

She giggles at my enthusiasm, then clasps her hands together. "Okay. You guys ready to go in? Let's go!"

We follow her as she weaves through the crowd and leads us around the back of the building. Three security guards with arms the size of bazookas guard a door that says PRIVATE: STAFF ENTRANCE ONLY.

Mandy shows them her pass that hangs on a lanyard around her neck, and they let us in with an intimidating dip of the chin. Her heels clickety-clack on the concrete floor as we walk down a narrow hallway. I can hear the hum of the crowd on the other side of the wall. I'm a bundle of excitement and giddiness and anticipation. There are so many panels to see, signings to attend, and Pop toys to buy and only a few days to do it all. I tap my fin-gers against my thumb anxiously and try to mentally use the Force to make Mandy walk faster—the faster we get inside, the more we can tick off our SupaCon bucket lists.

I nudge Jamie with my elbow. "I can't believe we're actually here!"

He pulls the lens cap off his camera and nods. "I know. This is crazy!"

Two weeks ago, we were at school.

Wearing my scratchy, heavy winter uniform, complete with long skirt, knee-high socks, and dorky necktie. Charlie, Jamie, and I were huddled in the cold library, cramming for midyear exams. Melbourne was rainy and cold and gloomy.

Now, we're in San Diego, the US of A, in the middle of summer, at the most famous pop culture convention in the world.

And it's all thanks to Charlie, her three-million-strong YouTube channel, and the little Aussie indie movie she starred in that is now becoming the breakout hit of the year.

"So," Mandy says, glancing back at us as she walks, "did you two grow up with Charlie?"

"Yeah." I'm not much of a talker when it comes to people I've just met.

Jamie shrugs and tilts his head to the side. "Sort of. I was born in Seattle. But my mom got a job in Melbourne about four years ago, so I've been living there ever since."

Mandy slows her pace to walk alongside him. "Well, welcome back to the States!"

"Thanks. Good to be back."

Charlie puts an arm around him and turns to Mandy. "Don't be fooled by his American accent; this guy is a true Aussie now. Right, Tay?"

"Yeah." I start chanting "One of us, one of us," and a chuckle sputters out of me, followed by an unintentional snort.

I am the Queen of All Awkward.

Mandy smiles, but looks at me like I'm from another planet. "So how did you all meet? At school?"

"Yep," Charlie says. "We're graduating soon. When you told me about my SupaCon invite, we decided to make it an epic trip, just the three of us. This is my graduation present to all of us. Kind of like a pregraduation celebration."

"And preparation for next year," Jamie adds. "When we all move to LA together. Charlie is going to be a huge star while Tay and I study hard."

He winks at me, and I feel my cheeks warm.

"Charlie's told me all about your grand plans in LA," Mandy says. "I'll be sure to work hard to make sure she becomes a huge star." She glances up at Jamie. "I really thought you guys were older. You don't look like high schoolers."

I assume that last comment was solely meant for Jamie because I know I look exactly like a high schooler. People constantly assume I'm much younger than eighteen. I think it's because I'm short, round, and have big, innocent eyes. Or maybe it's my enthusiasm for all things pop culture. Or my perpetual shyness. Or all the above.

Charlie looks like a normal eighteen-year-old to me, too. She's much taller than I am, and thin, sporting bright pink hair and a Last of Us video game T-shirt.

But I can't blame Mandy for thinking Jamie is older; he's showing some heavy stubble along his jawline from not shaving since we left Melbourne. Add to that his towering height and dark brown hair pushed into a laid-back mess (thanks to the long flight over the Pacific), and he could pass for twenty-one, easily.

He's got the whole Peter Parker thing down to a tee, including the camera hanging around his neck.

I watch Mandy out of the corner of my eye, trying to figure out how old she is. When Charlie told me she got a manager, I had pictured a middle-aged woman in a pantsuit and a mobile phone permanently attached to her hand. But Mandy is young, possibly in her early thirties, and is wearing a *Vampire Diaries* T-shirt under a blue plaid shirt. The lanyard around her neck boasts the SupaCon logo: an electric blue circle with sc in the middle.

She stops by a door. "Jamie and . . . sorry, what was your name again?"

"Taylor," I say. I'm not insulted that she forgot my name. I'm the girl no one ever notices. Not in an oh-that-poor-lonely-wallflower sort of way. I'm not sad about it. I'm invisible by my own design. My mum lovingly calls me Little Miss Introvert, and—even though my little sister sometimes jokes that parties are my kryptonite—I like being the people watcher standing on the sidelines.

"Taylor, right, sorry. You two can enter the main floor here. Charlie, we need to get to your first event."

Charlie nods and gives me a big bear hug. "Okay, you two. Have fun!"

"We will," I say.

"I'll text you when I'm done."

Jamie and I push through the door and into a swarm of people. I suck in a deep breath through my nose. "Whoa."

The day has hardly begun, and already the floor is bustling. I've never seen so many people in my life. A set of escalators nearby is packed with cosplayers who look as awestruck as I feel. Aisles of booths stretch across the floor, and the constant chatter of voices echoes off the high ceiling and wide windows that flood the venue in natural light. I read online that over one hundred thousand people walked through here last year, and as hordes of fans shuffle shoulder to shoulder around me, I'd say this crowd will top that easily.

A slow smile spreads across Jamie's face. "We're here," he says in a creepy singsong voice, like the little girl in *Poltergeist*—one of his favorite movies.

"Okay," I say. "This is a huge thing for us. Who knows if we'll ever make it back here. So let's make a promise to ourselves."

I turn to him and push myself to hold eye contact. "This weekend is all fun, all the time. No worrying. No complaining. No stress. Just fun, geekiness, and fandom. Deal?"

"Deal." He sticks his hand out, and I shake it. "That all sounds good to me. All I want to do this weekend is meet Skyler, buy comics, and geek the hell out."

I laugh. We both know that promise was more for my benefit than his. Jamie isn't the worrier; I am. But I'm determined to make the next four days different from all the others.

I slip my thumbs under the straps of my backpack and hitch it up a little higher.

"First things first," I say with a dorky grin. "I need to get on Tumblr and tell the fandom I'm here. Then we need to find the line for the Skyler Atkins signing."

QUEENOFFIRESTONE:
Guys! GUYS! I'm in the USA!

SupaCon, I am IN YOU!

I'm super jet-lagged, but I'm so excited I probably won't sleep for days anyway!

I can hardly believe it.

This is my first time overseas. I was so nervous about the airport, going through security and doing all that gave me some serious fucking anxiety. Am I the only one who feels like that? I mean, everyone else seemed so chill.

Sometimes I see people at the supermarket or somewhere else mundane, smiling and cheerfully making small talk with strangers and not looking tense or uncomfortable at all, and I just want to go up and ask them how they do it. How do they manage to do everything they need to do and go out in the world and be human without feeling the weight of it all crushing them into oblivion? I don't go into stores alone; I get overwhelmed. It's the checkout that's the worst; I'm too shy to talk to cashiers. Just the thought of doing it is exhausting.

I'm forever observing, trying to learn how to be an adult human being by watching others, and I'm constantly in awe of how easy some people make it look. And then I feel certain that something is wrong with me for not being able to do said normal, easy things with such ease.

I'm rambling. I'll stop now.

Anyway, I just wanted to update you guys. I'm off to meet Skyler at her signing! Ahhhhhhh!

Here's a gif of Skyler being adorable.

#QueenFirestone #SupaCon #gif #SkylerIsBae #OneTrueQueen

CHAPTER 2

CHARLIE

AFTER SAYING GOOD-BYE TO TAY AND JAMIE, MANDY AND I
stroll down the hall. We step into a large freight elevator that
takes us up to a spacious, round room filled with SupaCon staff
and celebrity guests.

"This is the green room," Mandy says. "All the guests will be
in and out of here all weekend as everyone goes from panel to
signing to lunch and whatever else is going on." Her phone
buzzes, and she steps away to answer it.

Discreetly eyeing the famous faces in the room, I wander
around the edge of the room and over to the snacks table covered in sweets and pastries. Everywhere I look, I see Hollywood
heroines and hunks, TV vampires and hunters, and fellow You-
Tube stars. Some are seated at tables while others stand in groups,

all swapping stories and laughing together. One face in particular catches my eye.

A short girl in a SupaCon staff T-shirt approaches to add another box of doughnuts to the catering table, and I greet her with a smile.

"Hey," I say, still eyeing the familiar face on the other side of the room. "Is that Alyssa Huntington over there?"

The girl glances behind her and nods. "Sure is! She's here to promote a new movie."

I try not to stare at Alyssa, but I fail miserably. "It's so weird to see her in person. I've been watching her videos for years. She's one of the reasons I started vlogging."

The volunteer gives me a sideways glance and runs a hand over the back of her neck. "It's funny you mention that, because I've been watching *your* vlogs for years! I'm such a huge fan of yours. And I loved *The Rising*, too."

I don't often get recognized by fans, so I'm taken by surprise. "Oh, thank you so much!"

She glances around the room before leaning in. "You know, I'm really sorry about you and Reese."

I cringe internally. "Oh, it's fine."

"Did he really cheat on you? Or were you already broken up when those photos were taken?"

My whole body tenses. I pick up a doughnut and bite into it too hard, hurting my jaw. I chew unnecessarily slow, hoping she'll change the subject before I have to answer the question. She doesn't, so I swallow, look away, and say, "Um, is it cool if we talk about something else?"

Her mouth drops open, and her eyebrows shoot up to her hairline. "Oh God, I'm so sorry. I didn't realize. . . . Are you still in love with him?"

I wave a hand in front of me and shake my head. "No, I'm not. Definitely not. It's just—that's kind of personal. And I was hoping SupaCon could be my way of showing everyone I'm fine, that I've moved on. You know?"

She nods and places a hand on my shoulder. "I totally get it. Good for you."

I search the room for Mandy and spot her standing by a window, texting on her iPhone with a worried look on her face. I excuse myself from the conversation and walk toward her.

"Everything okay, Mandy?"

She shoots me a glance and purses her lips. "Mhmm."

I raise an eyebrow. "You sure?"

"Yep."

I walk over to the window and peer down over the growing mass of people outside.

"This is going to rock," I say. "I can't wait to finally meet the fans. How many people do you think will be at the signing today?"

Mandy clears her throat, and I turn around to see her frowning at me.

"Mandy, seriously. *What* is going on?"

She sighs and puts her phone in her bag. "There's been a change in plans."

I shrug. "So?"

No amount of changed plans could possibly be *that* bad.

I'm at SupaCon. Nothing could ruin that.

"Reese was supposed to start filming his new movie last week, but it was delayed. So . . . he's coming. Here. To do the panel. He'll arrive tomorrow morning."

"Oh."

I was wrong.

There is one thing that could ruin SupaCon, even for me.

Reese.

I take in a deep breath through my nose and cross my arms over my chest. "Well, I guess we were bound to see each other eventually. May as well get it over with."

Mandy's shoulders tense, then she bites her bottom lip.

I let out a sigh. "What is it?"

"The studio wants you to act like you're back together. Just until the first box office results come in. It's still opening week, and they think a rekindling of your love will be a great boost to the numbers, what with all the shippers out there still broken-hearted."

I scoff at her. "So what am I supposed to do? Pretend to still be in love with the guy who crushed me?"

Mandy stares at me with a pleading frown. "I know it's not fair to ask."

"No, it's not." I'm fuming. "I'm not some prop for the studio execs to roll out when they need a showmance." I try to speak calmly. The last thing I want to do is look like a diva yelling at her manager in front of all my peers.

Mandy nods sympathetically, but I can tell by the look on her face that she's already said all this to them.

"What happens if I say no?"

"They've threatened to replace you in the sequel."

I flop onto a nearby couch and cover my face with my hands. I can't remember a time when I've been angrier.

"What do you think I should do?"

Mandy thinks for a moment, then looks me in the eyes. "I think *The Rising* is your big break into movies. No one expected a little Aussie indie film to have so much success. I think losing this could put your career at risk. And with Reese not doing the sequel, you're the lead. That's huge."

I push out a long, exasperated groan.

"But," she continues, leaning back against the glass and adjusting her shirt, "I also think that you have the talent and the fan power to keep you in the sequel—no matter what the studio says."

My shoulders relax. "Thank you."

She smiles with her lips closed. "I'll call them and tell them you're not doing the showmance."

I stare at Mandy nervously while she talks quietly—and tersely—on the phone.

I text Taylor and Jamie on the group text that we always use.

Charlie: Reese is coming tomorrow.

Taylor: For real? Ew. Don't worry, dude. Don't tone down your awesome just because of this.

Charlie: UGH. This sucks. SupaCon is supposed to be MY moment. I was going to prove to everyone that I'm fine without him. Everyone was going to see how awesome I am and realize I don't need to be hanging off his arm. People were going to stop feeling sorry for me and stop asking me about him. I was gonna rock it!

Taylor: You can still rock it! You won't just escape his shadow, you'll blast it to smithereens! BOOM!

Jamie: Yeah! Blow it up! And remember: don't let him mess with your head.

Taylor: Agreed. If he messes with your head, I'll mess with his face.

Mandy gets off the phone and walks over to me.

"How'd it go?" I ask, noticing her pursed lips and averted gaze.

"They're disappointed. But they know they need you, so they'll get over it."

"So I'm not fired?"

She shakes her head. "No. You're not fired. But they did request that you be polite and civil to Reese."

Of course they did. No one is allowed to upset Reese Ryan—a blockbuster magnet with wavy, surfer-blond hair, sparkling blue eyes, and a smile that makes girls all over the world weak in the knees.

I roll my eyes. "So he can be as douchey as he likes, but as long as I play the sweet little sidekick and bat my lashes at the cameras every now and then, they're happy."

Mandy slumps her shoulders, nodding. "Pretty much."

I grit my teeth in frustration and ball my hands into fists. "It's just so frustrating. It's been six months, and yet people still just see me as *his* ex."

"It will all blow over. Especially once the sequel comes out."

Mandy smiles, and I smile back at her. "Thanks for standing up for me."

"It's what I'm here for. Don't worry about Reese. It'll only be for one day, really. You'll probably only have to see him at the panel."

I nod. That makes me feel a bit better.

At least I have today to enjoy the con and have fun with my fans.

Someone taps on my shoulder, and I turn around to see Alyssa Huntington smiling at me. I gasp audibly and immediately regret it.

A spark of recognition flashes in her eyes. "It *is* you! Charlie!" She points at me, and I try not to explode at the fact that she knows who I am. We may run in the same online circles, but I've always seen myself as on the fringe of YouTube stardom and Alyssa as smack-bang in the middle of it. "I thought it was you. Your hair is different. But it's awesome!"

"Thanks! Yeah, I dyed it recently." I feel my cheeks turning the same color as my hot-pink hair. I'm still getting used to it. "I love your hair, too!"

She runs a hand over her buzzed head. "Thanks! I did it for a new movie I'm doing."

I try to think of something to say to keep the conversation going, but I'm lost. My brain has left the building. I've had fan art of this girl on my bedroom wall for three years, ever since she made her debut in the web series *Venus Soaring* when she was eighteen. Tay even wrote Alyssa Huntington fanfic for me. I've seen all her videos dozens of times, from her fun collabs with other YouTube stars to her in-depth interviews with female STEM leaders and political activists.

Now she's standing right in front of me, smiling like the sweetest person in the world.

And I'm not saying anything.

"I love your channel," I say. "And that TED talk you did on intersectional feminism blew my mind. My best friend, Tay, and I watched it, like, a thousand times."

She beams. "Thank you. I got trolled hard for that, so it really means a lot whenever someone tells me they learned from it."

I shake my head. "Seriously, you've done so much for me. You inspired me to speak out for myself. I would never have started my channel if it wasn't for you. I've worshipped you for years."

I wonder if I'm coming on too strong, but her wide smile puts my worries at ease.

A SupaCon staff member approaches Alyssa. "We're ready to go in about two minutes."

"Okay, thanks," Alyssa says. The staff member walks away, and Alyssa turns back to me. "I gotta go, but we should meet up while we're here." She pauses for a beat, tilts her head to the side, and adds, "How's Reese doing, by the way? I saw the trailer for *The Rising*; you guys look great in it."

I hesitate. I don't know how to answer that.

Is she asking because she genuinely wants to know how Reese is? Or is she asking to find out if Reese and I are still together or not? Does she have a girlfriend? I'm usually up to date with her love-life rumors, but I could have missed something.

All these questions run through my mind, leaving me frozen in place, smiling like a loser while she waits for me to answer.

"Um," I start. "Reese is fine, I guess. But we broke up six months ago."

"Oh God, sorry! I heard you got back together."

I wave it off. "Yeah, that rumor circulates about once a month."

She opens her mouth to say something, but the staff member calls her name, telling her it's time to start her panel. "Shit," she says. "I gotta go. But we'll meet up, yeah?"

I nod enthusiastically. "Yeah, for sure."

Her gaze lingers on me for a moment, and then she's gone. I watch her walk away and disappear through the double doors, then turn around to see Mandy grinning at me, and I burst into a fit of excited giggles.

"Did that just happen?" I ask.

"It happened," she says, her eyes wide. "It happened so hard."

CHAPTER 3

TAYLOR

QUEENOFFIRESTONE:

Hey guys!

Right now I'm in line waiting to meet the one and only Skyler Atkins!

Ahhhhh! FTFO!

I feel sick and excited and terrified. . . . Is that normal when you're about to meet your queen? I hope so, because I feel like I'm about to puke all over this guy standing in front of me.

But even puke-covered humiliation wouldn't bring me down from this high. I've waited for this day my whole life. Ever since I saw the first Firestone book in my school library and stayed up all night reading it. Skyler's books have been my world for over a decade. Queen Firestone made me feel like I wasn't alone. When the sixth and final book was released, I read it cover to cover in one sitting. And then I cried for days because it was over. (Shout-out to all the Firestoners who helped me through that week!) I guess you can tell how much this means to me, but in case it's not clear, here are my top three ways Skyler Atkins has changed my life:

1. She created a world I feel safe in. Let's be real; I don't feel safe in the real world. It's big and scary and confuses the shit out of me sometimes. But in Everland, Queen Firestone reigns and protects her queendom. She's a hero. She fights for those who don't feel strong enough to fight for themselves. I needed that growing up. Shit, sometimes I still need that now.

2. Queen Firestone is the best role model a kid can have. In the beginning of the series, she's scared. Fear rules her. Monsters killed her parents and hunted her, so she hid herself away from the world to protect herself and her sister, Crystal. But slowly, after she realizes it's more dangerous for her to hide

than to fight, she grows into a warrior, a queen, and a hero—but she's still afraid. She learns to trust her powers and her skills again, and she saves her people. But through all that, she's still afraid. That's what I like most about her; she isn't fearless. She's scared, but she keeps fighting. She has moments of doubt, when she runs away, but she comes back. She doesn't give up. Sometimes she fails, she falls down, she makes mistakes. She's real.

3. Reading the Firestone series introduced me to the power of words. I have trouble expressing myself through talking. My thoughts get jumbled, and I get flustered and freeze. I never ever end up saying what I want to say, and so for a long time, I just stayed quiet. But reading Skyler's stories inspired me to write, and I discovered I can say everything I want to say and more simply by finding a pen or a keyboard and going wild. I want people to look back on my stories a decade after they read it, and think, "Wow, I'm glad I had that story. It helped shape who I am." That's what Skyler did for me.

Crap! The line is moving forward! Gotta go!

I hit POST, close my Tumblr app, and slip my phone back in my jeans pocket. Someone taps me on the shoulder, and I glance behind me to see a short, thin girl smiling nervously at me.

"Hi," she says, pushing her black hair behind her ear. "Sorry. I really need to pee. Could you hold my place in line?"

I laugh and say, "Of course."

"Thank you so much," she says before stepping out of the line and speed-walking out of the hall.

I jump up and down excitedly next to Jamie. "I can't believe I'm finally going to meet Skyler Atkins!" It's all I can do to stop myself from squealing and flailing my hands around, but I don't want to seem weird.

"What are you going to say to her?" Jamie asks, stretching his long neck to get a better look at the stage. He's so tall he doesn't even have to stand on his tiptoes to see over everyone's heads.

"I've got it all planned out," I say. "I'm going to step forward, gently place my box set of books on the signing table, and give her my biggest smile. Then I'll shake her hand and introduce myself. I'll tell her that Queen Firestone is my hero and that reading the Firestone books got me through primary school, and the movies got me through high school, and th—"

"Hey," he says, looking down at me. "I thought *I* got you through high school." He winks.

I roll my eyes. "Okay, okay. I'll tell her that the movies and you and Charlie got me through high school."

The line moves, and I practically leap forward. And then it stops again. "Can you see her?"

"Nah. She's sitting down."

Jamie and I have been waiting in line for five hours. He lifts the flap of his shoulder bag and pulls out two Snickers bars. He holds one out to me. "You want one?"

I shake my head. "Too excited about meeting Skyler to eat."

He raises an eyebrow. "Did you eat on the plane?"

"A little of dinner. But I was too excited about coming to America."

"So you haven't had a proper meal since then? That's, like, fourteen hours without food!" He shoves the Snickers in my face. "Eat. You're gonna pass out."

I scrunch up my face and wave it away. "I'll eat after. We'll grab a late lunch."

He looks at me like I just said I don't know who David Tennant is. "You're crazy."

"I'm fine. I'm running on pure adrenaline right now. You can feed me when I crash later."

He presses his lips together tightly and nods, satisfied, then throws the second Snickers back into his bag.

The line moves forward again. I grin in anticipation and lean slightly out of the line and start counting.

"There are only fifty-three people ahead of us now!"

"You think Charlie will be able to wrangle up some of those VIP passes for us?" Jamie asks with a mouth full of chocolate and peanuts.

"Nah, you heard Mandy. I don't think we're important enough."

He swallows. "Speak for yourself. I'm very important. I have many leather-bound books, and my apartment smells of rich mahogany."

"*Anchorman*," I say with a half smile. "That's 5–4."

He furrows his brow. "Nuh-uh. We're even now. 4–4."

I adjust the heavy box set in my arms. Carrying six books in a limited-edition metal box for five hours seemed like a good idea when we arrived. But it will be worth it once Skyler signs it. "Nope. You didn't get my *Goodfellas* reference on the plane."

He leans in and looks at me with hooded eyes. "That's because your Joe Pesci impression sucks."

I glare at him. "How dare you."

He shoves the last piece of chocolate in his mouth and grins. A crumb falls onto his shirt—his favorite shirt, a dark gray tee with a Zelda graphic on the front—and he gasps.

"No!" He swats the crumb off and stretches his shirt out an inch from his chest to inspect the damage. It's all clear. He looks up at me. "That was close."

The line moves forward. I can't help it; I squeal like a kid in a candy store. "Eeeee! We're getting closer!"

Jamie squeezes his mouth shut, trying to hold in his laughter. "I've never seen you this excited before."

"Sure you have! What about the midnight release of Firestone Four in ninth grade?"

He smirks. "I stand corrected." He pauses, glancing down at me before looking straight ahead. "That was our first and last date."

I scoff. "It was not." I try to say it casually, but my reddening cheeks betray me. "Not our first date, I mean." That still came out wrong, so I try again. "I mean that was *not* a date. At all."

"Well, *I* thought it was a date."

"It was a group of friends going to a bookstore party to

fangirl over the new Firestone book. I made that very clear before the boxes were even cut open."

He rubs his nose at the memory. "I remember. My nose still clicks every time I sneeze."

"That was your fault."

He nods. "I know, I know. That was the last time I ever put my arm around a girl without asking her first."

"It just took me by surprise, that's all. I didn't know you had a *thing* for me."

He chuckles awkwardly as we shuffle forward with the crowd. "And I didn't know you had such a strong right hook."

I twirl a strand of my hair in my fingers as I wait for him to say something cryptic, like he sometimes does whenever we talk about the Date That Everyone Except Me Knew Was a Date.

I still wish someone would have told me everyone thought it was a date. I missed all the clues until it was too late. Even then, I didn't have the confidence to do anything about it. A few months later, Jamie started dating a girl from his photography class. It didn't last, but seeing them together made it clear that whatever feelings he had for me were long gone.

If I were to be honest right now, I'd say, "If I had known you had a thing for me, I would have let you put your arm around me."

But I won't say that.

There are a lot of things I won't say.

And soon, we'll both be at university, and even if everything goes according to plan and we're accepted into schools in LA, we'll get caught up in study and new friends and life, and all the things that I've left unsaid will haunt me.

That's why I need to meet Skyler.

If I can be brave enough to meet my idol, to talk to her, then I can do anything. I'll have what it takes to go out into the world, to university, on my own.

On my own.

Jamie's voice sounds far away when he says, "You know, I heard that Skyler isn't going to sign on to write the screenplays for the last two Firestone movies."

My head snaps up, and I look Jamie in the eye. My shocked expression breaks his serious one, and he grins cheekily.

"That is not even close to being funny," I say.

"Just trying to snap you out of whatever you were thinking about."

"What do you mean?"

"You looked so worried," he says. "Like you always do when you're having one of your Flash Forwards."

"Oh. Yeah." I push my glasses farther up the bridge of my nose with my index finger.

"Remember: no worrying allowed here."

I nod.

He started calling them Flash Forwards a few months after we met. No one else had ever noticed when I disappeared into overanalytic, panic-inducing daydreams before, but he did.

I hitch my box set under one arm and pull my phone out of my jeans pocket. My screen lights up with notifications from my thousands of Tumblr and Twitter followers. I open up Twitter and start scrolling through my replies.

"The fandom is going nuts right now," I say with a smile. "So many Firestoners are asking me if I've met her yet."

"I bet they're all so jelly," he says sarcastically. "They, like, literally can't even."

I gasp dramatically. "Jamie Garcia!" I nudge his arm with my elbow. "Don't make fun of them!"

He nudges me back. "I'm just kidding. You know I love Internet people, too."

"You know you're the only weirdo in the world who calls them 'Internet people.'"

"That's what we are. People who live in the Internet."

Someone taps on a microphone near the stage, making me jump. I slide my phone back into my pocket and stand on my toes, hoping to see Skyler up ahead.

"Hey, everyone," a voice says. I spot a short guy standing in front of the stage, holding the microphone. He's wearing a lanyard and a SupaCon T-shirt like all the other staff members I've seen running around.

Suddenly, a cluster of people form around the signing table.

"I think Skyler's leaving?" Jamie says, raising his eyebrows.

"To everyone still waiting, I'm really sorry," the guy on the mic says, "but we've run out of time. Ms. Atkins has a flight to catch that she's already running late for."

Gasps and moans fill the room. Some are annoyed at Skyler; others are ready to defend her.

I'm just in shock. "Wait, what?"

28

Jamie looks down at me, but I avoid his gaze. He opens his mouth, but no words come out. He must see the devastation in my face. "I'll be right back." He walks down the line and starts talking to one of the staff.

"What the hell?" a voice says from beside me. I turn to see the girl whose spot in line I was watching while she went to the bathroom. She looks at me in confusion. "What happened? Did I miss something?"

I nod solemnly. "Skyler's leaving. She has to get to the airport."

Her face falls. "Oh."

I huff out a sigh. "I know."

She shuffles from side to side and chews on the inside of her mouth, then holds out a hand to me. "I'm Josie. Thanks for holding my spot, though I guess it was pointless in the end."

I shake her hand and offer the politest smile I can muster, which is hard when I'm feeling so disappointed that Skyler's leaving. "No worries. I'm Taylor." I don't know what to say after that, so we both just stand there, looking around.

"I'm really bummed now," Josie says. "Skyler's my favorite author."

I slouch my shoulders. "Same. I can't even process this." We start talking about our most cherished moments in the books, but it still doesn't cheer us up.

Josie checks the time on her phone. "Well, I guess I better get back to my booth if there's not going to be a signing."

"You have a booth?"

She beams. "Yeah! I'm in the Artists' Alley selling my books. Come check it out if you're in the area."

I grin. "Awesome! I will."

Josie leaves just as Jamie returns, frowning. "I tried to find out if Skyler would be coming back at all this weekend, but the guy didn't know. The poor dude was pretty frazzled, though; everyone was getting up in his face."

I feel tears brimming in my eyes, blurring my vision. I stare down at the box set in my arms, trying to focus on the letters in the titles to stop myself from crying. The crowd starts to move together, and I look up to see the front of the line following Skyler and her handlers toward the back exit.

Jamie leans down and whispers in my ear. "I have an idea."

I watch him from the corner of my eye. "It's too late. She's leaving."

"Do you trust me?"

I tap my fingers on the side of the box nervously. "Of course I do." I unzip my bag and gently lower the set inside before zipping it up again.

"Then come on." He tugs on my elbow and starts pulling me out of the line and away from the crowd. Everyone, including the security guards and event staff, is distracted by Skyler as she makes a quick exit behind the stage.

Jamie takes me to a door marked STAFF ONLY and nudges it open. He peeks inside, then takes one last look at security before stepping into the forbidden hallway, pulling me in after him.

"Jamie!" I scold him. "You're gonna get us kicked out!"

He looks to his left, then his right, scanning the hall, then crouches to meet my eyes. "We'll be fine. You came all this way to meet her. And we're not leaving until you do."

We start running down the hall. The walls are an off-white color and completely bare, and all I can hear are our shoes colliding with the floor. We turn a corner just in time to see the back of Skyler's head, her flame-red hair swaying as she hurries up a set of stairs with her handlers.

"There she is!" I gasp. Suddenly, I don't care how reckless this is or that we could get kicked out—I have to meet her.

I'm so close.

If I miss my chance, if I chicken out now, I don't know how I'll find the courage to face next year. I'd never tell anyone, but the thought of moving to LA with Charlie and Jamie, away from home and my family, terrifies me.

We keep running, but two security guards walk out of a room up ahead.

Jamie skids to a stop. "Change of plan."

"What do we do?"

He takes hold of my hand. "Run!" We spin around and run back the way we came. We turn the corner again just as three event staff members enter from the signing hall.

"Shit!" I whisper.

Jamie pushes me into a nearby room, and it isn't until we're inside that I realize it's the men's bathroom. "God, it stinks in here!"

His mouth turns up into a crooked smile, and he puts a finger to my lips. "Shh!"

The bathroom door starts to open, and once again he's pulling me out of the way. We jump into the nearest stall, and Jamie swings the door closed and locks it as quietly as possible.

A cheerful whistle fills the room, followed by the sound of a man relieving himself.

I cringe and step as far back as I can without touching the toilet, hoping my trench coat isn't dragging on the floor. We're squished in tight, Jamie and I, our bodies pressed against each other unavoidably. He's thin, but tall and broad, and I'm just wide. My cheeks warm into a blush, and I try to look anywhere but at him, even though I can feel his eyes burning into me.

The bathroom door opens, and the whistling fades into the hall. I let out a relieved sigh.

"You know," Jamie says, still looking at me, "if we weren't in a pee-soaked toilet stall right now, this would be kind of romantic."

I roll my eyes and push him out of the way, unlocking the door and peering out. "Well, it *is* a pee-soaked toilet stall. And I need to get out of here before the stench makes me puke."

We sneak out of the bathroom and hurry down the hallway. I don't breathe again until we've made it safely back into the signing room, which is still emptying of Firestone fans. "That was so stupid of us, Jamie. Getting caught could have got us banned from SupaCon for all eternity!"

"I would have taken the blame," he says. "It would have been so worth it if you had met Skyler."

"That's another thing," I say, stopping to take my backpack off. "Skyler would not have appreciated being chased backstage by a couple of weirdos. I mean, she could have had us arrested for stalking or harassment or something!" I unzip my bag and make sure the box set isn't damaged from all the running.

I look up to see Jamie deep in thought. "I didn't think of that."

I stand up and throw my backpack over my shoulder.

He sighs. "Sorry, Tay. I just really hate seeing you disappointed. Besides, you never do anything reckless. Think of it as an adventure! Taking a risk every now and then is good for you."

I start walking, and he follows. "I don't do risk. I'm a teacher's pet who hates confrontation and fears authority of any kind, remember?"

He laughs. "How could I forget? Come on, all your favorite heroes are adventurers! Indiana Jones, Marty McFly, and I seem to remember Bill and Ted had quite the excellent adventure."

I narrow my eyes at him and smirk. "Bill and Ted's and Marty's adventures involved time machines. And I wish I had one right now so that I could go back to fifteen minutes ago and sucker punch you before you had a chance to drag me back there."

Jamie, doing his best Bill voice, says, "That would be most nontriumphant." I burst out laughing.

He grins most triumphantly, happy that I'm no longer annoyed at him. "All that adventuring made me hungry. Let's go grab some food. There's supposed to be a cool diner around here somewhere."

CHAPTER 4

CHARLIE

"HI THERE! WHAT'S YOUR NAME?" I ASK WITH A FRIENDLY smile and my pen hovering over a poster for *The Rising*. The girl on the other side of the table is starry-eyed and smiling so wide I can almost see every one of her multicolored braces.

"Cara," she says, but it comes out more like a giggle than a name. "You're my all-time favorite YouTuber. I've seen all your vlogs so many times!"

"That's awesome! Thank you for watching!" I wink at her and start writing a sweet little note on the poster, adding my autograph at the bottom. A bright flash of light takes me by surprise, and I look up to see Cara holding her phone up, taking a selfie with me. I look at the camera, smiling just in time for the second flash to go off.

"Here you go, Cara," I say as I hand her the poster. "Thanks so much for coming! Enjoy the movie!"

Cara looks like she is about to explode into a burst of confetti and fireworks. She hesitates, like she wants to ask something. And then she just lets it blurt out: "Are you and Reese back together?"

My heart stops.

It begins.

I swallow hard, all too aware that Cara—and Mandy and a few other girls within earshot—are watching me, waiting eagerly for my answer.

"No, but we're still good friends!" I say with my realest fake smile.

Cara gasps. She looks so happy, and it's hard for me to watch. "If you do get back together, will you get married?"

I have to stop myself from gagging. "Oh." I laugh awkwardly. "No, we're just friends. Definitely no wedding bells. Besides, I'm only eighteen! I don't even know if I want to get married."

Cara opens her mouth to ask another question, but I have to stop the madness before it becomes too much. "Thanks so much for coming, Cara!"

Cara grins before walking away in a daze.

I feel a tap on my shoulder and turn around to see Mandy looking down at me. "Five more minutes, then we have to go. You've got three interviews for *The Rising*, then the cosplay contest and promo party before you're done for the day."

I nod, but I can't help but feel guilty. I lean on my elbow to scan the line of people wanting their posters and merchandise signed. There have to be at least one hundred people still waiting excitedly. This is the first time I've ever done a fan event, and I don't want to disappoint anyone.

I look up at Mandy, who is eyeing me knowingly. She sighs and pulls out her phone. "Okay, I'll let them know we need to push it back another thirty minutes. But that's it!"

I give her a grateful grin. "Thanks, Mands!"

Mandy waves the next person forward. This girl is around the same age as me, with jet-black hair tied into a long braid and bright red lipstick.

"Hi!" I say.

"Hi," the girl says, her lips twitching. "I'm such a huge fan! I've seen all your videos! And I saw *The Rising* last night; it was so good!" She's speaking so fast I can hardly keep up.

"Wow!" I beam as I take her poster to sign. "Thank you so much for all your support. I'm so glad you liked the movie! What's your name?"

The girl doesn't answer. She's not even looking at me anymore. Instead, she's looking up, way over my head. Her mouth is hanging open in shock. "Is that . . . Reese Ryan?"

My stomach drops to the floor.

No.

I really hope the girl is mistaken, but then the others in line behind her start to squeal. Scream. Cry.

The full Reese Ryan effect is spreading right before my eyes like magic.

Or the plague.

"Shit," I utter under my breath. Slowly, I turn around in my chair, dreading seeing his face even while I search for it.

He's looking down at me from the second-floor balcony, flashing a toothy smile while waving to his adoring fans.

Every muscle in my face wants to glare at him, to give him a look that would turn him to dust right here and now. But I quickly remember that I'm supposed to be nice to him, and I offer him the warmest smile I can muster.

I can do this, I think.

I am an actress, after all.

He blows me an obnoxious kiss and winks at me, and I shoot imaginary death rays at him from my eyes.

He is actually *enjoying* this.

I suck in a deep breath. *Just pretend*, I tell myself. *Pretend it's Opposite Day. Or Bizarro World. Yes, that's it. I live in Bizarro World, where people say hello instead of good-bye, day is night, and I still think Reese is a good guy.*

But, if this truly was Bizarro World, Reese would be easy to get along with. He would be a kind, caring, genuine guy instead of a gigantic phony with narcissistic tendencies and a tiny penis.

Ha.

Now I really am smiling.

I wince from the loud screams echoing behind me and wave up at my ex-beau. He winks at me again and points to the left, toward a set of stairs, then disappears.

Please don't come down here.

Please don't come down here.

Oh God, please don't.

He comes down the stairs like he's running a sprint.

He is *loving* this.

He struts toward me, waving and blowing kisses to the fans

like he's on a late night talk show. With each step he takes, I want to run more and more.

Reese picks up his pace, running toward me and sweeping me up in his arms, spinning me around like we're in some cheesy rom-com.

He puts me down, but keeps his hands planted firmly on my hips. "How's my little Charlie?"

Ew.

I hold my fake smile and remove his hands from my hips as playfully as I can. "I'll be much better if you never call me 'your little Charlie' again."

"Oh, *someone* is sensitive today," he says, keeping his own fake smile glued to his face. He spins me around to face the cheering crowd and drapes an arm over my shoulders. "Smile for the fans!"

I smile. And wave. And think of all the ways I could completely annihilate him in front of everyone if I really wanted to. A swift elbow to the ribs would do it. Or a knee to his groin. Oh, how sweet that would be. But no, I have to think of the fans. And my career. *The Rising 2.*

And then the chanting starts.

"Chase! Chase! Chase!"

That's our ship name. The first time I heard it, about a year and a half ago, I thought it was cute. I wore it proudly like a badge of honor, like it proved we were destined for each other. It made me feel validated somehow. Worthy. Now it just makes me feel like a fool.

But still, I smile. And wave. And pretend it didn't take months to put the million pieces of my heart back together after what he did.

One of the fans starts running toward us, and then everyone follows. Suddenly I'm having flashbacks to the stampede scene in *The Lion King*.

Mandy appears in front of us. "Time to go!"

Reese takes hold of my hand while security and staff huddle around us and shuffle us up the stairs and back into a private room. The moment the door closes, and Reese, Mandy, and I are out of sight, I pull my hand away from his.

"What a rush!" he says as he pushes his hands through his sun-kissed hair.

I give him the full force of my glare. "What the *hell* was that?"

He shrugs. "What?"

"What are you doing here? I thought you weren't supposed to come until tomorrow?"

"The studio thought it would be a good idea to do the interviews with you today and interact with the fans."

My shoulders drop. "Great."

Mandy's phone rings, and she walks out of the room to answer it, leaving Reese and me alone. I sit in one of the two chairs ready for the upcoming interviews. A tall poster for *The Rising* stands proudly next to me. The image is of Reese running, his jeans and flannel shirt torn and bloodied. I'm right behind him, slightly back in the picture to let the audience know that he's the star.

I remember that day. Trying to run in skinny jeans, a push-up bra, and a crop top three sizes too small in the Australian summer heat while the director yelled at me to "run sexier."

But even with all that, it was still the most fun I've ever had. It doesn't get much better than playing make-believe for a living.

I notice Reese watching me, so I pull out my phone and start writing a text.

911. Reese. Here. Now. FML.

I hit SEND in the group text and look up to see Reese still staring at me.

"What?"

He raises an eyebrow. "Your hair is pink."

I run a hand through my hair self-consciously. "Yeah, I had to do it. I got a guest role in a sci-fi show, and they wanted an 'Asian girl with dyed hair'—original, I know—but I liked it, so I kept it."

"What show is that?"

"*Starscape.*"

Reese doesn't even try to hide his condescending smirk. "Well, any role is a good role, right?"

I roll my eyes. "Actually, I'm the first Chinese Australian actor to work on that show, so that's pretty epic."

He nods, but he seems distracted. "Cool."

I go back to pretending I'm doing something important on my phone. Neither Tay nor Jamie has replied yet. They're probably busy having a blast while I'm stuck with him.

Reese walks over and sits next to me. I can feel him watching me still, so I drop my head slightly and let my hair fall in between us, blocking him from my sight.

"So . . ." he says, clearing his throat.

I ignore him.

He sighs and leans forward, resting his elbows on his knees and looking down at the carpet. "Look. I'm sorry, okay? About, you know . . . But I swear, Lucy was just a one-time thing."

I turn to look at him, narrowing my eyes. "I thought her name was Sarah."

He squeezes his eyes shut. "Right. That's what I meant. Sarah."

I stand up, throwing him a disgusted look. "There was more than one?"

He just looks up at me and shrugs sheepishly.

I fold my arms across my chest. "Wow, you really are a dick."

Before he has a chance to try to defend himself, Mandy walks back in. She looks at me, then at Reese, then back at me before mouthing, "Are you okay?"

I nod.

She gives me a weak smile. "The first interviewer is here. I didn't get a chance to push it back, with the fan army out there converging on you. Are you both ready?"

"Ready as I'll ever be." I turn to Reese. "But we need rules. We're not together anymore, no matter what the studio or the fans say. You do *not* have permission to touch me, under any circumstances. If I smile at you, it's not an invitation. I don't care if the whole crowd at the panel tomorrow is chanting for us to kiss Wills-and-Kate style, it ain't happening."

I sit back down in the chair and start counting on my fingers. "No hand-holding. No hip-holding. No winking. No kiss-blowing. No bodily contact whatsoever. No pet names. And when the inevitable questions about our breakup or the chances of us getting back together come up, we just give the standard answer about that being our private business. If you're not down with any of that, tell me now. I'd rather walk into the studio and quit the sequel right now than sacrifice my personal space or comfort over this."

He raises his palms and nods. "Okay, okay! Jeez. I got it. No fun stuff."

I glare at him again, wondering how I didn't see this side of him while we were together. He was nothing but charming and sweet in the beginning, leaving flowers and notes in my trailer, running my lines with me for hours to ease my nerves, and treating my family like royalty when they visited the set. I still remember my sisters gushing over him, and my mother's surprised smile when he gave her a box of her favorite chocolates. That's how he got into my heart, by being kind to my family. And that's why it hurt so much when it all ended. He didn't just disrespect me; he disrespected the people I love most in the world. He hurt them, too.

My phone buzzes, and I see a reply:

Taylor: No way! Sorry, dude. Is he doing the interviews with you? It's okay, you've got this. You're Charlie Liang. He's just a douche with a teeth-whitening addiction and an inflated ego. You can tell him I said that. ;)

I snort out a giggle. Taylor always knows how to make me laugh.

Mandy makes sure we are ready, then opens the door to let the first reporter and camera crew in.

CHAPTER 5

TAYLOR

QUEENOFFIRESTONE:

So . . . I didn't get to meet Skyler. She had a flight to catch.

I'm devastated.

I was so close. There were only 53 people between me and her.

53!

FUCK. I don't even know what to say.

I'm just gonna sit here and eat some fries and try to

pretend I didn't just miss out on a once-in-a-lifetime chance to meet my hero.

Here's a gif of Queen Firestone from Firestone Two, when Crystal died and she did that epic ugly cry.

That's my feels right now, you guys.

That's my feels.

#FuckFuckFuckShit #Heartbroken #I'mTotallyNotCryingRightNow

I hit POST and put my phone in my pocket, then commence Operation Pretend I'm Totally Not Dying on the Inside. "I hope Reese isn't a douche to Charlie today."

Jamie holds his camera up and snaps a photo of me, then rests his arms on the table and leans forward. "Me too. But you know him. Once a douche, always a douche."

I tap my fingers rhythmically on my glass of Coke. "I know. But she was so looking forward to coming here. This was supposed to be her time to shine. It's not fair that he shows up and now suddenly she's got to accommodate him."

"It's more than unfair—it's archaic." Jamie shakes his head. "But she can handle it. She's smart. Much smarter than Reese."

The waitress walks over to our booth, carrying our food. "Veggie burger and fries?"

"That's me," I say, raising my hand like I'm in school. She places the plate in front of me.

"And double bacon cheeseburger with chili cheese fries." She slides the plate in front of Jamie, who gazes at his meal lovingly.

"Sweet lord, have I missed American burgers," he says, gently picking up his burger and admiring it up close.

I scrunch up my nose at it. "You're going to have a heart attack at eighteen."

He takes a huge bite and moans theatrically. Then he slowly raises his eyes to mine, deadly serious. "And it will be absolutely worth it." Grease runs down his chin, and he licks at it with his tongue. "Besides, I've been eating fish and chips and shrimp on the barbie for the last four years. I deserve this."

"First of all"—I cross my arms—"you know we don't call it 'shrimp.' It's prawns. Second, I have never eaten prawns, let alone put them on a barbecue. And last, we have plenty of good burgers in Australia!"

He raises his eyebrows and waves his burger at me, dripping mustard on the table. "It's not a burger if you put pineapple and beet on it. Weirdos."

Before I have a chance to defend my country's culinary preferences, he places his burger onto the plate. His eyes trace the table, and then the tables around us. He wipes his meaty mouth on a napkin and looks at me. "You don't have ketchup. I'll go find some."

He slides out of the booth and walks to the other end of the diner, on the hunt for tomato sauce.

A young couple walk in holding hands. The girl is in Queen Firestone cosplay, just like me. She slides into the booth in front of ours, and her boyfriend goes to the bathroom.

I look down at my fries, smiling to myself, feeling so lucky to be here at SupaCon, surrounded by people who are just as passionate about Queen Firestone as I am.

I contemplate eating a fry, but I decide to wait for Jamie. It's not right to eat fries without sauce.

I look up to see him walking back toward the booth, a full ketchup bottle in one hand and his iPhone in the other.

He's so distracted by something he's reading on the screen that he stops at the booth in front of ours and scoots in across from the *other* Queen Firestone cosplayer.

The girl is so surprised, she just stares at him. My hands cover my mouth as I try not to laugh.

The boyfriend walks out of the bathroom then, and approaches the table with a perplexed look on his face.

He stands over Jamie with his hands on his hips and clears his throat.

Jamie finally drags his eyes away from his phone and looks up at the guy, confused.

"Can I help you?" the guy asks.

Jamie lowers an eyebrow. "No?" he says, like it's a question, and I can't hold back my laughter anymore.

He looks at the girl sitting across from him, and his head moves back in shock when he sees she isn't me.

He jumps out of the booth so fast, anyone would think he had superspeed like the Flash. "Sorry, wrong booth. My bad!" He holds his hands up innocently before spinning around and sliding sheepishly into the correct booth.

I can't stop laughing.

"Why didn't you tell me I was in the wrong booth?"

"Couldn't." I gasp for air. "Laughing . . . too . . . much."

He narrows his eyes at me, but his mouth twitches. "Still, you could have texted me. Tweeted me. Sent a smoke signal even." He's trying hard not to laugh. "That poor girl probably thinks I'm a creep."

He slides the ketchup bottle to me, and I take it, stifling my laughter to a light snicker. "Thanks. No one's ever risked getting beat up just to get me tomato sauce before. I thought he was going to pound you into the ground like in those old *Looney Tunes* cartoons."

He smiles smugly and stretches his arms, resting them on the seat. "Well, you know, sometimes a guy's gotta do what a guy's gotta do to ensure a lady has all her condiments."

"The lady is grateful." I tip the bottle upside down and slam the bottom of it, letting the sauce fall over my fries.

He bows his head dutifully. "I am but your humble servant," he says in a terrible British accent. "Do with me what you will."

He raises his eyebrows suggestively and pairs it with a brazen grin. I feel my cheeks heat up and my heart somersault in my chest. My whole body tingles when he looks at me like that. I drop my eyes to my plate, hoping my face doesn't look as pink as it feels. I hate when he does that. I never know if he's flirting or kidding around, but either way it makes me feel foolish.

And hopeful.

And then foolish some more.

"You know," he says quietly. I think he's going to say something serious, so I lift my head and lock eyes with him. But something makes him change his mind, and he smiles again. "If you weren't so hopelessly addicted to ketchup, I could have avoided that entire ordeal."

I pick up a sauce-covered fry and hold it in front of my mouth. "If I'm a ketchup addict, then that makes you my enabler. And if you weren't glued to your phone, you would have known you were sitting in the wrong booth. What were you looking at anyway?"

"Oh!" he says, pulling out his phone. "Skyler tweeted something interesting. I was going to tell you, but Boothgate distracted me." He holds his phone over the table, and I look at the screen, reading the tweet.

@SkylerAtkins: Sorry SupaCon! Had to race to the airport
:(But I'll be back to have dinner with the winner of the
Queen Firestone SupaFan Contest on Sunday!

My eyes pop out of my head. "What's the Queen Firestone SupaFan Contest?"

He pulls his phone back and starts tapping at the screen. "That's what I was just about to find out."

I take a bite of my veggie burger while he googles. It's the best burger I've ever tasted, but I decide not to give him the satisfaction of telling him that.

I watch him as he reads intently. His dark eyebrows pinch

together. "It seems," he says, his eyes flicking up to me, "that it's a surprise Firestone event being held this weekend. They just announced it. It's a contest to find Queen Firestone's biggest fan."

My heart leaps into my throat. "That's me! I'm Queen Firestone's biggest fan!"

"Well, there are two rounds. Round one is a cosplay contest. Round two is a trivia quiz based on the Firestone books and movies. The winner gets to have dinner with Skyler, be her date to the SupaCon After-Party, *and* go to the premiere of the next Queen Firestone movie."

I lean back in the seat, my stomach doing queasy flips.

"Oh." My voice is just a whisper. If it was a fanfic or a fan art contest, I'd rock it. But a public competition? In front of actual *humans*?

No chance.

He tucks his phone back into his pocket and watches me carefully. "I think you should enter."

My jaw drops. "Me? No way. I can't do that." My glasses slide halfway down my nose, and I anxiously nudge them back up with my knuckle.

He leans forward, stretching his arms toward me over the table. "Why not? You know everything there is to know about Queen Firestone. I hear you quoting the books and movies every day. And your cosplay is kick-ass. You could win this, easy."

I shake my head, eyes glued to my half-eaten burger. I've lost my appetite. "I can't. What if it's on a stage? All those people looking at me? What if I make a mistake? I wouldn't even be able to breathe, let alone answer trivia questions."

"But this is your chance to not just *meet* Skyler, but have dinner with her. Party with her. Go to a premiere with her!"

I imagine myself standing on a stage, under the bright lights, all those faces in the crowd. Competing with other people.

Even the idea of winning is scary. Dinner with my hero? What would I say? What if she didn't like me?

No, this is all too much, too fast.

I shake my head again, this time more intensely.

"I'll go with you," he says, trying to convince me. "I'll be right there through the whole contest, cheering you on."

I feel him watching me, and the pressure is suffocating. My foot starts tapping the tiled floor, and I trace my index finger in a circle over the shaved left side of my head. Little movements that no one else in the diner will notice, but that bring me comfort.

"No," I snap at him. "You know I can't do stuff like that."

"You came *here*," he says. "To SupaCon. Even though it's a big deal for you. Even with the crowds, the noise, and everything, you haven't seemed overwhelmed at all."

I breathe out a long sigh, knowing he doesn't understand. "That's different. I planned this. I *prepared* for this. I knew this was coming for weeks. And coming to SupaCon is something I've always wanted to do. Just because I made it here doesn't mean it was easy. And just because I don't *seem* overwhelmed doesn't mean I'm not."

I feel guilty for snapping at him, but I don't know why he is pushing me like this.

My eyes burn with tears, and I stand up. "Can we just stop

talking about this?" I sidestep out of the booth and head to the bathroom. "I'll be back."

Rogue tears trickle over my cheeks as I lock myself in a cubicle. I've hardly slept. Hardly eaten. Flown fourteen hours to a new country. I'm surrounded by people and noise and nonstop newness. I didn't meet Skyler. Jamie thinks I'm an idiot for not wanting to enter the contest. Everything is out of place. I'm imploding, warping like steel under a searing flame. Tightening. Shrinking. Collapsing in on myself. Choking on tears and words I want to say but can't.

Most people think of anxiety as panic attacks. That's not entirely accurate.

I haven't had a panic attack in years. I started to recognize the signs and learned what I needed to do to stop it from spiraling. I learned how to internalize it to avoid public embarrassment. Anxiety isn't an attack that explodes out of me; it's not a volcano that lies dormant until it's triggered by an earth-shattering event. It's a constant companion. Like a blowfly that gets into the house in the middle of summer, flying around and around. You can hear it buzzing, but you can't see it, can't capture it, can't let it out. My anxiety is invisible to others, but often it's the focal point of my mind. Everything that happens on a day-to-day basis is filtered through a lens colored by anxiety. That nervousness that makes your palms sweat and your heart race before you get up and make a speech in front of an audience?

That's what I feel in a normal conversation at a dinner table.

Or just *thinking* about having a conversation at a dinner table.

The fear that other people feel on rare occasions, reserved

only for when they jump out of a plane or hear a strange noise in the middle of the night—that's my normal.

That's what I feel when the phone rings.

When someone knocks on my door.

When I go outside.

When I'm alone.

When I'm in line at a store.

Everything feels like I'm on a stage, spotlight on me, all eyes on me, watching, judging. Like I'm one second away from total disaster. It's invisible, it's irrational, it's never-ending. I could be standing there, smiling and chatting like everything is totally fine, while secretly wanting to scream and cry and run away. No one would ever know. In my mind, no one can hear me scream. I hide it because I know it's not understood or acceptable— because *I'm* not understood or acceptable. So here I am, hiding it. Standing in a toilet stall, trying to remember how to breathe.

I find my phone and headphones in my pocket and plug them in, turning up the Queen Firestone soundtrack and closing my eyes.

Breathe in. One . . . two . . . three . . . four . . . five. Breathe out.

I close the lid on the toilet and sit down, rubbing my palms over my gray-denim-clad thighs as I focus on the music.

Breathe in.

CHAPTER 6

CHARLIE

MY STOMACH RUMBLES AS THE INTERVIEWER BEGINS TO ASK his final questions, and I hope the microphone hovering above us didn't catch it.

"So, Reese," he asks, "your character goes through a lot in this film. He loses his parents, his siblings, his home, and eventually his whole country. How did you prepare for that kind of emotional journey in this role?"

Reese leans back in his chair, nodding slowly like he's really considering his answer. "It was tough. Obviously I've never experienced anything so horrible, so I had to get into a really dark headspace."

I listen as he goes on and on about his acting methods, catching glimpses of the guy I once thought I knew. Even after all this time, I can't figure out where the performance ends and the real

Reese begins. Maybe he doesn't even know anymore; he spends so much time on show for the world.

He finishes his answer, and the reporter turns to me. "Charlie, doing a movie with such intense action sequences must have taken a toll on your body. How did you stay in shape?"

I see Mandy rolling her eyes at the question, and I try hard not to do the same. This is the third interviewer in a row who's asked Reese an in-depth question about his job as an actor, and then asked me about my workout and diet regimen. I want to tell this guy to ask me something else, but I don't want to look like a bitch or get in trouble with the studio, so I grin and bear it yet again.

By the time I leave, I'm starving.

Charlie: Survived interviews with The Douche. YES! Where r u?

I send the text to our group chat, but Jamie replies in a private message.

Jamie: @ diner across the street. I think Tay's panicking.
She's been in the bathroom for 10 mins.
Charlie: B there asap.

Just then, Tay replies in the group chat.

Taylor: Hey! We're at the diner across the street. Come
hang out with us! :D

Classic Tay. Pretending she's chilled even when she's melting down on the inside.

Jamie sends me another private message: She's back now. I think she's okay. I tried to ask if she's okay but she waved it off. Said she's fine. I dunno.

Charlie: Don't bring it up unless she does. Try making her laugh.
Jamie: Already on it. She seems okay now.

A message pops up in the group conversation.

Tay: I know you guys are texting about me. I'm fine. Promise. Let's get back to having fun. WE'RE AT SUPACON!
Charlie: Sorry, Tay. Love you.
Tay: Love you back.

I open Twitter to catch up on the day's tweets. I raise an eyebrow when I see a familiar name popping up in my feed: Alyssa Huntington.

A blogger I follow shares a photo of Alyssa standing on a stage and waving. The caption reads: *Alyssa Huntington surprises fans at SupaCon!*

I smile like an idiot at the memory of our brief conversation.

I'm so engrossed by the tweets and photos of Alyssa that I don't watch where I'm going and slam right into someone when I turn a corner.

My phone drops to the floor, and I crouch down to pick it up, apologizing profusely.

"It's fine," the woman says, her hand reaching my phone first and handing it to me. But when I try to take it, she doesn't let go. "Oh," she says.

I look up to see Alyssa standing in front of me again.

She's staring straight at my phone.

The phone with pictures of her on the screen.

"Is that me?"

I play it cool even though I'm dying of embarrassment. "Oh, yeah. You're all over my corner of Twitter. A lot of bloggers and fans I follow were in the audience."

I take my phone and lock the screen faster than I ever have before.

Alyssa raises her eyebrows. "Oh, cool! I've never seen a crowd like that before. It was incredible. Us YouTubers have the best fans, don't you think?"

I laugh awkwardly. "Absolutely."

I'm barely even sure what she asked me. I'm too busy thinking, *Be cool. Be cool. BE COOL!* I mentally slap myself out of my starstruck stupor and speak. "Is this your first time at a con?"

"As a guest, yeah. But I've been coming to cons as a fan for years." She looks at me with unwavering focus as she talks, and it makes me feel secure and vulnerable at the same time. "What about you?"

"This is my first, as a fan and a guest. But I haven't had a chance to get on the floor yet."

She reaches out and touches my arm. "You have to. It's like another world out there. There's so much to see and do and buy."

The cast of *The Vampire Diaries* walk down the hall with a crew of staff, and we step aside as they stroll by. I grin at Alyssa and laugh. "This is so weird. How have I gone from shooting videos in my bedroom in Melbourne to talking to Alyssa Huntington while Stefan and Damon walk by?"

She laughs. "I'm with you. I can't believe this is real. I saw Felicia Day coming out of the bathroom earlier, and I nearly passed out."

I gasp. "No fucking way!"

Alyssa smiles a crooked smile and shoves her hands into her jeans pockets. She's watching me, looking deep in thought, like she's trying to read my mind.

"Hey," she says, motioning to the nearby venue door with her thumb. "I heard the food here sucks, so I was heading out to one of the local places. You wanna grab some lunch?"

Be cool, I tell myself again. I shrug and nod once, trying desperately to act casual. "Yeah, sure."

Our eyes lock, and Alyssa's lips part into a cheerful grin. "Cool."

We start walking toward the nearest backstreet exit, and I quickly type a message to Tay and Jamie.

Charlie: Alyssa freaking Huntington just asked me to lunch! Rain check on burgers?

Taylor shoots back a reply straightaway: WTF! That's awesome! Yes! GO! We'll see you later :D :D :D

Five minutes later, I'm sitting across from my personal hero, watching her order a cheeseburger and curly fries. Her new supershort hairstyle brings more attention to her deep brown eyes, peering out from black lashes and winged eyeliner. Her umber skin is adorned with black ink tattoos of birds in flight and flowers in bloom, with portraits, words, and symbols dotted down her arms and on the inside of her wrists. I know from her vlogs that she's smart, compassionate, outspoken, and everything I want to be. I can't believe I'm sitting at her table.

"So," Alyssa says after the waitress has taken our order and walked away. "I love your YouTube channel." She smiles.

I have to do a double take. "Wait, what?" I'm sure I misheard her. "*My channel?* You've watched my videos?"

She seems amused by my surprise. She laughs and leans forward, resting her arms on the table. "Yeah. I've seen all of them."

If a plane fell from the sky and landed on the diner right now, I would be less shocked.

She laughs again, the corners of her mouth reaching toward her smiling eyes. "Don't look so surprised!"

I realize my mouth is hanging open and snap it shut. I think back over the hundreds of videos I've made and hope I didn't post anything too embarrassing. "I don't know what to say. I guess I thought you were too big a star to even know I existed."

"Are you kidding? I've watched you from the beginning. Your reviews have introduced me to some of my favorite video games and comics." She lowers an eyebrow. "I'm a huge nerd, so your channel rocks my world."

I smile like a dork. "I'm a huge nerd, too!"

The waitress comes over with our drinks—two Cokes with ice—and proceeds to stare at Alyssa. "Um, hi. I love your videos so much! Do you mind if . . ." she says as she pulls a phone out of her pocket. "Can I take a selfie with you?"

Alyssa sits up straight and nods. "Sure!"

The waitress leans over the table awkwardly, holding her phone out as she tries to get both herself and Alyssa in the picture.

"Oh," I say, giggling. "Do you want me to take it?"

The waitress's eyes light up, and she hands me the phone. "Thank you!"

I hold the phone up and wait for both of them to smile before snapping a few pictures. "There you go," I say as I pass the phone back to the ecstatic fan.

"Thank you so much!" She runs back behind the counter and proceeds to go through the photos excitedly.

"Sorry," Alyssa says, her smile uneven and slightly embarrassed.

I wave it off. "Oh, please, it's cool!"

"I guess you're used to stuff like that by now, with all your vlogging fangirls."

I let out a laugh. "No way! That sort of thing never happens to me. Unless I'm somewhere like here, at SupaCon, of course. I'm not nearly as popular as you."

Alyssa's lips turn up into a half smile, and she looks out the window. "You will be. *The Rising* will make sure of that."

I'm sure she's flirting with me. At least, I hope she is. It excites and terrifies me all at the same time. I love everything about crushes. The butterflies, the possibilities, the giddy wonder of it all. But this is the first time I've liked a girl who might actually like me back.

The moment I first realized I'm into more than one gender was a quiet one. It was sudden and almost anticlimactic, so it's not a particularly exciting story. I was fourteen, and by that time I'd had more than one crush on a girl, mostly movie stars. But I never interpreted my feelings as a crush; I just thought I admired them a whole lot. It didn't occur to me that those feelings were similar to the way I felt about guys I liked.

I saw a post on Tumblr with the title "You Won't Believe These Actresses Are Bisexual" or something stupid like that. I didn't really know what that meant at the time, so I googled it. It didn't take long to recognize myself in many of the articles I found.

And that was it. But I've never actually been with a girl before. I've never even *flirted* with a girl before. This is all so new, and I'm not sure if I'm reading too much into this. Are we having lunch as friends, or could this be something more?

I've been crushing on her since I was fifteen. And I hope the sparkle in Alyssa's eyes is a good sign.

"So," she says again, breaking the short-lived but heavy silence between us. "Have you started filming the sequel to *The Rising* yet?"

I shake my head and take a sip of my Coke. "Not yet. Filming starts in a few months, in LA. There's a bigger budget, bigger studio, and a lot more pressure this time. And it all means many more eyes on me and my life." I feel the muscles in my shoulders tighten at the thought.

"Try not to let it get to you," she says, leaning forward again. "If you buy into the hype and the drama and the pressure, you'll break."

I move forward in my seat. I want to tell her that I've already been broken. That the last year didn't just break me; it crushed me. I want to tell her that I'm terrified of it happening again. But it still feels too raw, so I just ask, "How do you handle it all?"

She thinks for a moment. "I'm still learning. People keep telling me to ignore it, and I'm a pro at hitting the BLOCK button. But it's hard when you get racist, sexist, and homophobic comments slung at you every day. You probably get the same thing."

I nod, trying not to think of some of the terrible things people have said about me online. "It's infuriating."

She gives me a sympathetic frown and reaches out to take my hand. "Trust me, I get it. You're not alone."

I didn't know how much I needed to hear those words. We hold hands and sit quietly for a minute or two. The silence between us is comfortable, relaxed. It feels good to talk to someone who's in a position similar to mine, who's finding herself more and more in the public eye, and who's being herself in a world that tells her not to.

The buzz of her phone getting a text breaks our moment. She looks at the screen and gasps. "Crap! I've got a press thing in ten minutes." She looks up apologetically at me. "I'm really sorry, I gotta go."

I shrug it off and smile, even though I'm secretly disappointed to end our lunch. "It's cool. I should get back, too. I'm sure my manager is freaking out that I'm not there."

We slide out of the booth and walk to the counter, asking for our food to go and splitting the bill between us. While we wait for the waitress, Alyssa leans back against the counter to face me. She seems so laid-back and casual, not anything like how I'm feeling. She stares right at me, her lips curved up slightly, her eyes lingering on mine. I glance at the register, chickening out of the intense staring contest we are having.

"Thanks for the advice," I say, dragging my eyes back to hers.

"Anytime," Alyssa says as she takes her change and starts walking toward the door. "Us girls need to help each other out, you know?"

"I couldn't agree more."

We walk side by side down the street, heading back to the convention center.

Alyssa shoots me a sideways glance and clears her throat. "So, are you making any vlogs while you're here?" She slides her hands into her pockets.

"Yeah!" I have an idea and turn to look at her. "Hey, would you want to, maybe, do a collab?"

Her face lights up. "I'd love to! What do you have in mind?"

I think for a moment. "We could do a challenge, or a Q and A. They're always fun."

"Sweet!" she says. "How about I give you my number? Text me when you're free, and I'll make some time to meet up with you."

"Yeah, cool," I say, pulling out my phone. I'm trying so hard not to freak out or let my elation show.

We swap phone numbers and keep walking, pausing once we reach the staff entry.

"Cool," she says, her eyes lingering on mine again.

"Well, I guess I'll see you later."

I wonder if we should hug or if that would be too weird. My phone starts ringing, saving me from having to figure it out. It's Mandy.

Alyssa starts to walk away, waving and smiling. "See you later!"

"Bye!" I wave and then answer my phone. "Hey."

"Charlie, where are you? The cosplay contest and promo party start in five minutes."

"Oh, crap! I'm on my way."

CHAPTER 7

TAYLOR

QUEENOFFIRESTONE:

I just need to vent for a second. I think the craziness of coming to SupaCon just hit me. But I'm okay.

I must seem so weird to the people in my life sometimes.

But whatever they see on the outside is nothing compared to how I see things from in here.

Everything is just so fucking intense. All the time. It's like the brightness and sound is turned all the way up on the TV, and you can't ever turn it down. And the anxiety is a constant hum, a buzzing in your body and mind that never stops. Sometimes it feels like I'm allergic to the world, like I'm allergic to my own species. Being here, it's an assault on my senses.

But I'm okay.

I'm okay.

I have to be okay.

Anyway. Thanks for listening. Or reading, whatever.

I'll try to post SupaCon stuff later.

"Look at all this Firestone swag!" I skip toward the stall and stop at the first table. It's covered in Queen Firestone T-shirts, action figures, mugs, books, and jewelry. "I'm in heaven."

Jamie stands by my side and points to a nearby set of shelves. "There's even more over there."

He gives me a sideways glance, and I pretend not to notice it. I hate when he worries about me; it makes me feel like a child. But it's understandable, after my almost-meltdown back in the diner. He's seen me like that before, plenty of times, but it still makes him uneasy. He'll be treating me like a ticking bomb for the rest of the day. Unless I speak up.

"I'm fine, Jamie," I say with a sigh.

My eyes are glued to a T-shirt with the original Firestone One book cover art on it. "You don't need to worry about me."

He turns to face me as I pick up the shirt, rubbing my thumbs over the soft material.

"You sure?"

I press my lips together and nod. "Yeah. I think the jet lag caught up with me. But I'm good now."

His shoulders relax. "Good."

I spot another table of awesome shirts and run over to it, only to find they're all in men's sizes. "Seriously? Why do guys get all the best T-shirts?" I pick one up and stare at it hungrily. "Screw it, I'm buying this. It's mine." It wouldn't be the first time; most of my wardrobe consists of T-shirts and flannels from the boys' section—it's just what I feel most comfortable in.

Someone taps me on the shoulder, and I turn around to see another Queen Firestone cosplayer.

"Hi!" she says, smiling from ear to ear. "We're gathering up all the Queen Firestones just over there." She points down the aisle. "You wanna come with?"

"Um." I peer through the crowd. Over a dozen cosplayers are huddling together, some in the Queen Firestone trench coat like me, and others in her suit of armor.

My first instinct is to say no, but I know I'll regret it if I do. At the very least, it would make a great photo to share with the fandom on Tumblr. "Sure."

She grins and grabs my hand, pulling me through the crowd. "I found another one!" She giggles when we reach the others.

They pull me into the middle of the group, all complimenting me on my cosplay and asking me where I bought the trench coat.

"I made it," I say, feeling slightly overwhelmed.

"Seriously?" a suit of armor queen asks, her eyebrows raised so high they almost blend into her hairline. "Are you, like, a pro cosplayer?"

I laugh out loud. "No way! This is my first time cosplaying. I stayed up late every night for over a month watching how-to videos on YouTube and teaching myself to sew."

I thought about buying one, but the ones I found online were too small to fit me comfortably, and the crown on the back wasn't right, so I decided to make my own. I became so engrossed in it that some nights I sewed until sunrise without realizing, even forgetting to eat. Luckily my mum and sister were there to pull me out of my trance or I would have starved.

"That's so rad!" another trench coat queen squeals. "It looks just like the real thing! It has the sigil on the back and everything!"

I beam with pride. "Thanks!"

"Okay, queens!" a voice shouts over the chatter. "Smile!"

I look up and see dozens of cameras pointed at us. People passing by have stopped to snap photos on their phones, and a few others look pro, holding big Canons complete with flash extensions.

This is what it must be like for Charlie: cameras and eyes on her so much of the time.

"Whoa!" I say through a smile as the flashes go off. "This is awesome!"

"So is this your first SupaCon?" asks the girl who dragged me over here.

"It's my first any con."

"Oh, wow! Where are you from? England?"

"Australia."

Just then, a TV crew runs up to us. The reporter says something to one of the girls up front, and she nods excitedly. She turns to us and waves her arms around to get everyone's attention. *"Entertainment Now* wants to film us!"

A chorus of screams erupts, and I join in on the excitement.

The cameraman points his lens at the front and then pans around our group. When the red light flashes my way, I put on my best smile.

The reporter stands in front of us and starts asking questions, moving her microphone from girl to girl.

My smile vanishes, and my chest starts to tighten.

She's getting closer.

Any second now I'm going to be on television.

I listen to the questions she's asking the other girls, trying to prepare my arsenal of answers so I don't freeze up.

She steps back and calls out, "Who traveled the farthest to be here today?"

A flurry of answers are shouted.

"Omaha!"

"New York!"

"Toronto!"

And then the girl next to me takes my hand and lifts it up, pointing to me. "She's from Australia!"

Twenty Queen Firestones turn to look at me, and my breath gets caught in my throat.

The reporter pushes her way over to me, waving at the cameraman to follow.

I suck in a slow, deep breath and pray that I don't make an idiot of myself. I catch a glimpse of Jamie standing in the aisle, snapping photos of the whole scene. He lowers his camera, his jaw hanging open. But he's smiling.

Seeing his excitement strengthens my resolve, and I straighten my shoulders and smile.

"Hello there!" the cheery, red-haired reporter says with a sweet tone. "What's your name?"

It takes me a second or two to remember. "Taylor."

"And Taylor, how far did you travel to be at SupaCon today?"

"I came all the way from Melbourne, Australia."

I don't know if I'm meant to be looking at her or the camera, so I end up darting my eyes back and forth comically.

"Wow!" she says, like she's hearing it for the first time. "How long is that flight?"

"Um. I think it was about fourteen hours. We pretty much came straight here from the airport." I grin, pleased with myself for stringing multiple sentences together.

She turns to the camera. "Now *that's* commitment! What a hard-core fan!"

And then she hurries away as fast as she came, leaving all of us buzzing in her wake.

Our group begins to disperse, all the cosplayers going their separate ways with excited waves.

I walk straight up to Jamie, a huge smile on my face. "Did you see that?" I slap him playfully on the shoulder.

"I did!" he says with a crooked grin. "You're famous now! Better tell Charlie to watch out."

I laugh giddily. I feel another tap on my shoulder and turn to see that same Queen Firestone cosplayer smiling at me again.

"I'm Brianna, by the way." She adjusts the strap on her tank top. I notice she's showing less cleavage than I am and wonder if my top is too revealing. I decide it probably isn't, but hitch it up self-consciously anyway.

She sticks her hand out, and I shake it, hoping mine isn't too sweaty from on-air nerves. "I'm Taylor."

"Are you entering the SupaFan Contest?"

I scrunch up my nose. "Nah."

Her eyes widen. "Why not? You came all this way!" She taps my arm. "You should make the most of it! First prize is dinner with Skyler!"

"That's true," I say, smoothing out my coat. "Maybe I will enter."

"Great!"

One of the other girls starts calling her name. "I'll see you there!"

I wave as she disappears into a nearby aisle. Jamie looks at me, smiling smugly. "So you *are* going to enter the contest?"

I wave my hand dismissively. "Of course not."

He cocks his head to the side. "But you just said—"

"I know what I said."

He furrows his brow. "I don't get it."

I shrug. "I couldn't tell her why I don't want to do it. It sounds stupid."

"Being scared isn't stupid. It's normal."

I start walking and he follows.

"It's just that I know exactly how that conversation would have gone," I say. "I would have told her I'm too afraid to enter. She would have asked what I'm afraid of. I would have had to bring up the whole social anxiety thing, and she would have either encouraged me to enter anyway, completely disregarding my terror, or she would have nodded and excused herself."

He laughs and looks away. "You don't know that. She could have understood."

"History and experience have proven to me that it's very hard for people to understand, and all too easy for them to judge."

He shakes his head like he's disappointed. "But how will you know how people will react if you don't open up to them in the first place?"

I glance at him, confused. "Are you mad at me?"

His head snaps back in surprise. "No! Why would I be mad at you?"

I shrug my arms into the air. "I dunno! That's why I asked."

He laughs, but when he speaks, his voice is serious. "I could never get mad at you."

"Good, because I hate when people are mad." We wander around the busy floor, and I still feel slightly uneasy, so I try to lighten the mood. "I'm on such a high right now."

Jamie tsks and waggles a finger at me. "Now, Taylor, you're supposed to just say no."

I roll my eyes and elbow him in the side. "A natural high, idiot."

"Ow!" He pouts, rubbing his ribs.

He winks at me, and I poke my tongue out at him.

"Hey, Flirty McFlirtersons!" a voice shouts over the crowd, and I don't need to look up to know it's Charlie.

She struts toward us with a bright grin. A few heads turn as she walks by, escorted by Mandy and a SupaCon staff member. People recognize her and try to snap a sneaky photo.

"Hey!" I say.

"You know," she says when she's closer, "if you two were a couple, you'd fully be the superannoying type that call each other 'pookie' and walk around with your hands in each other's back pockets."

I give her a look that says "shut up!" and she winks at me mischievously. I feel like my whole body is blushing. Like all the blood is pressed against my skin, lighting me up like Kylo Ren's lightsaber. If there was one thing I could change about myself, it would be the blushing. It's my own personal awkwardness meter, and it's constantly going off, telling everyone exactly how I'm feeling no matter how much I want to hide it.

Jamie hides his hands in his pockets, and I think I see a hint of pink in his cheeks, too. "Where are you going?"

She starts moving again. She's being hurried through the hall by her little posse. "*The Rising* cosplay contest." She turns around and starts walking backward. "You guys coming, or what?"

"What about the VIP stuff?" I ask.

"No passes required for this! Come on!"

Jamie and I light up like little kids on Christmas and run after her excitedly.

CHAPTER 8

CHARLIE

THE CROWD CHEERS AS THE WINNERS OF *THE RISING* COSPLAY contest are announced. The floor vibrates beneath me from the applause.

"This is gonna be intense," Reese says.

I nod. "It's gonna be awesome."

A girl in a SupaCon shirt and a headset runs over to us. "Ready?"

"Yep."

Two other staff members are on either side, hands holding the edge of the tall paper wall in front of us, preparing to wheel it onto the stage.

The host speaks into the microphone, chatting to the winners excitedly. "Now, for the winners of *The Rising* cosplay contest, we have a special surprise for you!"

That's our cue. The set is pushed forward, and Reese and I walk behind it, hiding until we reach our mark.

Gasps echo through the crowd as they all wonder what the surprise could be. We reach the mark, get our smiles ready, and burst through the paper. The screams are deafening. I hate that I don't know if they're cheering for me or for "Chase." The host welcomes us while the two winners jump back and cover their mouths in shock. I see instantly why they won. It's like I'm staring into a mirror, seeing Ava and Will (me and Reese) exactly as we appeared on-screen, complete with torn jeans, dirt stains, and blood spatter. The only difference being that these two are both girls.

"You two look perfect!" I say, but they're still freaking out too much to comprehend what I'm saying. I try again. "I can tell you worked hard on your cosplay."

"Th-thanks!" the girl dressed as Will sputters. "We've seen *The Rising* three times already!"

Reese walks to the edge of the stage, waving to the crowd and blowing kisses like he's strutting down a catwalk. The girl dressed as Ava takes a step closer, and I notice tears streaming down her cheeks.

"Oh, sweetie!" I put an arm around her. "Are you okay?"

"I love you!"

"I love *you!*"

She wipes her cheeks and giggles uncontrollably. I can't help but giggle with her. I live for moments like these. Reese turns around to congratulate the winners, raising his eyebrows when he sees his role being played by a girl.

"You're a girl!" he says, pointing at her.

She laughs awkwardly and nods. "Yeah! It's a gender swap."

He considers her for a moment, and I pray he doesn't say anything sexist or demeaning. Even for him, that would be a new low.

He gives her a half smile and shrugs. "Cool!"

He hugs her, and she grins so wide I think she might burst. We spend the next thirty minutes posing for photos with the winners and the fans. To my relief, only three people ask if Reese and I are back together. But in my mind, that's still three too many.

When it's time to say good-bye and go backstage, I'm excited to spend a little time with my friends.

"Charlie!" Tay says when I hug her from behind. "How'd you do? Were they surprised?"

"Shocked."

Jamie gives me a hug. "We could hear them cheering for you. So cool!"

"I think they were just excited to see Chase reunited," I say sarcastically.

Tay furrows her brow. "Don't say that. They love *you*, not Chase."

I nod. "I'm so sorry you didn't get to meet Skyler, Tay." She had sent me a devastated text about it earlier, but I didn't have a chance to talk to her about it until now.

She sighs. "It's okay. Maybe it wasn't meant to be."

Jamie nudges her playfully, but he's frowning like seeing

her upset causes him physical pain. "You will meet her one day, Tay. I promise."

She lifts one side of her mouth into a sad smile and nudges him back. Then her head snaps up, and she looks at me with wide eyes. "How was lunch with your dream girl?"

I don't even try to hide my smitten grin. "It was amazing."

Tay giggles. "Are you swooning?" She looks up at Jamie, pointing at me. "Is she swooning?"

He nods. "She's swooning."

I shake my head, but it doesn't shake the smile off my face. "I am *not* swooning. I do not swoon."

Tay and Jamie glance at each other, then back at me, and both say, "Swooning."

Tay grabs my hands. "Did you ask her out?"

"No." I feel a little embarrassed when I say it.

Jamie cocks his head, confused. "Why not? You've liked her for so long."

My heart skips a beat, and I suck in a quick breath. "I have. I do like her. A lot. But I was scared, and I didn't know if she likes me as a friend or something more. It's so confusing!" I push a strand of hair behind my ear. "*But*, we did make plans to do a collab together for my channel. We swapped numbers."

Taylor grins. "Yes! That's so great, Charlie!"

I shrug. "It's not a date, though."

Jamie puts a hand on my shoulder. "But it could lead to one, if that's what you want."

Tay nods. "Exactly. After everything you've been through, this is a big step. You've got to move on at your own pace."

I glance over at Reese, who's downing a beer. "It would be easier to do that if *he* wasn't here. How am I ever going to set myself apart from him like this?"

"I think you're giving him too much credit," Jamie says, concern written all over his face.

"I just feel like I'm stuck with him. The more we're seen together doing all this press, the harder it makes it for the media and the fans to just see *me*."

Tay's eyebrows pinch together. "Who cares what they see. It only matters what *you* see."

"Whoa," Jamie says. "That's deep. Like, Yoda level."

Tay blushes and we laugh.

"Since when do you care what anyone else thinks?" Jamie asks, folding his arms and tilting his head to the side.

I throw my head back and let out a dramatic sigh. "I know, I know. This isn't like me. What's wrong with me?"

"Hey," Tay says, her voice low and serious. "Nothing is wrong with you. You've just gotten over a superintense, very public breakup. Anyone would have a little self-doubt after that."

I hear Reese's obnoxious laugh from the other side of the room and wince. His very presence is digging into me like a giant, egotistical, blond splinter.

"I just want him out of my life."

Tay sticks her bottom lip out into a sincere frown. "After SupaCon, that's it. You don't have any more events or commitments with him."

"But I'll still have *Chase*. People will still be tweeting me, telling me to get back together with him. Fandom blogs will mention the breakup, the humiliation, every time they write a post about me. It's never gonna go away."

Tay and Jamie exchange worried glances, and I feel pathetic.

"Charlie, it will go away," Jamie says.

Tay puts her hands on my shoulders and looks me deep in the eyes. "It will."

CHAPTER 9
TAYLOR

QUEENOFFIRESTONE:

You guys!

Thanks so much for all your messages. I'll try to get to them all later, but for now I just wanted to say thanks. I'm fine. I just had a moment. But I'm good now.

Guess what? I was on TV!

And I met a bunch of other QF cosplayers! I'm having a blast :D

I'll post more later, but right now I've gotta go.

Tay xo

"You want a drink?" Jamie asks. We're standing in the corner by the food, surveying the party.

"Yeah, thanks."

Jamie heads toward the bar to get us a couple of Cokes, and I scan the small gathering of people. I'd expected to see more familiar faces, like cast members from *The Rising* or some of the many celebrity guests gracing SupaCon this year. But it's mostly full of studio execs and other important people of the non-famous variety.

In other words, it's boring as hell.

Charlie is making her rounds, chatting with everyone. We had a few minutes to chat before she was pulled away to schmooze the suits. The whole room is revolving around her, like every single person is stuck in her orbit. It's quite a sight to see, one that makes me beam with pride.

After the struggle she's been through the past six months, she deserves this. I think she's slowly going back to her normal, confident self.

When we walk into a room, Charlie's the one everyone looks at. She's what people usually refer to as pear-shaped, I guess. Or is it hourglass? All these words people have for describing bodies seem a bit much to me. Whatever Charlie's shape is, it seems to be more socially acceptable than mine, judging by how people talk about her. People are always telling her she should be a model. But sometimes she gets a bit tired of people only seeing her for the way she looks.

Out the corner of my eye, I spot someone walking toward me

and turn to see Reese. I groan internally, but give him a wave as he approaches. "Hi, Reese."

He raises his beer as a greeting. "Hey." He looks me up and down, and I feel exposed. "What are you wearing?"

I fold my arms over my chest self-consciously. "I'm cosplaying. Queen Firestone."

He pinches his mouth to the side, studying me. "All right," he says, as though I needed his approval.

I breathe out a quiet laugh.

He takes a swig of his beer. It occurs to me that he's only nineteen, and I consider pointing out that the legal drinking age here is twenty-one, not eighteen like it is back home. But I don't want to sound like a Goody Two-shoes, so I keep quiet.

"So, how's school?" He asks this with an air of cockiness, and I'm not sure why.

"Good."

He looks around the room as if searching for someone more interesting to talk to, then seems to decide to give this conversation another try. I wish he wouldn't. I wish he could see that I'm the one stuck here talking to him, not the other way around.

"You think you'll get into uni?"

"Yeah," I say, then I think that might sound too boastful and add, "I mean, I hope so. I've applied to heaps of schools. I want to get into a creative writing course. Or screenwriting. Or both." I don't tell him that I applied to UCLA and other US colleges, because I don't trust him to be encouraging and I'm anxious enough about my chances of getting in already.

He struggles to swallow his drink, like I just said something hilarious and he's trying not to spit beer all over me. "You wanna be in movies?"

I shake my head profusely. "Not *in* movies. I'd like to write them. And books. I really want to write books."

Not that I've really thought about uni that much. I've tried thinking about it, planning for it, but every time I do I get a sick feeling in my stomach. But I have enough self-awareness to know that if I'm going to put myself through the stress and anxiety of going to class every day, it will need to be a class on something I care about. And there's nothing I'm more passionate about than books, movies, and storytelling.

"That's adorable."

I narrow my gaze. "Why?"

"Well, you're not in the business so I don't expect you to know why it's cute, but it is. You know you'll have to sleep your way to the top, right?"

"Um, sorry?"

He leans in, and I can smell beer on his breath. "How do you think Charlie got where she is?" He points at himself, arrogance practically oozing out of his pores.

I step back, glaring at him. "I know how Charlie got to be where she is. Through hard work and creativity and persistence and skill. It had nothing to do with you. In fact, dating you probably hindered her more than helped her."

I can't believe I said that. My gaze drops to the floor.

"Jeez," he says. "Someone can't take a joke. If you're gonna make it in Hollywood, you'll need to be less of a bitch."

My mouth falls open, and I keep my eyes trained on the carpet. If I move, I'll cry. And the last thing I want right now is for him to see me cry. He'll just take it as a sign that he's wounded me, when really it's just because I'm overwhelmed and don't know what else to do. Blood rushes to my cheeks, and I feel my hands begin to sweat and shake. But I don't say anything. Everything I want to say rushes through my mind, bottlenecking and getting stuck in my throat.

Reese turns to leave, but someone is standing in his way. I look up to see Jamie, his gaze locked on Reese.

Reese slaps a friendly hand on Jamie's shoulder. "Watch out, mate, she's in a mood."

Jamie puts the two glasses of Coke on a nearby table, shrugs Reese's hand off him, and stares him in the eyes. Reese tries to get past him, but Jamie puts a hand on his chest to stop him. "Hang on a second, man. I just wanna see if I understand this."

He looks at me, his jaw clenching when he sees the tears in my eyes, then looks back at Reese. "So, you insult Tay, basically tell her she'll only succeed if she puts out, then insult her best friend and take credit for her success. Right?"

"I didn't insult anyone."

Jamie rolls his eyes. "You know what? The fucked-up thing is that you really believe that. You really don't see how what you just did was a dick move."

Reese opens his mouth to say something, but Jamie holds up a finger. "Then Tay stands up for herself and for Charlie, and somehow that makes *her* a bitch? Do you see the flaws in your argument, Reese?"

Reese scoffs at him and points a thumb back at me. "You didn't hear her, man. She was rude."

Jamie raises an eyebrow. "Oh, I heard. I heard the whole thing. And I gotta tell ya, man, it sounded to me like you were the one being rude."

I see Reese squeeze his hand into a fist by his side, and my eyes flick over to Charlie, who's standing on the other side of the room. Mandy is talking to her enthusiastically, but Charlie's eyes are glued to Reese and Jamie. She knows something is going down. My breathing is getting shallower. I'm furious at Reese, but terrified for Jamie. With his movie star abs and bulging biceps, Reese is big. He could punch Jamie's lights out in a second.

"You're asking for it, Jamie," Reese says. He pushes Jamie, making him stumble backward. Jamie grits his teeth, but doesn't push back. He stands straight and firm, glaring at Reese.

Reese tilts his head to the side, seeming confused. "What, you're not gonna fight back?" He smiles.

Jamie crosses his arms over his chest. "Cool it."

Reese laughs. "What a fuckin' pussy." He shoves Jamie again, taunting him. I look on, horrified and unsure what to do. Everyone in the room is watching now.

"Reese!" Charlie yells. "What the hell are you doing? Leave him alone."

Reese pushes Jamie again, backing him into a table. Jamie's face is red with anger, and I can see Reese is hurting him.

Reese shakes his head. "Man up." He slaps Jamie on the face, and that's when Jamie retaliates.

Jamie shoves Reese. Taken by surprise, Reese tumbles backward, falling into a table and chairs. The table collapses underneath him, and the sound of plates and glasses smashing makes my ears ring.

I stand there, my hands covering my mouth and my eyes wide. Everyone freezes.

Jamie wipes a hand down his face and shakes his head in disappointment. He steps over Reese and reaches a hand down to help him up. "You okay?"

Reese takes his hand and lets Jamie pull him to his feet. Then he swings his fist back and punches Jamie in the face. I scream as his head snaps back, and he plummets to the ground.

I decide to take action.

I hurry over to Jamie, take his hand, and help him steadily to his feet. He glares at Reese, but I press my hands against his chest, which is hard and tensed in anger.

"Come on," I say. "Let's go. This party isn't cool enough for us." I try to speak with confidence, but my voice is shaking.

Jamie drags his eyes away from Reese and over to me, his expression softening. His right cheekbone is already red from where Reese hit him. I nod toward the door and take Jamie's hand. Every muscle in my body is tense as we walk away from Reese, but I don't look back. Charlie is staring at us, concern all over her face, and I give her a thumbs-up to reassure her that we're okay.

I pull Jamie out the door and into the hallway. "Are you okay?"

He nods. "I'm fine."

I stare at him squarely in the face. "That guy is a Neanderthal. I'm so sorry he did that to you."

He drops his gaze. "It's not your fault. It's his. And mine. I was trying so hard not to fight him. You know how I feel about macho dicks. But I couldn't just do nothing, either."

I realize I'm still holding his hand and let go. "He could have beaten you to a pulp." I feel my blood boiling and clench my fists at my side. "Ugh. I wish I could jump into a DeLorean and go back to ten minutes ago and stop that idiot from ever opening his ignorant, cocky mouth."

I glance at him, and he's watching me, the corners of his mouth pulling up slightly.

"What?"

He laughs, but flinches in pain when his cheek moves. "I've never seen you so pissed before. And yet in all your rage, you still managed to slip in a movie reference. You're good."

I laugh, shaking my head loosely. "You didn't need to do that, you know. Step in when Reese was being an asshole. I was fine."

"You weren't fine. I saw the look on your face, and I never want to see that look again." His jaw clenches.

I let out a long exhale. "It's not like it's the first time I've been called a bitch." I've lost count of the times people have called me a bitch or a snob, misinterpreting my shyness or lack of eye contact as disrespect or rudeness.

"Just because it's happened before doesn't make it okay."

"I know. And even though you didn't need to step in"—I pause, making eye contact with him—"I'm glad you did. You said everything I wanted to say, but couldn't."

"I don't know." He grins. "I think you got a few good verbal punches in yourself."

"Thanks," I say. "Hey, you wanna call it a day? I'm pretty wiped. I just wanna go to our hotel and watch a movie or something. And we should put some ice on your cheek."

He smiles. "That sounds perfect."

CHAPTER 10

CHARLIE

AFTER TAY AND JAMIE HURRY OUT THE DOOR, I WALK UP TO Reese, who's sulking alone at a table in the corner. I told one of the execs to call security, but he just shrugged it off. Reese gets away with his douchery yet again.

"Hey," I say, taking a seat next to him. "What the actual fuck?!"

He raises a hand to silence me. "Not now. I don't need to hear a lecture from you."

I roll my eyes. "Too bad. I don't need to see you picking fights and punching my friends, and yet that's exactly what you did. If it were up to me, you'd be outside on your ass with your VIP badge confiscated. What the hell is wrong with you? Jamie and Tay didn't deserve any of that."

He doesn't look at me. "Pfft, that chick is strange. And he's a prick."

"Yeah, because you're such a decent dude." I stare at the empty beer bottle he's clutching in his hand. "Are you drunk?"

He shakes his head, and his eyes widen. Slightly red and unfocused, they give him away. It's clear that this isn't his first drink.

He hunches over the table and stares at me intensely. "I miss you, Charlie."

I almost fall off my chair, I'm so surprised. "Um, what?"

"I miss you." He pulls his chair closer to mine, and I give him a perplexed look. "Charlie, breaking up with you was a huge mistake. I should have never let you go."

I cross my arms and lean back, feeling very skeptical of his intentions. "Then why did you?"

He rubs a hand over his face and leans back in his chair. "I'm an idiot. Obviously."

I scoff. "At least we agree on that."

"I'm being serious."

"Did it sound like I was joking?"

He groans and shakes his head at me, his blond locks falling in front of his eyes. He blows them back and puts the empty bottle on the table. "Charlie, I'm trying to tell you that I want you back."

My jaw drops. I don't know what to say, so I just stare at him, trying to search his face for the truth. I glance at the party on the other side of the room, making sure no one is overhearing this very strange conversation. If people found out about what he just said, I'd never be able to escape Chase.

"Charlie." He reaches a hand over the table, opening his palm for me to take. I don't. "Come on. I made a mistake."

"*Mistakes*. Plural. And you just added a huge one to the list with what you just did to my friends."

"Fine. Mistakes. I've made mistakes. But I've learned from them, and I'll never do anything like that again."

His hand is still out, and I still don't take it. I furrow my brow, still wondering if this is for real or if it's some horrible practical joke. "Are you being serious right now?"

He nods. "Yes. I should never have treated you like that. I was out of control. I wasn't used to all the attention, and I gave in to it. It was wrong. I'm sorry."

As much as I've wanted to hear him apologize, it's still hard. I close my eyes and take in a deep breath. When I open them again, he's looking at me like he used to when we first started dating. He's looking at me like I'm the only girl in the world.

I remember the first time he looked at me like that; we were in the middle of an intense scene in *The Rising*. It was the first day of filming.

We were running from thousands of zombies, down a closed-off Sydney street. My heel broke, and I plummeted to the ground, ripping a hole in my jeans and scraping my hands and arms. He stopped running, came back, and crouched beside me, wrapping one of his big, muscly arms around me and helping me up. His bright blue eyes were full of concern and care for me.

Looking back now, I see it was such a cliché, but it won me over instantly.

And then the roller coaster began.

Falling in love with Reese was like a tornado; everything around me was spinning, and there was nothing to keep me steady. So I got whisked off my feet. First love is crazy enough, but being in the public eye amplifies that crazy by a million. Sometimes I wonder if that was what doomed us: all the attention. It was a mistake to be so open about our relationship from the start. The public scrutiny and constant watchful eyes of camera lenses got to us very quickly. It made me shrink, and Reese expand. I spent more time at home, trying to avoid the spotlight, while he drank up the attention—even tipping off paparazzi to where we were going for dinner. It wasn't the first time fame poisoned a relationship, and it won't be the last.

"Charlie," he says, pleading with me. "Aren't you going to say something?"

Six months ago, this might have been enough. My heart was still broken then, and I thought he was the only thing that could put it back together.

But not now.

"Look, Reese, I really don't think you want me back. I'm not even sure if you ever truly loved me."

He clenches his jaw, and hurt flashes in his blue eyes. "How could you say that?"

"I can say that because I really believe that if you loved me, you wouldn't have done what you did. You wouldn't have paraded around with another girl while we were still together. You wouldn't have put me through all that heartache and humiliation. And you would have treated me better. Much better."

"Seeing all that tabloid shit hurt me as much as it hurt you."

I scoff. "Doubt it. I was the one who turned on the TV to see you making out with some slut." I pinch the bridge of my nose between my thumb and forefinger and blow out a frustrated exhale. "Sorry. I shouldn't have said that." Slut-shaming is something I've been on the receiving end of more than once. I've even spoken out against it publicly, and yet here I am contributing to it out of anger. This guy brings out the worst in me.

"You have every reason to be pissed." He finally slides his hand off the table, accepting that I won't take it. We're awkwardly silent for a minute, and then he can't wait any longer. "Charlie, do you want to be with me, or not?"

"No." I say it before he even finishes talking. My answer is quick, but certain. I don't even have to think about it.

"But what about us? What about Chase?"

I raise an eyebrow. "What *about* Chase?"

"Everyone wants us together. The fans, the studio. Us being together will make everyone happy. We'll be the most famous couple in the world."

I glare at him, disgusted. "I don't care about that. It won't make *me* happy. You don't treat me the way I deserve to be treated. You never did. And you just proved you don't care about anyone else, either. Anyone who goes around throwing punches only cares about himself. I have zero interest in getting back together with you."

"Come on," he says. "What are you afraid of?"

"I'm not afraid. I know what I want, and it's not this."

He reaches out and takes my hand.

I pull it away. "Don't. You don't get to hold my hand anymore."

He shakes his head and smirks. "Fuckin' hell, Charlie. Since when did you become such a prude?"

I clench my jaw so hard it hurts. "How are you not getting this? You cheated on me. You humiliated me. You constantly belittle me. And five minutes ago you beat up one of my best friends. Saying no to you doesn't make me a prude, Reese. And if you think it does, then you need some serious help."

I stand up, done with this conversation for good. "I'll get your manager. You need to go back to the hotel and sober up."

I walk away in a huff, trying to maintain my composure for the partygoers.

CHAPTER 11

TAYLOR

JAMIE STICKS THE KEY CARD INTO THE SLOT AND SWINGS THE door open.

I dump my backpack in the hall and start exploring our room. Jamie and I are Charlie's tagalongs, so the three of us are sharing a studio suite in a fancy-shmancy hotel a block away from SupaCon.

It's a simple but luxurious room, with a flat-screen on the wall, a couch and coffee table by the window, and two double beds. Our suitcases sit on the beds, having been brought up by the concierge earlier.

Jamie drops his shoulder bag on the couch and stretches. His T-shirt lifts slightly, exposing his lower abdomen and that sexy V some guys have. I try not to stare. I try *really hard* not to stare.

"You and Charlie take the beds." He sinks onto the couch and pats it. "I'll take the couch."

"What?" I ask, looking at the two big beds. "Don't be silly. Charlie and I can share. We share the same bed at sleepovers all the time."

He picks up the TV remote and shrugs. "Up to you. I don't mind."

I sit down on the bed, but my coat makes an offensive scrunching sound, and I stand back up again. "I'm going to get changed. This trench coat looks awesome, but it's not too comfortable."

"Cool. I'll find something for us to watch. You want something to eat? We could order room service?"

My stomach rumbles at the mere mention of food. "Yes. Definitely."

He reaches over to the coffee table and picks up the menu.

"I'll have—"

"Let me guess," he says with a crooked grin. "Vegetarian club sandwich with fries and extra ketchup."

I cock my head at him. "Yes. And a—"

"Coke. Vanilla, if they have it."

I cross my arms over my chest. "How the hell do you know all that?"

He laughs. "It's what you always get when you order room service at a hotel."

"*I* know that, but how do *you* know that?"

"You told me. Like a year ago, after you went on that trip to Sydney with your mom and sister."

"Oh," I say. "I don't know whether to be impressed or worried that you remember that."

"Impressed," he says. "Definitely impressed."

I shake my head and pick up my suitcase, heading into the bathroom.

When I come out, I'm swimming in comfort, wearing loose-fitting yoga pants and an old *Jurassic Park* T-shirt I got for Christmas one year.

Jamie is lying on the bed, one arm behind his head and the other holding the remote.

His mouth stretches into a grin. "Look what's on."

I turn to the TV and see Queen Firestone's snow-white face and gasp. "Firestone One!" I clap my hands and jump up and down. "Yes!"

"Come sit with me," he says. "Room service is on its way."

I climb onto the bed, stretch out next to him, and sigh. "Look at this." I gesture to the room. "We're in a fancy hotel room. My queen is on the TV. Club sandwich on its way. And two more days of SupaCon awesomeness ahead. It doesn't get any better than this."

He glances at me, his lips curving into an uneven smile. "Agreed."

I sit up, my eyes glued to the TV. "This is my favorite part!"

Jamie and I start quoting the lines, doing our best Queen Firestone impressions.

"I *am* queen," we say, our expressions smoldering and voices low. "And I will not lose twice."

I clutch my hands to my chest and fall back onto the pillow. "I can't believe we didn't meet Skyler today. We were so close!"

"I know. I'm shattered."

"Shattered doesn't even begin to describe it. I'm pretty sure I'm scarred for life." I say it with a smile, but I'm not joking. Missing my chance to meet Skyler is heartbreaking. I felt like my whole future was dependent on it, and now I'm lost.

Jamie frowns. "It's okay. You'll get another chance. Maybe she'll come to Oz for the premiere of Firestone Five."

My hope lifts. "You reckon?"

He nods. "It could happen. She's due for a trip Down Under. How about this—" He turns onto his side and props himself on his elbow, looking down at me. "Next time she comes to Australia, you and me will road trip to whatever city she's in and camp out in line to be the first to meet her. Sound good?"

I nod excitedly. "That sounds awesome."

"Good," he says, smiling. "It's a date."

The credits start to roll, but I'm not looking at the TV.

I'm looking at Jamie.

And he's looking at me, right into my eyes.

We're only inches away from each other. If he just dipped his head a little, we'd be kissing. If he just dipped his head a little. I swallow hard, feeling unprepared for whatever is happening. But I don't want it to stop.

A loud knock at the door makes me jump, breaking our gaze. Jamie rolls off the bed and walks to the door, mumbling something about timing. I sit up on the bed and cross my legs, trying to decide if that was an almost-kiss or just a plain old staring contest.

"I got it. Thanks, man," Jamie says at the door. He carries the tray of food over and rests it on the end of the bed. The room fills with the smell of fries, making my stomach groan in anticipation.

Jamie throws a cloth napkin over his arm and lifts up the domed lid, revealing my sandwich. "Dinner is served, madam."

I tuck my knees under myself and bow. "Why thank you, kind sir."

I open my can of Coke as he slides onto the bed next to me, shoving a fry into his mouth. His phone starts to buzz, and he runs over to the couch to find it.

"It's Mom," he says before answering it.

I take the chance to update my Tumblr.

QUEENOFFIRESTONE:
So, today has been weird. Good weird.

I know you're all living vicariously through me right now, wanting updates and pictures and news. And I promise I'll be doing all that, but right now I need to rest. I gotta recover from today so I'm ready to do it all again tomorrow. Anyone who knows me will tell you I have a tendency to overdo it sometimes, especially when I'm excited about something. I go all in. And if I'm not careful, I'll wipe myself out before the end of day one. I guess you could say I need to ration my energy. Anyway, hope you guys understand.

Let's round up the awesome from day one:

—I'm living my dream of going to SupaCon! I will never ever get over the fact that I am HERE.

—I was on TV in my Queen Firestone cosplay—which everyone is LOVING, btw! All those hours spent working on it and pouring my blood, sweat, and literal tears into it were so worth it.

—I *almost* met Skyler. I glimpsed her hair, you guys. I was in the same room as her. I'm still shattered that I didn't meet her, but I'm trying to see the positives here. I didn't meet her, but I got closer than ever before. That's something, right?

—I recognized the signs of panic and gave myself what I needed to calm down. This is amazing progress. A year ago I would never have been able to do that. I'm definitely counting that as a win. I also remembered to take my meds, something I was worried I'd forget about with all the chaos of this trip. So yay!

A bunch of other things happened, but I can feel my mind getting tired now so I'm switching off.

Stay awesome!

#SupaConRULES #GoodWeird #FirestonerCosplay

I hit POST and turn my attention back to my sandwich, catching some of Jamie's conversation.

"Already?" he says, pacing by the bed. "Okay. Yeah, open it."

There's a long pause, then excited screaming through the phone. Jamie smiles and rubs a hand down his face.

"Seriously?" He lets out a hearty laugh.

I take a bite out of my sandwich and watch him curiously. He looks at me, grinning from ear to ear. "Okay. Yeah. Mom, I gotta go. Okay. Bye."

He ends the call and drops his phone onto the bed, still grinning at me.

"What?" I ask, my mouth full of bread and vegetables.

"A letter from UCLA arrived. I got an early offer for next year."

I swallow. "For real?" I stare at him with my mouth ajar.

He nods, excitement all over his face.

"That's awesome!" I drop my sandwich on the plate and jump off the bed. I run over and wrap my arms around him, and he squeezes me tight.

"I can't believe it!" he says.

I rest my head on his chest. "I didn't even know you could get an acceptance letter this early." I should know that, seeing as I also applied there as part of our plan for all three of us to move to LA.

"Oh, yeah." He steps away and rubs the back of his neck. "I really didn't think I'd get in. I've told you that Mom and Dad went there, right? They've always talked about how I would go there one day. They're freaking out."

The reality of what this means starts to sink in. It's happening. It's almost time to leave high school, leave Melbourne, and start anew. "UCLA. So you're the first of us to know for sure that you're moving back here to the US!"

"I guess so." He smiles.

I sit back on the bed and rub my hands back and forth along my thighs.

"Don't worry," he says. "You'll get in, too. And Charlie will be doing her thing. It's going to be awesome."

I nod slowly. "Yeah, for sure." We're silent for a minute or two. I want to be happy for him, and for the most part I am, but I can't deny that it makes me nervous.

I knew this moment would come. All anyone has been talking about this year is graduation and university and the future. But I thought this particular moment wouldn't come for at least another six months. It's not supposed to happen yet. We're still supposed to have time.

The door clicks and Charlie flies into the room, snapping us out of our thoughts.

"Oooh," she coos. "Do I smell fries?"

"Hey!" I stand up and give her a wave. She points down at my plate and rubs her stomach, and I laugh. "Go ahead."

"Thanks!" she says as she falls onto the bed. "I'm starving."

She takes a bite of a french fry. "Jamie, are you okay? I'm so sorry about Reese."

I jump up. "The ice!" I run to the minifridge and pull out some ice, wrap it in a hand towel, and hurry to Jamie. I hold it up to his face, gently pressing it against his cheek.

He watches me while answering Charlie. "I'm fine. But I really, really hate that guy."

Electricity rushes over me as he looks into my eyes, making me feel too exposed. I give him the ice and turn to Charlie. "Reese is the biggest tool. But you don't need to apologize, Charlie."

She takes another bite. "What happened, anyway? One minute you guys were all talking, then the next Reese was on the ground."

I wave a hand dismissively, wanting desperately to forget it ever happened. "It doesn't matter. He was just talking shit."

"As usual," Jamie adds.

Charlie cringes. "You won't believe this." She gulps. "But he told me he wants me back."

"Huh?" Jamie says, like he thinks he misheard her.

"No fucking way," I say, sure I heard her right but still unable to process it.

Charlie nods. "Yep. He wants to get back together."

"And you said . . . ?" I drag the *said* out, narrowing my eyes at her.

"No! Of course I said no."

I exhale in relief. "Thank God."

Jamie runs the tips of his fingers over the stubble along his jawline, looking confused as hell. "How did he think you would even consider getting back with him?"

Charlie shakes her head. "I think he was drunk. Anyway, once this weekend is over, I don't want anything to do with him. I just want to get to LA with you guys, film the sequel, and leave him behind for good."

"Speaking of moving to LA," I say, wiggling my eyebrows at Jamie.

Charlie tilts her head to the side. "What?"

I nudge Jamie with my shoulder. "Tell her!"

He tells her about UCLA, and she screams. Holding my smile, I get up and walk into the bathroom while they celebrate together. I lock the door and lean over the sink, staring at my reflection.

"It's okay," I whisper to myself. "You'll be fine. This is good for them. You'll get in, too." I suck in a deep breath. "You won't be left behind."

I run my hands through my hair absentmindedly, stroking the shaved part to feel the tiny spikes. I force a smile at my reflection, trying to cheer myself up, and then just end up analyzing myself. I try not to, but it's hard when I'm already feeling low.

I think I'm what people refer to as curvy, even though I don't really have a waist. But I do have a stomach. And boobs. And hips. And thighs. And a slight double chin that I'm self-conscious about and try to hide in photos by tilting my head a certain way. I was always the so-called "chubby" kid. But most of the time, I was oblivious to the way I looked as a child, too busy building LEGO castles and playing video games. But then I started secondary school, and all the girls around me started talking about diets and pinching their stomachs to compare fat rolls with each other. Everyone around me was growing into shapely teens while I sort of just rounded out more. I started seeing body-shaming at school and on TV, and I could have gone down the path of deep self-loathing, but then I met Charlie.

Charlie is a lot of things, but insecure isn't one of them. At first I was intimidated by her outspoken personality and Beyoncé-level confidence, but she took me under her wing, and I quickly learned that she's sweet, kind, and fiercely protective of those she cares about.

On the first day of year seven, the teacher sat me next to her. She smiled and introduced herself, and I didn't utter a word. Class was about to start, but someone knocked on the door. A woman tapped on the glass and smiled in my direction, and I heard Charlie gasp. It was her mother, smiling and waving and beaming with pride. She opened the door a crack and whispered something to Charlie in Mandarin, and Charlie leapt up, whispered something back, and closed the door. The teacher asked her if everything was okay, and Charlie explained that her mother just wanted to see her in her first secondary school classroom. I remember being horribly embarrassed for her at the time, but now it just seems sweet.

When she sat back next to me, I built up my courage, leaned in, and whispered, "Are you okay?"

She smiled and said, "I'm fine."

Another girl at our table stared at her with wide, horrified eyes. "Aren't you embarrassed?"

Charlie gave her a quizzical look. "No. Why? My mum's proud of me. I'd never be embarrassed about that." She laughed, and I laughed with her.

We became inseparable. We had sleepovers, and we'd spy on her two older sisters at her house and watch movies all night at my house. She gave me a crash course in the wonders of online fandoms and video games and always knew which YouTubers to watch.

I've always likened her to a wildfire: unstoppable, constantly moving wherever the wind takes her, and lighting a spark everywhere she goes. And then there's me, the girl who's plagued by worry and anxiety, the proverbial wet blanket. We tend to balance each other out quite nicely.

Don't get me wrong; that's not all we are. Like everyone, who we are isn't set in stone. Sometimes I'm the wildfire, when I want to be.

Once, when Charlie and Reese were beginning to crumble, I stood up for her. Charlie and I were in her room watching one of Alyssa's videos. Alyssa was interviewing a popular feminist blogger about something called intersectionality. Reese walked in as the blogger started talking about bisexuality, and he groaned. Charlie closed her laptop and asked him what was wrong.

"I'm not a homophobe or anything," he said, holding his palms up. "I'm all for gay marriage and all that, but bisexuality? I just don't believe it's real."

I held my breath, having known about Charlie's sexuality for years by then.

Charlie stood up and crossed her arms. "What do you mean?"

He shrugged and spread out on her bed like I wasn't even there. "I just don't believe in bisexuals."

"What do you mean you don't *believe* in bisexuals? They're not mythical creatures," I said. "They're real people, just like you."

He squirmed uncomfortably, and Charlie sighed. "Reese, I'm bisexual. Do you believe in me?"

He sat up and stared at her like he was suddenly seeing a whole different person. "You? But you're with me."

"So? I'm still bi."

He narrowed his eyes at her, and they were silent for a while, like they were both waiting for the other one to apologize. I wondered if I should leave but was too scared to move.

When Reese finally said something, I wished he hadn't. "But how could you possibly know you're bi? Have you ever been with a girl?"

I remember seeing the frustration written all over Charlie's face, and I spoke up. "How did you know you were straight before you were with a girl, Reese?"

His eyes widened, and he jumped up from the bed. "Look, like I said, I'm all for equality and gay rights and stuff. That's all I'm gonna say." And he left the room.

Charlie fell onto the bed in a huff. "He's all for equality, but he doesn't even believe bisexuality exists." She rubbed her fingers over the space between her eyebrows like she had a headache. "You can't pick and choose whose equality you support. That's not equality." She said it quietly, as if only to herself.

"Are you okay?" I asked, worried at the way Reese seemed to get into her head and make her doubt herself. She nodded, opened her laptop, and pressed PLAY on the video. She never mentioned it again. Six months later, she and Reese broke up.

I hear the door to our hotel room open and close, so I compose myself and go back out there. When I do, Charlie is gone and Jamie is sitting up against the headboard with his plate in his lap, taking a bite of his burger.

"Where's Charlie?"

"She got called to Mandy's room to prepare for the panel tomorrow. We need to get that girl into Project Leda so she can clone herself; that way she'll be able to do all this press stuff and still have time for us."

I laugh and sit on the bed to finish my sandwich. "It's all pretty cool, huh? The three of us moving to LA?"

"Yeah, it's awesome." He's watching me. I can feel it. "But it's also kind of sad."

My head snaps around to look at him, and his eyes drop to his plate.

"I mean," he says, "leaving home, being away from family. And it's scary starting college, especially in a new place."

I sigh in relief. "You think so, too?"

He raises his eyebrows. "Of course I do. I was really scared moving to Melbourne and starting a new school, and now it's happening again. The last four years have been fun, so it sucks a little to think that's all gonna change soon."

I pick apart my sandwich, tearing off a piece of bread and rolling it into a ball before popping it into my mouth. We sit quietly, eat our fries, and watch TV. I stare at the screen and think about us. Jamie came into the picture in year nine, two years after Charlie and I became best friends, and soon we were a trio of BFFs.

I started having a crush on him the first time I saw him, on his first day at our school after moving from Seattle. He was reading the first Queen Firestone book while sitting on some steps one morning before school. He wore a burgundy beanie and a *Star Wars* T-shirt, and I was hooked. It wasn't until a month or two later that he actually spoke to me. I heard his American accent and fell hard. Visions of us getting married and moving to the USA, right between the Hollywood sign and the Empire State Building (at fourteen, geography wasn't really my strong point), and we'd live happily ever after.

It didn't really work out that way.

Aside from that weird nondate, nothing else even slightly romantic happened between us. Instead, we discovered a shared love of sci-fi movies, the Firestone books, and Nintendo, and became insta-friends, and it's been that way ever since. In movies, college changes everything. Couples break up, people change, friends stop hanging out.

Friends. Stop. Hanging. Out.

That's what really scares me.

I remember what I said before: "It doesn't get any better than this." With everything about to change, maybe it *won't* ever get any better than this. I'm beginning to realize just how important these two weirdos are to me. Every now and then, I glance at Jamie. All these years, I thought one day we would be more than friends. It seemed impossible and inevitable at the same time. But now it's painfully clear that that is never going to happen.

When making friends is the hardest thing in the world for you, you don't risk it all by telling one of them that you're in love with him.

CHAPTER 12

CHARLIE

THE SOUND OF QUEEN BEY'S "RUN THE WORLD" WAKES ME UP at nine a.m. I press my face into the pillow and reach a hand out, fumbling around the bedside table to turn my alarm off. I hit snooze and roll over, but sit up when I see Jamie and Taylor sleeping in the same bed. The room was so dark when I came in last night that I just assumed Jamie was on the couch.

They must have fallen asleep watching TV while I was with Mandy. I can't help but smile at how adorable they look, facing each other, close enough to touch, but not making physical contact. It sums up their relationship perfectly: both wanting to be close, but not close enough that it gives away how they really feel about each other.

I pick up my pillow and throw it at them to wake them up. It lands on Taylor's head, but she doesn't even flinch. Jamie rubs his eyes and gently lifts the pillow off her head, then throws it back at me, hitting me in the face. I fall back on the bed, laughing.

"Guys," I say. "Wake up! I have the morning free before the panel. Let's do something!"

Jamie props himself up on an elbow. "Like what?"

Tay wakes up then, groaning and muttering something about going back to sleep.

I jump off my bed and onto theirs. "Come on, we've hardly had a chance to hang out this weekend." She opens her eyes, and I give her my best pout, making her laugh.

"What do you want to do?" she asks with a yawn, and I grin.

An hour later, we're fed, showered, caffeinated, and exploring the aisles of SupaCon. We're only on the floor a few minutes before Tay grabs my arm with both hands and squeezes so tight I think she's going to rip it off.

"Charlie," she whispers, her eyes wider than her smile. "Look!" She points over the crowd.

Through the window into the street, I see something gold and sparkling and bigger than my house. "Is that . . . ?"

Tay nods so fast she reminds me of a bobblehead. "A Queen Firestone *jumping castle!*" She spins around to find Jamie, who's perusing a *Naruto* box set at the Viz Media booth. She pokes him in the ribs and grins. "Jamie, look!"

He follows her direction and laughs when he sees it. "You've died and gone to heaven, haven't you?"

She nods frantically again. "You comin'?"

"Nah. I'll catch up. I'm in my own version of heaven: manga and anime!"

"Have fun!" Tay says as she grabs my arm and pulls me outside through the crowd.

When we join the line, I notice the two teenage boys in front of us glancing back at me. At first I think they're just admiring my Ms. Marvel T-shirt, but then one turns around and says, "Are you Charlie Liang?"

I freeze for a moment, trying to remember where I've met them before, but then I realize they recognize me from my work, and I beam with pride. "Yes! I am! Did you see *The Rising*?"

His friend elbows him in the side. "I told you it was her!"

The first boy gives me a sheepish smile. "I didn't recognize you; your hair is so different. And no, we haven't seen *The Rising* yet, but we're going next week, and we can't wait!" He sticks his hand out. "I'm Eric, and this is my boyfriend, Jayesh."

"We watch your channel all the time," the second boy adds when I shake his hand.

"That's so cool! Thank you!"

I introduce Tay just as Jamie joins us.

"Are you vlogging while you're here?" Jayesh asks.

We move forward in line. "Hopefully. I might be doing a collab with a pretty big YouTuber."

Their eyes widen. "Who?" they ask in unison.

I tell them I shouldn't say, and they start rattling off names. When they say Alyssa Huntington, I give my best poker face—but it fails miserably.

"Oh my God!" Eric says. "I love her! You two would rock a collab!"

I lift my index finger to my lips and smile. "Don't tell anyone. Nothing's official yet."

Eric puts a hand over his heart. "Your secret is safe with us."

The five of us chat while we wait, then I take a few selfies with them, and before we know it, we're all climbing into the castle.

Inside it's dim and disorienting, and Tay grabs my hand. Jamie launches forward, bouncing so hard it sends us into the air.

Eric and Jayesh bounce by us hand in hand, then Jamie flies toward us, missing us by an inch and landing on his face. Tay reaches down to help him up, and all of us are laughing so hard we can't talk. The three of us jump around in a circle, holding hands and spinning too fast for people who just had breakfast. I notice Tay keeps letting go of my hand to hold her shirt down, and I hope she's not feeling too self-conscious. But the smile on her face tells me she's having fun, even if she is. As everything blurs around me, I think I see a familiar face in the crowd outside. I'm so distracted I lose my footing and slip onto my butt with my head still spinning.

I reach up and slap Tay on the thigh. "Hey, am I seeing things, or is that . . . ?"

She gasps and falls to my side, trying to catch her breath. "Alyssa . . . Huntington . . . outside!"

Jamie sits beside her, still laughing.

"Alyssa Huntington is right there," Tay says. "She's watching us."

She's far away, but she sees me. I can tell by her smile. "I should probably wave or something, right?"

Tay and Jamie nod, so I wave. Alyssa waves back, and I hear Tay squeal.

"Get the hell out there!" Tay says.

"Nah," I say. "We're hanging out. I've gotta go do the panel in, like, five minutes anyway."

Jamie wonkily stands up and proceeds to bounce so close to me that I'm soaring into the air. "I'm gonna keep doing this until you go talk to her."

Tay laughs and stands up to join him in pushing me out of the castle.

"Okay!" I say. "I'm going, I'm going. I'll see you after the panel."

"Cool," Tay says, edging me farther outside. "Go get her!"

Alyssa says something to her handler as I walk toward her. The handler nods, and Alyssa takes a few steps forward to meet me.

"Hey," she says with a flirty smile. "You look like you're having fun."

I point my thumb toward the castle. "You should get in there; it's like being a kid again."

"I would, but I'm on my way to a fan meet-up." She looks back at her handler, who gestures to his watch, and she nods. "You wanna come?" She says it casually, but the way she watches me and waits for an answer makes me think there's nothing casual about it.

I frown and slide my hands into my pockets. "I can't, sorry.

I've got a panel for *The Rising* soon. I should probably make my way to the green room."

She shrugs it off. "That's cool."

I desperately want to see her again, so I push away my nerves and go for it. "But I'm free later today, if you still want to do that collab?"

A wide smile spreads across her face. "Love to." Her handler steps forward and taps her on the shoulder, and she takes a step back. "I'll text you."

I let out a happy sigh. "Okay, great. See you later!"

She winks. "Can't wait."

I watch as she walks away, replaying her sexy wink over and over in my mind.

I take a seat at the long table, impressed that whoever provided my nameplate managed to spell my name right. I smile and wave at the crowd as they cheer for us.

The crowd quiets down, and the moderator begins the discussion. Tim Richards, the director of *The Rising* and its upcoming sequel, is seated next to me. Reese is supposed to be here, but Mandy told me he's unwell. The audience has been told he has another commitment, but really he's sleeping off the beer. Whatever the reason, I'm glad to finally be free from him.

Sitting here in front of all these fans, I feel both honored and completely out of my depth.

Just be cool.

The first question is addressed to Tim.

"Is it true that there will be a sequel?"

"Yes."

The audience cheers for at least thirty seconds. Once it's quietened down again, he continues. "We're very excited to announce that there will be a sequel. I've read the screenplay, and I'm very excited about it."

Question number two is for me, and they waste no time getting to the topic that's on everyone's minds. "Charlie, will both you and Reese be returning for the sequel, even though you're no longer an item?"

I smile, trying to hide my nerves. "I'll be returning for the sequel, but Reese won't be." I get the feeling she wants me to elaborate, but I end it there.

Tim leans forward. "I'm assuming everyone here has seen *The Rising,* but in case you haven't, I'm about to give away a major spoiler, so cover your ears." He waits, and a few people cover their ears. "Reese's character, Will, died at the end. He won't be coming back—zombie or otherwise."

A few chuckles can be heard in the audience. The moderator ushers in the next question, which is for me: "What do you think of all the fans who still support the Chase ship so strongly?"

I bite my bottom lip and shift uncomfortably in my chair. "I find it very flattering that the fans care so much about us. We shared so much of our relationship with the fans, and the fans really connected with that. A lot of those fans felt like they were a part of it—which I understand, because I've felt that way about couples myself—but when we broke up, I was surprised to see people so devastated. People uploaded YouTube videos of themselves crying. It was really hard to see." I clear my throat. "I just hope everyone can move on, because I'm really happy. And it's no secret that Reese has well and truly moved on."

The audience laughs. I probably shouldn't have said that.

Just then, I spot Alyssa poking her head through the staff doors at the back of the room. She grins and gives me a wave before disappearing again.

Her pop-in was so quick that I wonder if I imagined it, but then my phone vibrates on the table, and I see a text.

Alyssa: Couldn't stay, on my way to another meeting. You look good up there. The spotlight suits you ;) I'm free in an hour if you want to do the collab. Hilton Hotel, room 546.

If I wasn't on a stage in front of over a thousand people right now, I'd do a happy dance.

CHAPTER 13

TAYLOR

ABOUT TEN MINUTES AFTER CHARLIE LEAVES, JAMIE AND I climb out of the jumping castle, exhausted but energized from laughing so hard.

"Where to now?" I ask, surveying the crowded street.

"Come on," he says. "I've got something I want to show you." He leads me back into the main hall and past the many aisles until we reach the end. "I saw this when I was looking at the SupaCon map earlier. Stand right here and close your eyes."

He gently covers my eyes with his hands and turns me around. His touch makes my heart dance. He removes his hands. "Open."

My eyes snap open, and I see a narrow, winding aisle packed with people. An archway at the entrance reads FIRESTONE LANE in gold cursive letters.

I squeal. I decide here and now to never hold back my excited squeals again.

"Holy awesomeness, Batman! I read about this on the SupaCon blog last week. It's even bigger than I imagined. Do you want to go in?" I ask him, my eyes wide and pleading.

His lips pull up into a smile. "Do I want to spend the next five hours watching you gaze lovingly at all the swag in there? Sure, why not." He nudges me. "Of course! Why do you think I brought you here?"

I squeal again. I reel my smile back and put on a serious face. "Come with me if you want to fangirl," I say in my best Arnie voice, and then I laugh at my own hysterical wit.

He shakes his head and laughs. "Okay, Taylornator. Just promise me you won't overdose on Queen Firestone swag," he jokes. "I don't know CPR."

I take his hand and pull him toward Firestone Lane. "I can't promise anything."

Stepping under the arch is like walking through a portal into another world—my favorite world. "It's like we're *in* Everland! At the village market!" I clap my hands rapidly and begin a slow walk past the booths, wanting to soak in every bit of it. Everything is so beautiful that I don't know where to look first. Two little girls engage in a sword fight in front of a booth selling cosplay daggers, swords, and armor.

"I am the one true queen!" one yells.

"Nuh-uh!" the other argues. "I am!"

I stop at a table covered in silver jewelry and gemstones, picking up the ones that sparkle the brightest.

"Tay!" Jamie calls, and I glance around to see him poking his head out of a rack of clothes across the lane. "So much swag!"

I hurry over, ecstatic to find dozens of Firestone shirts in my size. After some serious browsing and decision-making, I choose three: two black graphic tees with Queen Firestone on them and one long-sleeved tee that says SKYLER IS MY ONE TRUE QUEEN.

I look in my wallet, trying to figure out how much I can afford to buy. "It's a good thing I left room in my suitcase for purchases."

We wander up and down the lane for another hour, until we're so hungry we can hear our stomachs over the crowd. On our way to the cafeteria, Jamie stops me.

"Tay, look," he says, nodding toward the comic book section. He lights up with excitement.

"Let's check it out," I say, knowing comics are to him what books are to me. We make a beeline for the nearest aisle, and he's instantly drawn to the Marvel booth. I keep walking and find Artists' Alley. I notice a familiar girl sitting quietly behind a table lined with a colorful selection of graphic novels and go in for a closer look.

The girl eyes me nervously for a moment, then smiles. "Hi."

"Hey!" I say, suddenly remembering who she is. "Remember me? Taylor? I minded your spot in line at the Skyler signing."

Recognition flashes in her eyes. "Oh, right! Hi!"

I pick up one of her novels. A girl with glasses is drawn on the cover, standing in superhero pose and smiling. From the title, it appears her name is Valentina, and the writer and illustrator is credited as Josie Ortiz. "Wow, you made this?"

She gives me a warm smile. "Yes."

I stare at the cover, in awe of her talent, but the words along the bottom make my heart stop: *The world's first graphic novel starring an autistic female protagonist!*

I hold the book out excitedly. "Shit! This is about an autistic girl?"

"Yeah," she says. "It's loosely based on my life."

I do a double take. I want to leap over the table and hug her, but I hug the book instead. "Um," I start, dragging my nails down my arm gently. "I have autism spectrum disorder, too."

Her eyes light up. "Oh, really? Are you an Aspie girl, too?"

I nod and look down at the floor. "Yes. I've never met another Aspie girl before. . . . I mean, that I know of. I guess I probably have, just not another girl who *knew* she was on the spectrum." I'm rambling, so I stop myself. "Does that make sense?"

Josie giggles a little. "Yes, it makes perfect sense." She stands up and steps closer to the table. "I actually just spoke about this on the Diversity in Media panel. When did you realize you're on the spectrum?"

"Only about six months ago. So it's still very new to me. I'm a bit confused by it all."

She seems to know exactly what I mean. "Yep, it can be an adjustment. I found out about two years ago, and I'm still learning. I was misdiagnosed with bipolar first, then my therapist suggested Asperger's, and it all just kind of clicked."

"Yeah, it was similar with me," I say. "I started seeing a psychologist to help with my anxiety, and she figured it out."

She breaks into a knowing smile. "I've got anxiety disorder, too. Mostly social anxiety, and complex PTSD from being bullied as a child."

"Really?" I ask. "But you just said you did a panel in front of all those people—"

She lets out a sigh and nods. "I know. I almost vomited before it started." I must be staring at her with a panicked expression, because she laughs. "It's okay. I didn't vomit."

I shake my head. "I could never do anything like that."

"I thought the same thing right up until I was sitting on the stage. But I adore my art, and it was such a great chance for me to show it to people. And I love SupaCon and feel welcome here—so that helped. My excitement won, and it makes the anxiety something I'm willing to put up with for today. But on other days, the anxiety, the meltdowns, the PTSD, they'll win. But not today. I just try to focus on that and take good care of myself, especially after. Social hangovers suck."

"Social what?"

"Social hangovers. It's like a normal hangover, but instead of being caused by too much alcohol, it's caused by too much social exposure and overstimulation of the senses."

I gasp. "I totally get those!"

She giggles. "Yeah, I think it's pretty normal for people on the spectrum or with anxiety."

"How do you cope with it?"

"Well, I've tried everything. Medication and therapy are great. I tried natural therapies, too. Yoga, acupuncture, meditation, aromatherapy. And a lot of it helped me relax. But it wasn't until I joined a few fandoms online and started taking illustration seriously that my anxiety really started to become easier to manage. It sounds so clichéd, but once I started doing more things that made me happy, it made everything else a little easier to deal with."

I hold my palms up. "Wait . . . are you saying that geeking out helps you cope?"

She nods. "Like nothing else."

I shuffle side to side for a moment, trying to think of what to say next. I want to keep talking to her; there's so much I want to ask, and then it all just surges out of me. "At first, I hated it. I felt like there was no hope, that no matter how hard I try, I'll never fit in and everything would always be hard for me." My bottom lip starts to quiver, but I keep going. "I fight every day, and too many times it's just not enough and the fear wins. I'm so fucking weak and everything is so fucking intense and sometimes I really hate it."

I gasp, covering my mouth with my hands as the tears pour out of me. I didn't mean to say all that. I feel exposed.

Tears fill her eyes, too. "Can I hug you?"

I nod, unable to speak. She walks around the table and hugs me. "I get it. Believe me, I know exactly how you feel." She lets go and steps back, wiping her eyes. "But please, please don't say that you're weak. You are not weak. People like us"—she pauses to clear her throat as more tears spill from her eyes—"we're brave. We're the ones who get up and face our worst fears every day. We keep fighting."

She crosses her arms and glances away. She's getting frazzled, and it's my fault.

"Let's say . . ." She pauses, looking back at me. "Let's say someone is terrified of heights, and in order to get out of the house every day she has to walk across a tightrope from fifty stories up. Everyone would say, 'Oh, she's so brave. She faces heights every day.' That's what we do. We walk a tightrope every day. Getting out the door is a tightrope. Going grocery shopping is a tightrope. Socializing is a tightrope. Things that most people consider to be normal, daily parts of life are the very things we fear and struggle with the most, and yet here we are, moving forward anyway. That's not weak." She reaches out and takes my hands. "We are the brave ones."

I don't know what to say, and even if I did, I don't think I'd be able to say it.

Her words have changed me, sparked something in me that I didn't know was there before.

"Are you okay?" she asks.

I nod and try to smile to reassure her.

"Listen," she says. "Everyday things can be harder for us, but that doesn't make us wrong or less than others. It took me a long time and a lot of self-loathing to learn that. Everyone has their strengths. And everyone has their kryptonite."

My throat aches from crying, so I just nod and whisper, "Thank you."

I buy the graphic novel, and Josie signs it for me. Then she reaches into her handbag and pulls out a card. "Here, this has all my deets on it. E-mail, Twitter, Tumblr, Insta, et cetera. I hope you stay in touch."

"I will." I give her my social media handles so we can follow each other.

Jamie walks over, carrying a bag full of comics. "There you are!"

I show him *Valentina*, pointing to the part where it says she's autistic, and his eyebrows shoot up. "That is so cool."

"This is Josie, remember from the Skyler signing? She created it."

Jamie introduces himself, picks up a copy from the table, and buys it then and there.

CHAPTER 14

CHARLIE

I STEP OFF THE ELEVATOR AND SCAN THE NUMBERS ON THE doors, searching for room 546. When I see it at the end of the hall, I take in a shaky breath, smooth a hand over my hair, and walk toward it, knocking lightly.

The door opens, and there she is. Dressed in a loose-fitting white T-shirt and leggings covered in a purple, starry galaxy print, she looks very relaxed and mind-blowingly gorgeous.

"Hey," she says with a smile.

"Hi."

She steps aside and holds the door open for me, and I walk in coyly.

"Can I get you a drink?" she asks, closing the door behind me. "I've got soda, juice, water . . . or I can order some room service?"

"Um, just water is fine, thanks." I look around her room. It's huge—much bigger than mine. It's ultrasleek and modern, all whites and grays and sharp angles, with wide windows overlooking the city. "Wow, what a view!"

"You should see it at sunrise," she says as she opens the fridge and pulls out a bottle of water. "Here you go."

"Thanks," I say. "So, where do you want to shoot?" I tap on my shoulder bag, filled with all my equipment.

She looks around. "Well, the light is best in this room. Maybe we can sit on the couch and set the camera up here?" She gestures to the coffee table.

"Yeah, sounds good." I place my bag on the floor next to the couch and start setting up. "I was thinking we could do a Q and A tag? Where we have about ten questions and we take turns answering them?"

Alyssa sits on the couch and crosses her legs. "Awesome."

"Those videos are always pretty popular, plus they're a lot of fun."

Plus, it's a great way for me to get to know Alyssa better, without it being too obvious that I'm interested in her.

I set up my lighting and pull the camera and tripod from the bag. "So," I say, glancing up at her from behind the tripod. "Are you enjoying SupaCon?"

Her face lights up. "Absolutely! This is my fifth year in a row, and I love it more and more every time." She leans forward, resting her arms on her knees. "But I miss being able to walk around the floor unrecognized. Hardly anybody knew who I was the first few times, but now . . ."

I nod. "Maybe you should cosplay it up. Pull a Bryan Cranston and wear a mask of one of your characters so no one knows it's you."

She laughs. "That would be awesome."

I place the camera on the tripod and press the ON button to adjust the picture. I can see Alyssa on the screen, watching me. Her eyes run down my body, and I shiver as though her gaze was a physical touch. I swallow hard and look up at her. "Okay, you ready to start?"

"Let's do it."

I hit RECORD and sit down next to her, pulling my phone out of my pocket and searching for random Q and A lists.

"All right," I say. "I've found a set of questions to answer. They're completely random, so if you don't feel comfortable answering one, just say pass and we can edit it out. Cool?"

Alyssa nods. "Cool."

I put my phone on the couch next to me. "Okay, I'm gonna do a quick intro. I'll say where we are, introduce you, you can wave or say hi or whatever you like, and then I'll introduce the tag and we'll start."

"Yep." She adjusts her position on the couch to be closer to me.

"Usually," I say, smiling nervously, "when I do collabs, the other person hides until I introduce them. But if you don't want to—"

"I can do that," she says, and then proceeds to slide off the couch onto the floor beside me. We both giggle at how awkward it all is.

I look straight at the camera and smile.

"Hey, everyone!" I wave at my millions of viewers. "I'm Charlie Liang, and I'm here at SupaCon! Today, I'm doing a very special collab with a very awesome person. You'll know her from her vlog, *Alyssa Says*, web series like *Venus Soaring*, the indie movie *Dear Ruby*, and her latest film, the terrifying horror movie *Stranger*. I'm so excited to be here with the one and only Alyssa Huntington!"

I hold my hands out, and Alyssa pops up, waving excitedly at the camera.

"Hey!" She sits next to me, this time even closer than before.

I try not to read too much into it; she could just be making sure she's in the shot.

Then she puts an arm around me.

Don't read too much into it.

"I'm so pumped to be here." She turns to me, her face only inches from mine, her eyes on my mouth.

Don't. Read. Too. Much. Into. It.

"What are we doing today, Charlie?"

I've completely forgotten.

"Um," I look down, searching for a clue to help me remember what this video is about. I grab my phone. "We're doing a Q and A session!"

I unlock the phone and see the list pop up. "Okay, so we each have to answer these questions as quickly as possible, saying the first thing that comes to mind. I haven't read these questions, so they'll be a surprise to both of us." I glance at Alyssa. "You ready?"

She slides her arm away and rubs her hands together. "Ready."

"Question one: What's your favorite TV show?"

Alyssa waves a hand like it's a no-brainer. "Easy. *House of Cards*."

"Ooh, that's a good one!" I say. "Mine is *The Walking Dead*."

Alyssa grins. "I love that show, too!"

"Question two: What's your favorite food?"

"Pizza," she says. "For sure. Love pizza."

"Mine is a Chinese dish that my mum makes. It's mapo doufu with tudou piar and mifan." Alyssa raises her eyebrows, impressed. "Basically, it's spicy tofu with sliced potatoes and rice. It's simple, but always reminds me of fun times sitting around the dinner table with my family."

"That sounds so good."

"It is! Okay, question three: Last book you read?"

Alyssa thinks for a moment, then looks at the camera. "*I Am Malala*. It was brilliant."

"I loved that book so much. The last book I read was *You're Never Weird on the Internet (Almost)* by Felicia Day, and it was so funny and insightful."

"Oh, I really want to read that!"

"Get it. She's so cool."

We giggle a little, and I try to compose myself. "Question four: What's your biggest fear?"

"Hmm," Alyssa thinks, pressing her lips to the side. "Losing the people I love."

I give her a sideways glance and am taken aback by the emotion on her face. I clear my throat and nod. "That's mine, too."

She locks eyes with me and gives me a small smile. I look

down at my phone and read the next question. "Question five: If you could have any superpower, what would it be?"

"That's a good one," she says, sitting back against the cushion and putting her arms behind her head. "Invisibility."

"I think mine would be to fly. Or read minds."

She smirks and looks at me. "Yeah. Mind reading would definitely come in handy."

Her gaze lingers, and I wonder if there's a subtle message in her words. I want to ask her whose mind she would like to read, but then I remember the camera is rolling and keep going.

"Question six: What's your ideal day?"

Alyssa leans forward, thinking. "I'd be in a new city. Maybe Paris or Copenhagen, with a clear schedule. I'd spend the whole day wandering around, going to museums, art galleries, restaurants. Seeing the sights, talking to locals, immersing myself in the culture." She sighs a happy sigh, and she looks like she's a million miles away.

"Wow," I say. "That sounds like a dream."

"Mhmm." She snaps out of it and turns to me. "What about you?"

"Well, I was going to say a day at Universal Studios followed by a movie marathon with my BFFs, but . . . I think I like your ideal day better."

This girl is a dream.

"Question seven," I say. I look down at the next question and hesitate, but decide to ask anyway. "Have you ever been in love?"

Alyssa's gaze falls to the coffee table, and she smiles to herself. "Yes. Once."

I feel her glance at me as she waits for my answer.

"Yes." I want to add "unfortunately," but I don't want to upset the Chase shippers. "Question eight: When you were a little kid, what did you want to be when you grew up?"

Alyssa smirks. "An astronaut. Or a scientist."

"Oh, that's awesome!"

"Yep." She straightens her shoulders proudly. "I was a huge science geek growing up. What about you?"

"I wanted to be a pro surfer when I was really little, then a fashion designer, but then I discovered YouTube."

Alyssa does a double take. "You can surf?"

"Yeah, I love surfing."

"That is so freaking cool," she says, looking impressed, which was exactly the reaction I wanted. "I've always wanted to learn how to surf."

I see my chance and take it. "You should come to Australia; I'll teach you."

"Done."

"Question nine: What's one thing you can't leave the house without?"

"I have two things: my cell phone and"—she tugs on a silver chain around her neck and pulls a silver crucifix up from under her T-shirt—"this necklace. It was my mother's. I never take it off."

"It's beautiful," I say with a smile, sensing its importance to her.

"Thank you."

"Okay, last question!" I scan the list for the final question, but pause when I see it. "Um, actually, that's it! We're done."

Alyssa cocks her head. "There's still one more. I can see it there."

I keep my eyes on the screen and close the window. "It's cool, we don't have to."

She chuckles. "What was it? Is it embarrassing?"

I glance up at her. "That depends."

She tilts her head toward me. "Tell me."

I laugh nervously. "Okay. It was: Do you have a crush?"

She laughs, too, nodding her head like she understands why I didn't want to ask it. "Yes."

"Yes what?"

She looks at the camera, her expression serious even though her mouth is still pulling up slightly. "Yes, I have a crush."

She turns to me, resting an elbow on her knee and her cheek on her hand. "Your turn." She raises an eyebrow, challenging me to answer the question.

I swallow and squeeze my eyes shut. "Yes."

Alyssa throws herself back against the couch, laughing at my total embarrassment. "I think you're blushing."

I touch my hands to my cheeks. "Am not."

"Mhmm." She smirks. She reaches up and takes a hand away from my cheek. She holds it there, and I look down at our hands, intertwined on the couch.

My heart is racing.

My mouth is dry.

I'm very aware of how soft her skin is on my own, of the way she's looking at me behind her long lashes, and of the blinking red light of my video camera.

She leans in, one hand holding mine and the other stroking a lock of my long pink hair between her fingers.

I close my eyes just before her mouth brushes against mine. My mind goes blank, my heart stops, and my breathing falters as I kiss her back. Her lips are even silkier than I imagined, soft and plump as they move over my mouth, my cheek, my neck, and then back to my mouth again.

It's a kiss that makes the rest of the world fall away. My universe consists only of her lips on mine.

We break away much too soon, then she exhales and slowly opens her eyes. "I have wanted to do that for over a year."

I gasp. "Seriously?"

She nods. "I told you; I've been watching your vlogs for a long time."

That reminds me of the video we're currently still making.

I glance over at the camera and grin sheepishly. "We should probably edit that last bit out."

Her lips twitch into an uneven smile. "Definitely."

CHAPTER 15

TAYLOR

QUEENOFFIRESTONE:

Okay, so I know I usually only post fandom stuff and
I've been posting a lot more personal things here this
weekend, but I've been learning a lot about myself here
at SupaCon. Things have been on my mind, and I feel
like if I don't let them out, I'm going to explode.

I just met someone like me. Another Aspie.

In one brief conversation, she made me see that there's
nothing wrong with me. I'm a perfectly normal Aspie
girl. I just feel broken because I'm trying to fit into a
nonautistic world. I'm a square peg trying to squeeze
myself into a round hole.

Up until now, I've done whatever I can to be normal and avoid leaving my comfort zone. But I'm starting to see that if you surround yourself with like-minded people, people who support you, then that comfort zone gets bigger and bigger.

And soon your comfort zone is the size of SupaCon.

For the first time in my life, I don't feel like I have to try to fit in, because I'm surrounded by people who are as passionate and excited about the same things I am.

For the first time, I'm not totally alone in my weirdness.

My weird is normal here.

My weird is embraced, accepted, and expected.

You guys, I'm starting to love my weird.

P.S: Everyone go follow @josiedrawscoolstuff and buy all the things! She rocks!

#AspieGirl #SupaConIsMyHome #LoveYourWeird

I hit POST and look up at Jamie, who's sitting across the table from me, reading Josie's book. "Is it awesome?"

"The awesomest," he says. "I can already see a few similarities between you and Valentina."

I pop an onion ring into my mouth. "Like what?"

He thinks for a moment. "Well, like in this scene. Valentina is drawing, and she's so focused on it that her abuela has to call her name three times before she hears her." He looks up at me and grins. "That's like you when you're writing. It's like you get sucked into a wormhole."

I laugh, and notice that even laughing feels different now. Lighter. Easier. Meeting Josie changed so much for me. "So," I say, tapping my feet on the floor while I sit. I take in a deep breath. "I think I'm gonna enter the SupaFan Contest."

His head snaps up. "Huh?"

"I want to enter the contest."

He sits up straight. "You do?"

"Yes."

He cocks his head to the side. "What made you change your mind?"

I shift awkwardly in my seat, already feeling nervous about my decision. "Talking to Josie." I know if I delve deeper into it with him, I'll cry, so I leave it at that.

Jamie smiles and pulls his phone out of his jeans pocket to check the time. "We better eat fast, then. I think the sign-up closes at three, and it's almost two thirty."

"Where do I sign up?"

"I'll check," he says as he unlocks his screen. "I saved the entry details on my phone in case you changed your mind." I wait hopefully as he reads. He runs a hand through his hair and grimaces. "It's on the other side of the building. In one of the smaller halls."

"Can we make it?"

He looks at the map on his screen, his eyes narrowed and forehead wrinkled as he tries to find the fastest route. "We can."

We quickly finish our meals, pay, and hurry back to the con.

"Follow me," Jamie says as we enter the building. He starts weaving through the crowd, and I follow close behind him. His long legs make him hard to keep up with, so I reach out and clutch his shirt so I don't lose him. He feels me holding him and glances back over his shoulder, winking at me.

Ten minutes later, we're running up to the hall entrance, where a woman waits with an iPad. "Are you here to sign up for the Queen Firestone SupaFan Contest?" she asks, a cheery smile plastered on her face.

"Yeah," I puff, catching my breath.

She asks my name and taps it onto the screen. "Okay, Taylor. You're all signed up! There are two rounds in this contest. Round one is called Queen of Cos, and it starts in about an hour. It's a cosplay contest. Do you have a Firestone costume?" I nod. "Great! Round two is called One True Queen; it's a trivia game based on the books and movies. That's at ten a.m. tomorrow."

I swallow the nerves trying to bubble up from inside me.

She gives me another smile. "Do you have any questions?"

Yes. About a million. But I shake my head. "No, I think I'm good."

"Great! See you back here in an hour." She starts talking to the next person wanting to sign up, and I turn around to leave.

Jamie is grinning at me. "Are you excited?"

"That's one word for it," I say. "I'm crapping my pants."

He laughs. "You'll be fine. You know everything about the books, movies, and Skyler. You're pretty much a pro fangirl."

I giggle. "I totally am."

"Okay," he says. "Let's get you back to the hotel to get your Firestone gear. You've got a cosplay contest to win."

An hour later, I'm backstage. My fingers are twirling my hair, pulling and twisting and smoothing it out again and again. I keep my head down, but sneak glances at all the other contestants. Most are wearing the same outfit as I am: the long black trench coat, torn gray jeans, Doc Martens, and a dark charcoal tank top. But few trench coats have the silver crown sewn into the back like mine. I'm hoping that gives me an advantage, but I have no idea how these contests work. Thinking it will help to know what to expect when we go out there, I peek around the wall.

The hall is filled with people.

The lights are bright.

The chatter is loud.

I step back. Peeking was definitely a bad idea.

"I can't do this," I whisper. I spin on my heels and start to leave, my heart racing in my chest.

"Taylor?" a cheery voice calls. I turn to see Brianna walking toward me, in full Firestone cosplay. "Hey! It's me, Brianna!"

"Hey," I say, pulling my hand away from my hair and shoving it into my pocket.

"Are you nervous? I'm so nervous!" She clasps her hands over her heart and flops her tongue out. "I think I'm going to pass out I'm so nervous."

I force out a friendly chuckle. "Yeah, same."

She scrunches her face up into a smile. "I'm so glad it's not just me!" She swoops an arm into mine and huddles closer. "Let's stick together, you and me. We can be nervous wrecks together."

I pat her hand and nod. "Deal."

I can't bear to tell her I'm chickening out, so I stay. And as silly as it sounds, just having her say that we can stick together makes me feel a little better. Three teens in SupaCon staff T-shirts hand out square cards with numbers on them. I get number forty-four out of fifty. Brianna gets number forty-three. I hold my card against my chest to stop my hands from shaking. The woman with the iPad appears again, this time wearing a headset, and calls for us to be quiet so she can give us instructions. I fantasize about running away, just turning around and running as fast as I can until I'm back in our hotel room, lying on the bed with Jamie and watching movies. A voice in my head keeps telling me I can't do this, and if I could quit without embarrassing myself, I'd listen to it.

"Okay," headset woman says. "One by one, you'll go out onto the stage. Walk to the gold star in the middle of the floor, pause, hold your number in front of you so the judges can see. Then keep walking to the other end of the stage. If you want to pose or twirl or do something to get the audience cheering when you reach the middle, go for it. As long as it's not obscene or offensive, of course." She makes eye contact with a few people in the group. "Judges will be choosing winners based on craft, performance, and the way the audience reacts to you, so make sure they remember you if you want to get through to round two." She pauses to say something into her headpiece. "Everyone ready? Good."

One by one, contestants start walking along the stage.

Brianna goes before me, and I watch as she struts confidently across the stage, trying to soak up some of her courage. She twirls like a ballerina when she reaches the star, holds her number card out, and ends it with a bow. I'm instantly jealous of how well she's doing.

Then it's my turn. I shift into autopilot, and everything that follows is like an out-of-body experience.

I enter the stage and suddenly become horrifyingly aware of how I walk.

I try to swing my hips more but then stop, worried that I just look stupid.

I'm so focused on trying to walk normally that I completely miss the star.

When I realize, I gasp, spin around and run back a few steps.

The audience laughs. I laugh, too—even though I'm dying inside.

I look down, making sure my feet are directly on the star, and hold my number card out. I even manage to give a big, toothy grin like I'm in a beauty pageant.

And then I walk as quickly as possible off the stage, feeling like I'm in over my head.

"That was so smart!" Brianna whispers to me. "Pretending to forget to stop on the star. It was so cute and awkward. The audience loved it! They'll definitely remember you after that."

I snort with laughter. "Yeah. Go me." I realize I should say something complimentary about her stage walk, and add, "They'll remember you, too. Nice touch with the bow."

She grins. "Thank you!" She holds up her hands, her fingers crossed. "Let's hope we both get in!"

I cross my fingers, too, as the last few contestants join us backstage, all of them breathing a sigh of relief once their walk is over. It's comforting to know I'm not the only one filled with nerves.

"And now," Brianna says as the fiftieth contestant exits the stage, "we wait."

Ten minutes later, after anxiously chatting with Brianna about our shared passion for Queen Firestone, which greatly calmed me down, cheery iPad woman tells us only ten contestants will be making it through to the next round. I'm eager to find out if I'll be one of them, even though a huge part of me would be relieved if I'm not. We're called onto the stage and told that winners should step forward when their number is called.

"The contestants going through to round two are . . . seven."

A girl in a Queen Firestone armor costume jumps forward, giggling uncontrollably as the audience cheers.

"Please hold applause until all numbers have been called," the host says. "Eleven. Eighteen. Twenty-two. Twenty-eight. Thirty-one. Thirty-six. Forty-three." Brianna squeals and steps forward, beaming with pride. "Forty-four. And forty-nine."

Electric excitement surges through me. I look at Brianna, who's waving me forward, and I move up and stand next to her.

"We're in!" she whispers excitedly, giving me a thumbs-up.

I stand there, smiling out over the crowd, and see Jamie sitting in the front row, grinning from ear to ear. He sees me smiling at him and winks. Once we're free to leave, I run down the stairs of the stage. Most of the audience has already left, but Jamie is waiting for me, leaning against a door frame.

"Hey, loser," I say as I skip over to him.

He tsks and shakes his head. "She wins one cosplay contest and suddenly everyone else is 'loser,'" he teases.

"Not *every*one else. Just you." I give him a mischievous smile.

He rolls his eyes and pushes himself off the wall. "I know you love me."

My heart does a weird double thump in my chest before I realize he's joking. My cheeks don't get the memo, and they burn red hot. His eyes flick to my cheeks, but he doesn't point it out or laugh at me, which is greatly appreciated. He looks away and smiles. "Come on, we can celebrate your win in the *Star Wars* aisle. There's a Hoth-themed ice cream parlor there."

As we walk through the crowd, I can still feel my stomach twisting in knots from being in front of all those people. But a strange high fills me, too, like adrenaline mixed with elation. It feels weird, but good.

CHAPTER 16

CHARLIE

I'M SITTING ON ALYSSA'S COUCH, PRETENDING TO BE FOCUSED on editing the video.

But really, I'm focused on her.

She's standing by the television, looking over the room service menu and humming to herself. "What do you think? Nachos? Salad? Club sandwich? Pasta?"

My stomach rumbles. "Nachos would be amazing right now."

She nods. "Agreed."

She turns around, and my eyes dart back to the laptop screen. When I glance up at her again, her smile widens, and my heart skips a beat. She picks up the phone and orders lunch while flicking through channels on the TV absentmindedly, stopping on an old episode of *The Simpsons*.

"Okay," she says after hanging up. "Lunch is on its way. How's the video coming along?"

"Almost done editing. It always takes forever to upload, so I'll just ask my manager to upload it for me later."

I keep my eyes on the screen as Alyssa walks over and sits next to me, putting her feet up on the coffee table. She seems so relaxed, and I feel so on edge. No one has ever made me so nervous before. I look at her from the corner of my eye; she's watching the TV. Bart says something funny, and she throws her head back in laughter. Her smile goes all the way up to her eyes and makes me smile, too.

"Who was it?" I ask, without fully intending to. My question surprises both of us.

Alyssa leans back. "Who was what?"

My mouth suddenly feels dry, and I clear my throat. "The person you were in love with." The invasiveness of my question makes me backtrack. "Sorry, you don't have to answer that. It's none of my business."

She shakes her head. "No, it's okay. She was a girl I met in college. We were together for two years. But when I started getting more involved in YouTube and acting, I moved to LA, so we broke up." I get the feeling there's much more to that story, but I don't want to pry any further.

"What about you?" she asks. "Was it Reese?"

I purse my lips and nod. "Yep. Unfortunately."

She offers a sympathetic smile. "That didn't end well, did it?"

I let out a laugh. "That's an understatement."

She opens her mouth to say something, but then closes it again. I tilt my head to the side. "What is it?"

She hesitates again, but obliges me anyway. "I'm just gonna be blunt. What did you see in him? In the few times I've met him, he's just been so egotistical. And you're so . . . *not*."

I cringe. "I guess I didn't see it." It comes out more like a question. "Or he didn't show me that side until I was already in too deep. We met on set, playing a couple, so I think it was a mix of falling in love with the character he played and being swept up in the idea of being with *the* Reese Ryan. Being wanted by a guy that everyone else wanted to be with. Ugh, that sounds pathetic, doesn't it?"

She frowns. "No. It's not pathetic. I can relate. My ex-girlfriend wasn't a movie star, but to me she was . . . everything. Everyone wanted to be with her, too. But she chose me. I didn't like myself much back then, and having her look at me the way she did made me feel like I was worth something."

"And when you broke up?"

She sucks in a deep breath. "I didn't see how much of my self-worth had been tied into that relationship until it was over. The hardest part wasn't leaving her behind; it was feeling like I'd left pieces of myself behind. The only pieces I liked."

I take her hand in mine and shuffle closer. "How did you get through it?"

"I threw myself into work. Getting to LA was a new chance for me. I made a promise to myself to not get involved with anyone for a while, until I felt like I could give myself to a relationship without *losing* myself to a relationship."

I clutch a hand to my heart. "That's what happened to me.

I lost myself in Reese. My whole world became about how he was feeling, what he was doing, what he was thinking. All I cared about for almost a year was doing whatever I could to be what he wanted. Why did I do that to myself?"

It is a rhetorical question, but she answers it anyway. "Love is intense. You break down all your walls to let someone in. But if they're not good for you, they can tear you up from the inside. And you think what you have together is love, so you let them."

Our gazes linger on each other, and I feel lucky to be allowed to look at her like this. To take in every shade of brown in her eyes and discover the tiniest of smile lines around her mouth. My eyes wander over her shoulders and onto the tattoos covering her arms. I absentmindedly trace my index finger over a particularly eye-catching artwork of a woman with strong eyebrows and three huge flowers in her hair. Alyssa swallows hard at my touch.

"Who's this?" I ask, looking at the tattoo.

"Frida Kahlo. My favorite artist. She was amazing."

I slowly move my finger up to another portrait inked onto her soft skin. It's of a black woman wearing a NASA astronaut suit. "And who's this?"

"That is Dr. Mae Jemison, the first black woman in space. She's also a dancer and a professor, has nine doctorates, speaks multiple languages, and guest starred on *Star Trek*. I could literally talk about her and Frida for hours."

"Go on, then."

She tilts her head, and her eyebrows pinch together suspiciously. "You want to hear me ramble on about art and science?"

I lean my elbow on the back of the couch and get comfortable next to her. "Yes."

There's a powerful dreaminess in her eyes as she talks. Her passion is crystal clear and so beautiful to witness that I don't dare interrupt. She tells me about the nights she spent as a child reading books about the stars and the planets. About how her dad would buy her a new kid-friendly science experiment kit every year for her birthday and then spend all day doing them with her. About the time a boy in her science club told her girls couldn't be astronauts. She went home and told her mother, a graphic designer, who made her a T-shirt with GIRLS CAN DO ANYTHING! printed on it. She wore it proudly to school the next day. She told me about the time her parents drove hours across the country to introduce her to someone they wanted her to know.

"When we walked into the lab," she says with a smile, "there was a black woman standing there in a lab coat and gloves, working. I'd never met a black female scientist before. I was so excited. She took us out to lunch and answered all my questions. When we were saying good-bye, she gave me my own lab coat. I still have it."

"Why did you leave college before finishing your degree?" I ask. "You seem so passionate about it."

She looks at me with determination in her eyes. "I'm going back. I needed to get away from there, from that relationship I was in. Then my acting career started taking off, so that's kept me busy. But I'm getting that degree. I've actually been thinking about taking a break and going back to finish. Acting and vlogging is fun, but it's not my dream."

She starts telling me about her college days, and I sit and watch and listen to her. And then suddenly, she's kissing me again. It's different from before. The hesitancy and first-kiss nerves are gone, and now she's not holding anything back. Neither am I. She tangles her hands in my hair, and I slide an arm around her waist, ushering her closer. Her lips are so soft; I could kiss them for hours and still want more.

There's another knock on the door, and she groans. "Sorry. Be right back." I pull her back and wipe my lipstick off her mouth, then she smiles and runs to the door. I try to compose myself, flattening my hair with my hands. Alyssa opens the door and a hotel staff member walks in, pushing a cart.

"Oh," she says, remembering. "Nachos!"

He places the plates on the coffee table, then he and Alyssa walk back to the door.

"How do they look?" she asks after she's closed the door.

I lift the lids and practically drool at the sight. "Um, only *amazing*."

She sits down on the rug next to the coffee table, and we start eating.

"So." She pulls a nacho from the cheesy pile. "What are you doing tonight?"

I take a bite, the chip crunching in my mouth, and wipe at a drop of salsa that fell onto my chin. "Dunno. What about you?"

She scratches her arm nervously. "Do you, maybe, want to have dinner with me?"

Surprised, I choke a little on the nachos and cover my mouth so I can cough.

She sits up straight. "Oh my God, are you okay?"

I cough again and nod, giving her a thumbs-up.

"Fine," I croak. I clear my throat and try again. "I'm fine."

"You sure? You want some water?"

I shake my head. "No, thanks. I was just surprised."

She cocks her head. "Surprised?"

"That you asked me out. I wasn't expecting it."

"Oh," she says, somewhat confused.

I feel like she's misunderstood me. "I mean, I was *hoping* you would ask me out," I say, and her shoulders relax. "I just wasn't expecting it right then, when I had a mouthful of guacamole."

She lets out a breathy laugh. "Oh, okay. I'm with you."

We sit quietly for a few beats, then she lifts a shoulder to her ear and raises an eyebrow. "So . . . do you want to have dinner with me tonight?"

I slap a hand over my eyes in embarrassment. "Oh God. Yes. Sorry. Yes, I do. I really do." I peek out from behind my fingers to see her giggling at me. "Ugh. Can you tell I'm nervous?"

She shrugs nonchalantly. "A little. But it's cute."

I roll my eyes at myself. My stomach does a flip at the thought of going on a date with Alyssa Huntington—and then it hits me.

A date.

With one of the most famous YouTubers in the world. An up-and-coming movie star with a fan base quadruple the size of mine. She can't even go on the con floor without being swarmed by fans. There are fan blogs dedicated to her love life, shipping her with any girl she's seen in public with.

I'm not ready for that kind of attention again. Not after Chase.

The risk of getting my heart broken and splattered on screens all over the world is too high. I can't go through that again.

I swallow nervously. "Um . . . can I make a request?"

"Sure."

"Can we, maybe, not go anywhere too public?"

Hurt flashes in her eyes. "Why? Because we're two women?"

I wave my hands in front of myself, shaking my head. "No! Not at all. I'm very out and very proud. I just . . ." I sigh. "My relationship with Reese was incredibly public, right from the start. Nothing was private. It was hard. And then it all ended up blowing up in my face. I couldn't escape it. I really like whatever is happening between you and me, and right now I'd really like to just keep it ours, away from everything else. Does that make sense?"

She nods, but seems unsure. "It makes sense." She comes and sits next to me on the couch. "But only because this is still new. If whatever this is becomes something more, I don't want to hide it. Okay?"

"Okay."

She reaches out and takes my hand, smoothing her thumb over my palm softly. "And I really like what's happening here, too."

Her gaze lingers on mine, and I feel my heartbeat picking up. A mix of emotions swirl inside me like a whirlpool. It's confusing, exciting, and terrifying all at once, and I don't want it to stop. I feel like a giant mess of contradicting thoughts and feelings, all moving so quickly I can't grab hold of any of it.

Whatever this is between Alyssa and me, it's glorious, it's

unexpected, and it's all happening so fast—and yet not nearly fast enough.

My phone buzzes. It's Mandy. "Sorry, one sec." I get up and walk over to the window to answer it. "Hey, Mands."

"Charlie, can you meet us at the front of the con? *Entertainment Now* wants to do a piece on you and Reese going through the new *Rising* live-action experience."

I glance over at Alyssa.

I don't want to leave. But I have a job to do. "Sure. Be there in ten."

When I hang up, Alyssa is frowning. "You gotta go?"

I pout. "Sorry. I've got some more press to do."

"That's fine. I've got a new script to read, anyway." She stands up and takes my hand. "I'll see you tonight. Pick you up at eight?"

"Sounds perfect!"

I give her my hotel and room number, pack up my laptop and filming equipment, and start to leave.

"Can't wait to see you again." She kisses me, and now I *really* don't want to leave.

She walks me to the door, opens it, and leans casually against the frame. I have to force myself to step into the hallway. "I'll see you later."

"Later." She watches as I walk away. I know because I look over my shoulder way too many times to still be cool. I step into the elevator and wait until the doors close before I swoon all over myself.

CHAPTER 17

TAYLOR

I'M BUYING A REY ACTION FIGURE IN THE *STAR WARS* AISLE when we get a text from Charlie.

Charlie: Hey! You guys free? Studio wants me & Reese to do The Rising live-action experience. Wanna join? It's got zombies!

I text her back: That. Sounds. AWESOME! Where? When?

Jamie and I meet Charlie outside the entrance to the maze. I'm still buzzing after making it through to the next round of the SupaFan contest. Usually, running through a maze with zombies on my tail would probably be something I'd say no to. But I feel like I've chugged five Red Bulls, so I figure, what the hell?

"Hey!" Charlie beams when she sees us. "How's your day been?"

"I entered the Queen Firestone SupaFan Contest!" It comes out louder than intended, and I laugh.

Her jaw drops. "And?"

"I made it through to round two!"

"That's bloody awesome, TayTay!" Charlie high-fives me and hangs an arm around my shoulders. She gives me a weird look, like she wants to tell me something, but then glances quickly at Reese and decides against it.

I poke her in the stomach. "What?"

She takes me and Jamie by the hands and pulls us near the doorway to the maze, away from everyone else.

Jamie is standing close behind me, leaning a hand against the wall. "You've got big news, don't you?" he asks with a cheeky grin.

"The biggest!" She makes a squealing sound in the back of her throat. "Alyssa kissed me!"

Jamie and I gasp. I grab her hands and squeeze my lips shut to suppress my scream. "Seriously?"

She nods. "And that's not all. She asked me out. We're having dinner tonight!"

I look up at Jamie. His eyes are shooting out of his head and his mouth is hanging open into a smile. "You're going to dinner with Alyssa Huntington?"

"I am."

We want to talk more, but Mandy calls us over.

Charlie squeezes our hands. "Don't tell anyone yet. Not even

Mandy. I don't want this getting online, not after the circus I've been living in since me and Reese. I really, *really* like Alyssa, and I don't want the media or the fans involved until I'm ready."

We nod. "Of course," I say, sliding my thumb and forefinger over my lips in a zipping motion.

Mandy comes over. "Everyone ready? *Entertainment Now* is here. They want to film you running through the maze. It'll be great publicity for the movie."

"We're gonna be on *Entertainment Now*?" Jamie asks.

"Well, maybe in the background. The cameras will be on Charlie and Reese."

Jamie's shoulders sink in disappointment, and I elbow him in the side. "Cheer up! You're about to be thrown into a zombie apocalypse! This is your dream!"

He chuckles. "True."

Mandy drags Charlie away to do a quick premaze interview with Reese and the *EN* reporter.

Jamie taps my shoe with his and tilts his head toward mine. "You sure you want to do this?"

I put my fists on my hips and stick out my chest, striking a Wonder Woman pose. "I can handle it. I'm SuperTay!"

He presses his lips together and puffs out his cheeks a little before bursting into laughter. "More like SuperDork."

I glare at him, holding my pose and trying not to laugh. "I could survive in there longer than you."

He lifts his chin and raises an eyebrow. "You wanna bet?"

"Let's do it," I say.

The corner of his mouth lifts into a half smile. "Okay. We'll race. The winner gets to hijack the loser's Twitter and tweet something embarrassing."

I narrow my eyes at him. I have way more followers than he does, and I'm not exactly fast on my feet. My reputation in the fandom could be at stake. But I'd love to smash that smug look off his face, and right now I'm feeling pretty invincible. "Deal."

Five minutes later, Reese, Charlie, Jamie, and I are standing in a dark room with the EN crew, waiting for the double doors to open into the maze. Creepy groaning and gurgling sounds are rolling out of speakers in the ceiling, and shadows are moving slowly over the boarded-up windows. I'm already scared, but I'm determined to make it to the end of the maze ahead of Jamie.

"Ready?" a voice calls from outside the doors.

"Ready!" Reese calls back.

I roll up the sleeves of my coat and move my weight from one foot to another, staring at the door. Jamie is next to me, glancing down at me every now and then with an evil grin. He's trying to psych me out. The sound of metal scraping against metal startles me, and the doors blow open with a loud *whoosh*. Light floods in, and Charlie is the first to launch into the maze. Reese is hot on her heels, with the reporter and cameramen racing to keep up.

Jamie and I make a run for it, trying to push each other out of the way and take the lead. I'm so focused on what he's doing that I don't see the zombie waiting in the wings. It leaps out at me from the right, and I jump back into Jamie's chest, screaming. He holds my shoulders and pulls me away, turning me around so he's between me and the zombie, which is chained to a wall and out of reach.

"Whoa," Jamie says, crouching slightly to look into my eyes. "Are you okay? Do you want to go back?"

I shrug his hands off me and hold my chin up high, acting calm even though my heart is pounding. "No. I'm fine." I smile up at him wryly. "And I'm going to kick your ass."

I burst into a sprint, leaving him behind. I glance over my shoulder to see him still standing there with a dumbfounded grin on his face. Then he starts running after me, and I scream a little, surprising myself. Charlie and Reese are nowhere to be seen, but I spot a cameraman running awkwardly ahead and assume he's following them.

We're in an alleyway—or a set that looks exactly like an alleyway, at least. Faux brick walls on either side of me, Dumpsters and rubbish bins every few feet. Broken windows and graffiti all around me. I keep running, knowing zombies could be anywhere and Jamie is gaining on me. The alley divides into two, and I stop to decide which path to take. They are identical, like mirror images of each other. I hear Jamie coming up behind me.

"What took you so long?" I turn around to see a gross, rotting face glaring down at me. One of the zombies. Even though I know it's only an actor wearing incredibly impressive makeup, I still scream. My feet start moving, and I choose the alley on the left.

It's a dead end. The far wall is a huge billboard-style image of the Sydney Opera House, the kind they must use in movies to make it look like they're in Sydney instead of on a Hollywood set. A lightbulb goes off in my mind, and I realize this is an exact scene from *The Rising*. In the scene, Charlie's Ava gets cornered by a horde and has to squeeze through a gap between buildings to get out.

A screech echoes behind me, and I spin around. Five zombies are closing in on me.

I run to the end of the alley and search for the elusive gap, finding it tucked away in the corner. It's dark, but much wider than the gap in the movie. I start running through it, discovering it's more of a tunnel than anything else. After turning a sharp corner, I suddenly find myself in some sort of factory or warehouse. The only light is from flickering fluorescent bulbs hanging from the ceiling. Shabby wooden walls are on either side of me, and I swear I can hear heavy breathing coming from somewhere. Something drips onto my forehead, and I look up to see a prop corpse hanging from a chain attached to a pipe.

"Ew!" I gasp and wipe the fake blood from my face. I edge forward, my arms outstretched in front of me to guide my way. I hear a shrill scream and recognize it instantly: it's Reese. I laugh quietly to myself and make a mental note to watch the next episode of *Entertainment Now* so I can see his face.

A hand grabs hold of my shoulder and I jump five feet into the air. I try to run, but it's got my arm. I hear a groan in my ear and feel warm breath on my neck.

"Raar!" the voice says. "Brains!"

I squeeze my eyes shut as a series of loud shrieks burst out of me.

"Tay!" Jamie says, laughing. "Relax! It's just me."

I turn to face him, exhaling a long sigh. "You scared the crap out of me, you asshole!"

I clutch my heart and feel it racing in my chest, then punch him in the arm.

He bites his bottom lip to stop his laughter. "Sorry."

I keep walking, and he squishes in alongside me. "How freaking awesome is this? I never want to leave."

"That's good," I say. "Then I'll definitely win."

A bald zombie with a disgusting gash in his skull leaps out from behind a corner, and Jamie and I stumble backward, screaming and grabbing hold of each other.

"Fucking hell," I say as the zombie disappears.

"Hey," Jamie says, still clutching my arm. "I know we're racing and all, but how about we call a truce on that? Just until we get out of this maze section. I don't want to go through this alone."

I nod repeatedly. "Yes. A thousand times yes."

Our fingers dig into each other's sides. Even with the threat of zombies all around us, I'm keenly aware that this is the longest Jamie and I have ever held on to each other.

Sure, sometimes we flirt—or attempt to flirt—but we generally avoid physical contact. As we huddle together through the shadows, I decide to let myself enjoy it. Even if it's just two friends helping each other through a fake apocalypse.

After all, SupaCon is about having fun.

CHAPTER 18

CHARLIE

"I THINK WE TOOK A WRONG TURN," I SAY AS REESE AND I FUMBLE through the darkness. A minute ago we were running down a replica Sydney street, now I'm not sure where we are. But it's dark. And we've lost the *Entertainment Now* crew. And I'm stuck with Reese.

Again.

"It's a maze," he says, his voice flat. "They're all wrong turns."

I roll my eyes even though he can't see it. "There's at least *one* right way to go here."

"Whatever."

I bite my tongue, resisting the urge to ask him what his problem is. I hope he's being extra snooty because he's still slightly hungover, and not because he's bitter after I turned him down.

"I thought about what we talked about yesterday," he says, and I cringe. "And I've decided I don't want you back."

I roll my eyes again, this time so hard it hurts. "Good for you."

"It *is* good for me," he says, the sarcasm so thick I can feel it. "You and me, it was fun while it lasted. But it wasn't enough."

I hear what he's trying to say: *I* wasn't enough. Not so long ago, hearing those words would have cut me deep. But I can see through him now.

"You're right," I say. "It wasn't enough."

His silence tells me he wasn't expecting me to react that way.

He takes another swing. "Yeah. You just looked so hot. I had to take another shot."

He wants to break me. I won't break. I am unbreakable.

I spin around in the dark, looking up at where I think his face is. "Shut up, Reese. Don't talk to me like that." I clench my fists together. "I don't get why you do shit like that."

"Do what?" His voice is strained, defensive.

"Act like such a macho prick!"

"Excuse me?"

"Don't you hear the nastiness in some of the things you say? Do you forget that I *know* you? That I know who you are underneath all that bravado?" I poke him in the chest. "I know you, Reese. Better than most. You don't have to play this with me."

"I'm not playing. It's not some macho act. I'm a guy."

I push out a frustrated groan. "You're infuriating, that's what you are."

His incessant need to "act like a man" was something we fought about when we were together. He would be sweet, sensitive, and emotional with me when we were alone. But the moment we were around other people, he'd turn into some wannabe jock character straight out of a teen rom-com.

There's nothing more disheartening than thinking you know someone—on a deep, soulful level—only to find out they're someone else entirely. I started questioning everything. I didn't know if the Reese I knew was real, or if the Reese I saw at parties and in the press was real. To make things worse, every time I brought it up with him, he would say it was all in my head. He had me questioning my own sanity. But once I learned he had cheated on me, I knew it wasn't my imagination. I realized he was too caught up in society's game of fitting in, and that's a game I've never been willing to play.

No one ever wins.

He breathes out a long, slow exhale. "Look, whatever, I'm sorry. You know how much pressure I'm under. People are watching me all the time. All the roles I play are big, tough guys. I gotta live up to that."

"Reese, being mean to people doesn't make you any more of a man. It just makes you mean." A creepy growl echoes through the building, and I lower my voice. "And you're not the only one under pressure. It's no excuse to act like everyone else is beneath you."

He exhales through his nostrils in a huff. "I don't do that."

"You do. You know, you'd be much happier if you just stopped caring what other people think and were yourself."

The hypocrisy of my words hits me hard, and I get an icky, squirmy feeling in my stomach.

Reese groans. "How about you just stay out of my head?"

"Believe me," I say. "I'd love to stay away from more than that. And once SupaCon is over, I can."

"Good."

"Great."

A bright white light shines directly on us. I squint and cover my eyes with my arm.

"There you two are!"

It's Candice, the *Entertainment Now* reporter, and her two cameramen. "We lost you!"

My eyes adjust and I see I'm standing just inches away from Reese, so I take a step back.

Candice pauses a few feet away, eyeing us suspiciously. A pleased smile creeps across her face. "Did we catch you two canoodling?"

"No," we both say, our voices stern and obviously irritated.

She flinches a little, but quickly recovers with a smile. "Shame." She waves us over. "Come on, what are you waiting for? Let's find our way out of this zombie-infested maze!"

The tension between us is thick, but neither of us lets it get in the way of our work. Reese and I catapult ourselves through the maze. A zombie leaps out, and Reese screams so loud it hurts my ears. He laughs and pulls out his phone to Snapchat while we run.

"Is this bringing back some happy memories?" Candice asks.

I can't hide the contempt from my face, and she sees it as an opportunity to bring up our relationship yet again. "Or perhaps some sad memories, Charlie? Is it tough being back here with Reese after such a public breakup?"

I bite my tongue, resisting the urge to throw a sarcastic comment in her face. "No, it's fine. We had so much fun filming *The Rising*, and this is just as fun." I smile, right on cue.

"What about you, Reese?"

He flashes her that pearly grin. "Charlie and I had some good times together on sets like these. Lots of great memories. And even though things with us didn't work out, we'll always have those memories."

Candice looks at him like he's the sweetest pear on the tree, then looks at me like I'm so lucky to be in his presence. "Don't you just wish all exes could be as great as him?"

This time, I hide my contempt but not my amusement. I laugh, shaking my head. "Yeah. He's something."

Three gross zombies appear from around a corner, and I'm grateful to them for saving me from this conversation.

CHAPTER 19

TAYLOR

"SO," JAMIE SAYS, PEERING DOWN AT ME AND CLEARING HIS throat. "I think I've come up with the perfect Twitter hack."

"Oh yeah?"

"Yep. It'll say, 'Gary Busey is my new bae. He's so much hotter than Jensen Ackles.'"

I gasp. "You wouldn't!"

He narrows his eyes and grins. "Oh, I would." He leans closer. "And I'll be sure to include a ton of typos."

My jaw drops. "Oh, you are going down!"

A loud screech erupts from behind us. We snap our heads around to see three zombies coming after us. Jamie starts running, taking my hand and pulling me with him. He looks back at me and smiles, laughing as we speed down the dimly lit path.

We reach a crossroads. Jamie looks back and forth. "Left, right, or straight?"

"Um . . ." A zombie materializes from the left, and then another two come at us from straight ahead.

We look at each other and both say, "Right."

We run past a wire fence with over a dozen zombies behind it, all reaching out for us. One clutches my trench coat and pulls me in, and I scream, slapping it away. Jamie reaches out and wraps his arm around me, stepping between me and the fence. I watch him out of the corner of my eye as we shuffle through the dark hallway. He gives me a sideways glance and smirks a little when he sees me watching him, and I quickly look away.

"Hey," he says.

I keep my eyes down. "What?"

"Look."

He points to a door. We walk toward it, and he pushes it open. It leads to a quiet suburban street set. It's night, lit by a lone street lamp, and there are three houses on either side of the road. A crashed RV has been dumped at the end of the street. A few straggler zombies roam the area.

"Should we go into suburbia or take our chances in the maze?" I ask.

He glances behind us and his eyes widen. "Suburbia."

I look over my shoulder and see a horde following us. We run into the street, stopping and starting as we try to figure out which way to go.

"I remember this," he says. "In the movie, isn't this where Reese's parents live?"

"Yeah." I point to the first house on the right. "I think it's that one. His mum and dad were zombies, remember? He saw them through the window."

"Right. He did that awful crying face. Let's stay away from that house."

I look around. "How the hell do we get out of here?"

He keeps his eyes straight ahead as we walk, but takes my hand. I try not to read too much into it, but my mind immediately disobeys. I wonder if he meant to take my hand, or even realizes he's doing it. It seemed like a very purposeful action, like he thought about it first. Or maybe I'm just overanalyzing it.

I'm good at that.

He looks at me. "Is this okay?" He nods to our entwined hands.

"Oh," I say, pretending I didn't even notice. I shrug. "Um, yeah. Whatever."

I see something move on the front porch of the house to my left and stop walking.

"What is it?" Jamie asks, stepping closer to me.

I point to the zombie as it stands up and stumbles down the steps. More zombies emerge from inside the houses. There must be more than fifty. They've been waiting for us. I start to laugh hysterically because I don't know what else to do.

"Come on," Jamie says, and we run straight down the street. The RV is pushed up against a black wall, and with nowhere else to run, we jump inside.

"Look!" I point to another door, with warm light leaking in underneath it. "I think this is the exit." I open the door and we jump out.

Jamie scratches his head. "Where are we?"

"We're in the library scene," I say, looking around the rows of bookshelves. Battery-operated candles on random shelves are all that light the room. "Which aisle?"

"Hmmm." He surveys each one carefully. "Right."

He holds out a hand for me and smiles when I take it. He definitely meant to do that. Now it's impossible not to read too much into it. We wander down the aisle to the right just as the door swings open behind us. I press my back against the shelf to hide, and Jamie does the same. Peering over my shoulder, I see Charlie, Reese, and the *EN* crew climb into the room. I'm about to step out and let them know we're here when a loud rumble shakes the walls.

One after another, zombies pile out of the RV and into the library. Charlie shrieks and they start running down the middle aisle. I press my palms to Jamie's chest and push him as far back as we can go, until we reach yet another dead end.

"Shit!" I whisper.

A chorus of groans and footsteps passes us on the other side of the bookshelves, chasing the others. Jamie and I squeeze together against the wall, covering our mouths to keep our laughter from being heard. I'm irrationally terrified that they'll find us. Once the zombie stampede passes us by, I realize Jamie is standing so close I can almost hear his heartbeat. Goose bumps spread all over my body, and my breathing becomes shallow. My back is against the wall, and he's looking down at me.

"You okay?" he asks. His voice is quiet, soft, and thick with something I don't recognize. I lock eyes with his, and a shiver runs down my spine.

"Mhmm. Fine." My voice is a shaky whisper.

The danger has passed. We don't need to hide here anymore, especially not in such close proximity. But still, neither of us moves.

He sees something on my forehead and frowns. "Are you bleeding?"

He touches the space above my right eyebrow gently with his thumb.

A few heartbeats pass before I reply. "It's fake blood."

My eyes are still watching his.

He looks relieved. "Oh."

His thumb lingers there for a moment, then he traces it down the side of my face, stopping at my cheek.

I don't know what to think. I'm almost certain I know where this is leading, but I dare not move or speak or even blink for fear that I'll somehow mess it up. That he'll stop touching me, stop standing so close to me, stop looking at me like I'm the most incredible sight he's ever seen. He strokes my cheek with his thumb, and I close my eyes instinctively, savoring the feel of his touch.

When I open my eyes again, he's looking at my lips. He sees me looking at him and gives me a sweet half smile. Then he leans in and touches his lips to mine. At first I'm so frozen that I don't kiss him back, but then my brain realizes what's happening, and I manage to move my lips with his. And the moment I do, it triggers something in him. He presses one hand against the wall behind me and the other to my lower back, pulling me into him. Inspired by his passion, I drape my arms around his neck. My head dips back, and I stand on my tiptoes to kiss him harder. He slides his other hand down the wall and around my waist, running his fingers up and down my back.

All the times I've imagined this moment collide into this one spectacular kiss.

All the years I've spent waiting for this have been worth it. Thoughts of what this kiss will mean for us try to intrude, but I push them away. For once, I don't want to think about the past or the future. I just want to be here, in this dark little aisle behind a row of prop books, kissing the boy I've always loved.

When we eventually pause for air, the inevitable awkwardness hits.

He presses his lips into a sexy smile and looks down at me with hooded eyes. "Hey."

"Hey," I say softly. I scratch the space behind my ear nervously, and then start to laugh. "This is so weird."

His smile fades, and he looks wounded.

"Oh," I say, covering my thoughtless mouth with my hands. "Ahhh. No. I didn't mean it like that. I mean, this is a little weird. But good weird."

He raises an eyebrow, and I continue to word-vomit all over him. "I meant it's weird that this is happening here, in the middle of a fake library in a fake zombie apocalypse." I suck in a deep breath and try to compose myself. "So, to summarize: the kissing is good weird. Kissing *here* is just weird."

His lips turn up into a crooked grin. My inability to funnel words from my brain to my mouth amuses him.

"The library may be fake," he says. "And the zombie apocalypse may be fake. But this," he puts his hands on my hips and kisses me again. "This is real."

I don't mean to, but I snort with laughter. He hangs his head and rubs a hand over his face, laughing with me.

"I know, I know," he says. "That was a terrible line."

"So cheesy," I say.

He nods, hiding his whole face in his hands now. "I panicked. I didn't know what to say."

I squeeze my lips shut, trying to force my laughter back down. "Hey, I don't judge. I'm the one who said this was 'good weird,' remember?"

He lets his hands drop back to my hips and lowers an eyebrow. "I don't think I'll ever forget that." He kisses me one more time. "Or that."

I giggle, and he hangs his head again. "Dammit! I did it again, didn't I? This is what you've done to me. One kiss from you, and suddenly I think I'm Ryan Gosling in *The Notebook*."

"Oh God," I say. "I hated that movie."

"I know." He sighs.

He locks eyes with me, and this time I kiss him.

CHAPTER 20

CHARLIE

REESE FINDS A DOOR THAT LEADS OUT OF THE MAZE, AND Candice continues the interview while we walk into a fake suburban street, complete with houses and gardens.

"So, Reese, is there a special girl in your life right now?"

"No," he says matter-of-factly.

"What about you, Charlie? Any special guys?"

I smirk. "No. No special guys."

But one very special girl.

"Well, I'm sure the Chase fans will be very excited to hear that you're both single, and here together no less!"

"We're not here together," I say. "I mean, we're here, but we're not together." I laugh awkwardly.

A gurgling sound rumbles from our left. Saved by the zombie.

Dozens shuffle out from behind the houses, forcing us to run down the street and take shelter in an RV.

"Hey," Reese says once we're inside. "Is that a door?" He shoulders it open and we jump out.

"Oh, sweet!" he says. "Library scene!"

"Wow," I say as we enter the library. "This is almost an exact replica of the movie set."

Reese and I creep forward, with Candice and the cameramen following closely behind. I think of the last time we were on a set like this. Reese and I were fighting about something stupid—I don't even remember what, but I know I was hurting. I had been hearing rumors about him with other girls, and instead of confronting him about it, I started petty fights over nothing. Up until that time, insecurity had never been a huge problem for me. I had my moments, sure. I never quite felt like I fit in anywhere, but my parents and sisters taught me to be proud of who I am. I learned early on that I would choose being different over being part of the boring crowd any day.

But when I started dating Reese, something changed. I began doubting myself. For the first time in my life, I started to wonder if I was good enough. The days we spent in this eerie library set were when the cracks started to show.

That was when everything started to unravel.

My bottom lip starts to tremble as all those painful emotions come flooding back to me. "I have to get out of here."

A chorus of groans erupts, and we turn to see a horde following us. I go full steam ahead, choosing the middle aisle, not waiting for Reese to catch up. If those cameras weren't on me right now, I'd lock him in here and throw away the key. Pretending to be friends with him for the sake of the studio and the fandom has been much harder than I expected. He's just a living, breathing, smiling reminder of how much I lost myself while I was with him—and how hard it was to find myself again after we broke up.

That's why I need to keep my relationship with Alyssa away from the media until I'm ready. My heart can't take a beating like that again—especially such a public beating. I reach the door and push it open, and the temperature rises about ten degrees. We're in a small classroom, from the scene with Reese and me making out after school. It was one of the first scenes in the movie, but one of the last we filmed.

I squeeze my eyes shut, wishing I was anywhere but here.

"What is this? Ghosts of Heartbreaks Past?" I mumble.

"What was that, Charlie?" Candice asks, sticking the microphone in my face.

"Nothing."

Reese stands next to me. "I remember this day."

He looks down at me, and I can see the guilt in his eyes. That was the day the first photo was leaked of Reese kissing another girl. I'd seen it online—someone tweeted it to me—that morning, and then I had to spend the rest of the day making out with him. If that happened now, I wouldn't do it. But I was broken down then. I couldn't find my voice to say no. I'm not sure I even knew I *could* say no, that I didn't have to do anything that would make me uncomfortable. I've been running from that day ever since. Running from Chase.

And now, I'm going to run again. I keep my eyes forward and force myself to move, heading straight for the exit. I burst through, shielding my eyes from the bright sunlight washing over us.

I'm surrounded by the sound of screams and people calling my name. My sight adjusts, and I see that we're back outside. "Whoa!"

Word must have spread that we were in *The Rising* maze. Hundreds of people are waiting for us, squished behind a row of barricades. "How did they know we were here?"

Reese stands next to me, his chest out and hands on his hips like Superman. "I Snapchatted, remember?"

"Oh, right." I grin at all the excited faces. "I'll take the left, you take the right. We'll cover more ground that way."

And I won't have to spend another second with you. We split up. I start talking to the crowd, posing for selfies with my most favorite people in the world: fangirls.

"You are my people," I say as I pose for a group selfie.

Candice rushes over. "Charlie, what's it like to have all these people screaming your name?"

I laugh. "It's really flattering. I'm still getting used to it, but this is fast becoming one of my favorite parts of the job. I feel like everyone here is my best friend. They all know me so well from my vlogs, and to see them here supporting my movie is just so amazing. I'm eternally grateful."

The crowd on Reese's side starts cheering, and I look over to see he has taken his shirt off. Candice is gone so fast I can almost see dust swirling behind her.

I laugh and roll my eyes. "Typical Reese."

"Are you guys back together?" a voice asks from behind me.

I turn around to keep posing for pics and shake my head. "Nope, just friends."

"But everyone online is saying you're together." The fan looks behind me, toward Reese. "You *are* here together."

"We're here, but not *together*."

It occurs to me that scrawling "Chase is dead" on my forehead would make my life so much easier.

He frowns, and I give him a hug. "It's okay. I'm happy. Reese and I aren't good together, anyway."

"You are!" he insists, nodding. "You're the best together."

I know he means well, so I smile. Another fan holds her selfie stick out, and I get into position.

"I'm glad you're not together anymore," she says. I glance at her, surprised, and she laughs. "Not in a mean way. You just didn't seem very happy then. You seem much happier now in all your videos."

Her words sting because I know they're true.

I nod. "Thanks. I am."

CHAPTER 21

TAYLOR

WHEN JAMIE AND I EVENTUALLY TEAR OUR LIPS AWAY FROM each other and find our way out, Charlie is waiting for us. There are people everywhere.

"Hey!" she says with a wave. "I was just about to send in a search party to look for you! Did you get lost?"

Jamie glances down at me, pressing his lips into a line. At first I think he's giving me the chance to tell Charlie—to make the move that will officially make us a "thing"—but then I worry that he's hesitating because he doesn't want Charlie to know. I start to freak out.

"Um," I start. "Not exactly."

My overanalytic mind takes approximately 3.1 seconds to come up with a thousand ways that our one kiss could ruin everything. Sitting pretty at number one is the very real possibility that I won't get into UCLA—or any college—and Jamie and Charlie will be moving across the Pacific Ocean without me and never coming back. Hot on its tail at number two is the risk of getting my heart broken a million other ways, in which case I would lose one of my best friends.

Am I supposed to tell Charlie? What if he wants to keep it a secret? Was it just a kiss to him? There are so many reasons this might not last. He would know that. So maybe this was just a momentary lapse in judgment? A mistake? I have no idea what I'm doing. How could this ever work? Why didn't I think of the consequences before I kissed him back? This could end badly. All these thoughts and more explode in my mind like fireworks, freezing me in a panic.

Charlie narrows her eyes, looking back and forth between Jamie and me. "Am I missing something?"

I chicken out. "Nah. We're just slow, I guess. You wanna grab something to eat?"

I sneak a look at Jamie. He's frowning, and a wave of nausea rushes over me. Is he mad at me now? I have no idea what's happening. I should never have let him kiss me.

Charlie isn't convinced, but she lets it go. "Yeah, I could eat."

We start walking to the diner Jamie and I went to yesterday, none of us saying a word. Everyone around us is laughing and talking and enjoying the vibrant SupaCon energy, but all I feel is awkward tension. In the few minutes it takes us to walk to the diner and find a booth, I've made myself sick with worry. Suddenly this feels like the longest and most exhausting day of my life.

The instant we sit down, Charlie's phone buzzes. She looks at the screen and sighs. "It's Mandy. Be right back." She slides back out of the booth and goes outside to take the call.

Jamie and I sit across from each other silently. I massage my fingers in my lap and keep my eyes on my hands. When I finally look up, he's watching me, his forehead wrinkled in confusion.

He smiles, but it doesn't reach his eyes. "You didn't tell Charlie," he says.

I swallow. "I didn't know if you wanted me to or not."

His eyebrows lift. "Why wouldn't I want you to?"

My eyes drop back to my hands, which are beginning to sweat. "Lots of reasons. We're best friends, for one."

He leans forward over the table and opens his hands to me. "So?"

I shrug. "So, why tell Charlie about something that maybe shouldn't have happened?"

He sinks back in the seat, wounded. "You don't think it should have happened?"

"Do you think it should have happened?"

"I asked you first," he says, then sighs. "Yes. I think it should have happened. I wouldn't have kissed you if I didn't want to."

The tears are coming, but I push them back. "But aren't you scared?"

"Of what?"

"The future? What could happen? All the ways this could go wrong?"

He chews on the inner corner of his mouth and thinks.

"I guess. I haven't really thought that far ahead. But I'm more afraid of never knowing how awesome it would be . . . to be with you."

Oh God. I've completely misinterpreted this. I rest my elbows on the table and drop my head in my hands.

"What's wrong?" he asks, reaching over and placing a hand on my arm.

I sigh. "Everything is changing. This"—I point from me to him—"this was my safe place. Our friendship is one of the few parts of my life that is comfortable and easy and free. And now this has changed, too. From now on, it's all going to be uncertain and new and just, changed."

He looks at me with concern. "But, it's good change, right?"

I think for a beat. "I always thought it would be. But it's been less than an hour since we kissed, and I've already screwed up."

"Hey," he says sternly. "You haven't screwed anything up."

A group of teenage boys burst into the diner, filling the room with banter and laughter. They squeeze into the booth directly behind me, and I shrink under their loud presence. I drop my hands onto the table and stare at Jamie, trying to get my mind straight.

He glances disapprovingly at the boys behind me. "Do you want to switch tables?"

I shake my head. I don't want to switch tables. I want to go home.

"This is all too much," I say, just as someone behind me says something funny and their whole table roars with laughter. Everything is loud. I feel like a train is barreling toward me, lights blinding me, sound deafening me. I can't think.

"Sorry? I can't hear you," Jamie says.

"It's too much!" I yell. I slide out of the booth and walk out of the diner just as Charlie is coming back in.

"Tay?" she says as I walk past her. "Where are you going?"

"Hotel," I snap, then immediately regret it.

She starts to follow. "Are you okay?"

"I'm fine," I say, feeling my mouth begin to dip into a frown as the tears threaten to spill. "Tell Jamie I'm sorry."

I speed-walk away from her, fumbling in my pocket to find my headphones as I push through the crowds. I rush back to our hotel room and slide my key card into the door. The moment I'm safely inside and finally alone, I let the tears come. I try not to think, because I know any thoughts I have will be cruel and only make me melt down faster. I rip off my coat and throw it on the bed, then proceed to tear off all my other clothes, too. I pick up my suitcase and go into the bathroom, lock the door, and turn the shower on. Before I step under the water, I switch off the lights.

The darkness envelops me and I exhale, feeling my shoulders relax instantly. I carefully step into the shower, close the door, and sit down under the stream, closing my eyes and leaning my forehead against the tiled wall. The hot water washes away my tears and my tension, and I wait until I can breathe again.

I lose track of time, but when my heart is calmer and my mind clearer, I turn off the water and wrap a towel around myself. I pull a fresh pair of jeans and a black T-shirt that says STRONG FEMALE CHARACTER out of my case and get dressed, all the while wondering how I'm going to fix the mess I made.

When I leave the bathroom, the sun is setting out the window and Charlie is sitting on her bed, watching *Entertainment Now*. She gives me an uncertain smile. "Hey."

"Hey."

She pats the space next to her, and I sit down. "They're about to show us running through the maze."

I look at the screen and see Charlie and Reese start running. Jamie and I aren't shown. Even though it was only a couple of hours ago, everything was different then. Simpler.

Charlie puts it on mute and turns to face me. "Are you okay?"

I keep my eyes on the TV. "You don't have to mute it. This is a big deal. We should watch it."

"My parents will record it. Plus, YouTube is a thing. Don't change the subject."

I side-eye her. "I'm fine."

She raises an eyebrow. "Mhmm. Except that you're not."

I glance around the room. "Where's Jamie?"

"Down at the con doing some serious retail therapy. He's going to need another bookshelf in his room for all the Marvel comics he's buying right now." She forces a laugh, then turns serious. "He didn't want to come up. He thinks you're mad at him."

I scoff. "Why would *I* be mad at *him*?"

"He thinks you felt pressured to kiss him. That you didn't really want to do it. Is that true?"

My eyes pop out of my face, and I shake my head adamantly. "No! No. I didn't feel pressured at all. Are you kidding? I've been wanting him to kiss me for four years!"

"*I* know that. But he doesn't. He feels horrible."

I drop my face into my hands and groan. "*I feel horrible. I thought . . .* I got confused. I thought he thought it was just a kiss, then I thought of how he's going to UCLA, and I might not get in, and even if I do, am I brave enough to move to another country? And he's had girlfriends and dates before, and I haven't, so I don't know what I'm doing. Then on top of all that, I thought he was mad at me for not telling you after we kissed." I suck in a deep breath through my teeth.

Charlie rubs my back. "He's not mad at you, Tay. He's in love with you."

My head snaps up, and I look her in the eyes. "He told you that?"

She smirks. "He doesn't need to tell me. It's been pretty obvious for a while. He's crazy about you."

I smile like an idiot. Then frown like an even bigger idiot. "Do you think I've screwed this up?"

"What? You and Jamie? Not a chance. You guys have practically been a couple for years, just without the fun stuff." She winks at me and nudges my shoulder, and I blush.

"I just," I say, biting my bottom lip. "I just don't know if I'm going to be good at any of it."

Charlie holds back a giggle. "At what? Sex?"

I gasp. "What? No! At being a girlfriend!"

She laughs. "Oh. What do you mean?"

I rub a hand over the back of my head, trying to figure out how to explain it. "Like, sometimes I don't think I'm being a girl right. I have an undercut and wear clothes I've bought from the boys' section, and I don't wear makeup or do my nails. I watch horror movies and play video games and burp and swear and don't talk about my feelings or any of that crap. I'm like Sandra Bullock in *Miss Congeniality*, only before the makeover."

"So?" Charlie shrugs. "Gracie Hart rocks. Besides, there's no one way to be a girl, Tay. You don't need to fit yourself into what society tells us a girl should be. Girls can be whoever they want. Whether that's an ass-kicking, sarcastic, crime-solving FBI agent or a funny, gorgeous, witty beauty queen—or both at the same time." She swings an arm around me and pulls me in. "Are you happy the way you are? Are you comfortable? Do you feel like yourself?"

The corner of my mouth lifts into a half smile. "Yes. Yes. And yes."

"Then that's all that matters. Fuck everything else." She thinks for a moment. "Are you really worried you won't be a good girl-friend?"

I hold my hands up. "I seriously have no clue what I'm doing."

"News flash," she says with a laugh. "Neither does Jamie. Sure, he's had dates and a girlfriend before, but this is *you guys*! It's different and new for both of you. Besides, one of the special parts of new relationships is that you get to figure it out together. But you'll never be able to figure anything out if you don't *talk* to each other."

I nod. "What do you think about all this? About me and Jamie?"

Her head dips back and she laughs. "Dude, you guys have been my OTP for, like, a year."

Just then the door opens and Jamie walks in, albeit a little hesitantly.

Charlie waves at him. "Speak of the geek."

"Sorry," he says as he starts going through his backpack. "I just need my phone charger. I'll just be a sec—" He sees that I've been crying, and it's like I can see his heart break. "Is that because of me?"

I wipe my tears. "No. It's because of me." I turn away. "Don't look. I don't want you to see my messiness." I hate crying in front of people.

Charlie hands me a tissue from the box on the bedside table. "We're all messy. What kind of friends would we be if we demanded you only show us your prettiness? This isn't Instagram—it's real life. And real life is messy."

"It's okay," Jamie says. I turn around as he pulls his charger out and stands up. "I'll go."

"No!" Charlie and I both say at the same time.

Charlie stands up. "I'll go." She gives me a stern look. "You two need to *talk*."

Jamie looks at me. "Are you sure?"

"Jamie," I say. "It's fine. Stay. Sit."

Charlie leaves, and Jamie comes and sits next to me, launching into an apology.

I hold up my hand to stop him. "Don't apologize. I didn't feel pressured to kiss you." I focus my gaze on the floor and suck in a breath. "I *wanted* to kiss you. I only freaked out because I misread a few things and thought it meant nothing to you, and that just led me into a spiral of anxiety and a teeny bit of a meltdown. It's no one's fault. It just happens sometimes. This has been a big few days for me, a lot of stuff to process. But I'm all right."

Out of the corner of my eye I see him watching me. "So"—he breathes—"you're not pissed at me?"

"No."

"You wanted to kiss me, too?"

"Yes."

His shoulders drop in relief. "Good. You're hard to read, you know."

I dip my head back and laugh. "*I'm* hard to read? The whole freaking world is hard to read."

He laughs. "I'm glad you're all right. And for the record"—he leans sideways and nudges my shoulder with his—"that kiss wasn't nothing to me. It was everything."

I nudge him back. "It was pretty everything to me, too."

He lowers his head and looks me in the eyes, raising his eyebrows as if he's surprised.

I smirk. "So, there's that."

He smiles, nodding slowly. "There's that."

CHAPTER 22

CHARLIE

I LEAVE TAY AND JAMIE IN THE HOTEL ROOM, SMILING TO myself. I've been waiting for them to get it together and realize they're head over heels for each other. I don't know how much longer I could have watched their incessant Ross-Rachel, will they/won't they storyline unfold without doing something drastic. I turn the corner toward the elevators and almost walk right into Alyssa.

"Oh! Hey! What are you doing here?"

She looks at her watch. "Ah . . . don't we have a date? Am I early?"

I slap a hand to my forehead. "Shit! I'm so sorry. I forgot."

She recoils slightly, and I can see I've hurt her. "No, I mean, I didn't *forget*. I just lost track of time. Tay, my best friend, she had a bit of a rough moment today, and she needed my help."

Dressed in skinny jeans, a purple crop top, and matching ankle boots, Alyssa looks like she just stepped off a movie poster.

"You look beautiful," I say, and immediately feel embarrassed that I said it out loud.

She smiles. "Thank you. You look . . . dystopian." Her eyes run over my T-shirt and jeans, spattered with fake blood from the zombie maze.

I look down at my outfit and laugh. "Yeah. I did *The Rising* live-action experience. It got a bit bloody."

I try to wipe some of the blood off my arm, but it's stuck on my skin and clothes like glue. "Um, I can't really go back to my room to change. Tay and Jamie are sorting some things out in there."

She waves it off. "All good. You look great just as you are."

She smiles flirtatiously, and I try not to openly swoon right in front of her. "Are you sure? You're so . . . pretty, and I'm all messy."

She holds a hand out for me. "I don't mind messy."

I take her hand, and we walk to the elevator. "Where are we going?"

"You'll see."

We walk the short distance to SupaCon, and she leads me around the back of the main building.

"Isn't the con closed for the day?" I ask.

She winks and squeezes my hand. "Not for us."

I follow her inside and down the mazelike aisles until we reach a huge section set up to look like an arcade. A sign above the entrance reads: ARCADIANA.

Alyssa ducks behind a counter, and a second later the games come alive. Lights flash and sounds erupt from the machines, taking me back to my childhood running around arcades with my sisters. I burst into a fit of giggles and can't stop.

I turn to Alyssa, who's smiling proudly. "My favorite vlogs of yours are the video game reviews. You always get so hyperactive playing the games—it's kind of adorable." She looks around the empty convention hall. "So I pulled some strings so we could come here after hours. All the classics are here." She glances at me. "Did I do good?"

I give her an excited grin. "You did awesome."

She smiles wide and pulls a cooler bag from behind the counter. "Here's something I prepared earlier." She opens the lid and pulls out a bottle of champagne and two glasses. "Shall we?"

I frown. "I don't drink. Plus, I'm not legal here. Eighteen, remember?"

"Oh, right." She puts the bottle back in the cooler and reveals two glass bottles of cola. "Coke?"

"Sure." I laugh. "You really came prepared." I scan the arcade, getting more ecstatic with every old-school game I see. I'm in heaven. "Look at all these! Pac-Man. Donkey Kong. TMNT. Tekken. Mario Kart!"

"I know," she says. "I think I'm drooling."

"Where do we even start?"

She smirks. "I think I know."

I follow her gaze to a game in the center row.

I gasp. "Is that a game of *The Rising*?"

"Yep."

She moves out from behind the counter and I pull on her hand, and we run toward it.

I marvel at it. "I didn't know it was going to be an arcade game! I didn't even know the video game was out yet. Look!" I point to the screen. "It's me! I'm in a game!"

Alyssa pulls a roll of quarters out of her bag and tears it open. "We gotta play this. Like, right now." She pops a coin in, and the music starts.

I pull the plastic red handgun out of the holster and get ready. A selection of avatars appear, and I'm thrilled to see I'm one of them. Me. The geek girl from the suburbs of Melbourne. The youngest daughter of Chinese immigrants. The only openly bi kid at school. The drama freak who makes vlogs in her bedroom.

I'm the hero.

Finally, I feel like the rest of the world is starting to see me the way I've always seen myself.

"Oh, this is so cool!" Alyssa says.

"Right?" The game starts, and avatar me is standing in a deserted Sydney street.

Alyssa jumps and points to the left side of the screen. "There's a zombie!"

I fire, shooting the rotter in the head. My character starts walking forward, her gun in front of her. My heart starts beating faster, but it's not because of the zombies hiding around every corner.

It's because Alyssa's hand is on my lower back. She's standing so close that I can feel her breath on my neck. A zombie bursts through a broken window and launches at me. I'm so distracted by Alyssa that I shoot in the wrong direction and miss, leaving the zombie plenty of time to attack.

"Aaand I'm dead."

"Oh, come on, Charlie!" Alyssa shakes her head, suppressing a smile. "You can do better than that."

"Hey!" I shoot her a mock glare. "You're making it very hard to concentrate."

She holds her palms up innocently and gives me a crooked grin. "I'm just standing here."

"Exactly. You're very distracting."

She looks at me with fire in her eyes, and I do what I've wanted to do since I first saw her in the hallway earlier.

I put an arm around her and pull her in, crushing my lips into hers. Alyssa doesn't hold back, sliding her arms around my waist and lifting me off my feet. Her tongue is in my mouth, and she tastes like Coke and sweetness. A zombie screeches through the game, startling us. We both look at the screen just as I get torn to shreds.

Alyssa gives me a sideways glance and smirks. "Oops. I guess that was my fault?"

I raise an eyebrow. "Worth it."

Round three starts, and I tear myself away from Alyssa and get back into position, ready to kill some zombies. After we both take turns kicking some undead butt, we move on to the classics. She crushes me in Donkey Kong and Need for Speed, but I triumph in Mario Kart and Mortal Kombat. Then we wander hand in hand back over to the counter. I sip my Coke as she pulls a picnic blanket from behind the counter and lays it on the floor in the middle of the arcade.

"What's this?" I ask.

She gives me a cheeky grin and winks. "Dinner."

Someone calls out Alyssa's name, and she tells me she'll be right back. When she returns, she's carrying two pizzas.

I dip my head back and laugh. "We're having pizza?"

She laughs. "You seem surprised."

"Not surprised. I just wasn't expecting all this; an arcade all to ourselves," I say.

She lowers an eyebrow. "But you like it, right?"

I nod enthusiastically. "Yes! Of course, yes. No one's ever done anything like this for me before."

"I've never done anything like this for anyone before," she says, seeming a little surprised herself.

We sit down on the blanket. Alyssa puts her hand out on the blanket, and I take it. She gives me an apprehensive smile, and I squeeze her hand. "This is the most awesome date in the history of the universe."

"This looks so good," Alyssa says as she flips open the pizza boxes. "I didn't know what you liked, so I ordered one cheese and one pepperoni."

"Yum! I love pepperoni."

We dig in, and I watch her as I chew. I can't believe I'm here, on this incredible date with her.

She notices me staring and wipes the corner of her mouth self-consciously. "Do I have sauce on me?"

I smile. "No. You're fine."

"What is it?"

I swallow and put the slice of pizza back on my plate. "I just can't believe I'm here with you."

"Why is it so hard to believe?"

I think for a beat. "You're just so . . . *cool*."

She laughs like I said something hilarious. "Trust me, I'm not. Maybe the characters I've played have been cool. But in real life, I'm a huge nerd."

I lean in and whisper. "Haven't you heard? Nerds are cool now."

She chuckles. "I guess my high school didn't get that memo. You should have seen me. I had no friends. I spent all my time in the library reading comic books, or in the science labs talking to the teachers. I was so shy I could hardly speak to other students. I've never once felt cool in my life. Except for maybe right now."

"Hey," I say. "I happen to think hanging out in libraries and science labs is very cool."

I try to picture this fun, confident, secure woman as a shy, insecure teen, and I just can't. "Were you really too shy to talk to people?"

She nods. "Painfully shy. I just didn't think people would like me, so I hid away whenever I could."

"How did you get here?" I gesture to where we are. "I mean, you don't seem shy or insecure at all."

She smiles, but her gaze falls to her lap. "I'm still shy. I just work harder to overcome it now." She clears her throat and locks eyes with me. "I've learned that I'm worthy of holding my head high and feeling good about myself. And I don't really care what other people think anymore." Her lips press into a hard line, and suddenly she looks to be a million miles away.

"Can I tell you something?" she asks.

"Anything."

"Remember that ex I was telling you about? The one from college?"

I nod.

"I don't really tell anyone this because it always makes me emotional, but here goes. Me and her—her name was Julia—I didn't expect it to be anything serious. We lived in the same dorm building and started fooling around. I'd been out for a while, but she was still sorting out some stuff so she wanted to keep our relationship secret. I loved her, so I went along with it. I just wanted her to be happy, and she always said she'd be ready to be more open soon. But after being together for a year and a half, she'd hardly even look at me in public, let alone hold my hand. It messed with my head, the weird back and forth we had. When we were alone, she adored me. But the moment we left my room, it was different."

She puts her slice of pizza down, and sensing the story is about to take a turn, I do the same. "Then a casting director who'd seen my videos asked me to audition for a movie, and I got the role. But I had to go to LA to shoot it. I asked her to come with me; she said no. I asked if she would visit me; she said no. I asked if I could come back and visit her; she said no. She thought people would get suspicious. That's when I realized that she was never going to be comfortable with me. In her mind, we were doing something wrong. She cared more about what others would think than she ever cared about me. So I left."

Alyssa pulls her knees up to her chest and clears her throat. "About a year ago, a mutual friend of ours died in a car accident. I went to the funeral, and Julia was there. It'd been so long; I just wanted to talk to her, see how she was. But when I walked over to her and said hello, she pretended she didn't even know me. That hurt. Then I met her girlfriend. She was so different from me. I sat there in the church, staring at the back of her head, trying to figure out what she had that I didn't. Trying to make excuses for Julia, to understand why she would want to hide me for so long, but then be so open with her new girlfriend. I started to ask myself if maybe it was just . . . *me*. It hit me then that no one who knows and loves Julia will ever know that she once knew and loved me. I left before the service was over, got back in my car, and cried all the way home."

Somehow, Alyssa says all that with only a few stray tears. I, on the other hand, am a blubbering mess.

She wipes her cheeks and gives me a sad smile. "That's when I realized I don't want to get to the end of my life and discover I spent all of it hiding who I really am. All that time I spent mentally bashing myself and hiding away, I could have used to do things that made me happy or to be with people who loved me and weren't afraid of it. So now, I try to focus on the parts of me and the parts of my life that I love, and not take anything for granted. Life's just too damn short, you know?"

I blink away the tears and nod.

She clears her throat again. "Still think I'm cool?"

I smirk. "The coolest."

I take in the sights all around us. "Look at this. Right now, we're eating pizza in an arcade at SupaCon. *This* isn't just cool. This is legendary." I pick up my slice of pizza and lift it to my mouth. "I never want this to end."

When I glance up, mouth full of pizza, she's looking at me with a half smile. "Neither do I."

CHAPTER 23

TAYLOR

"I'M GLAD YOU'RE FEELING BETTER," JAMIE SAYS.

I'm resting my head on his chest, and he's stroking my hair while we watch a rerun of *Supernatural*.

"Much better," I say, stifling a yawn. "Now that the chaos has settled."

"Chaos is what killed the dinosaurs, darling," he says in his surprisingly good Christian Slater voice.

I sit up and lean against the headboard. "*Heathers.*"

I glance down at him, then back at the TV, and smile.

He sits up next to me. "What?"

"Nothing." I smile again.

He raises an eyebrow. "Are you fantasizing about Destiel right now?"

"Hey, don't knock Destiel." I laugh. "Okay, I was just think-ing. I've never been able to tell you this before, but seeing as things are . . . changing: you're pretty cool."

He narrows his eyes. "Are you mocking me?"

"No! I'm totally serious. I mean, you've read all the Firestone books almost as many times as I have. You have an epic collec-tion of *Star Wars* T-shirts. You watch *Supernatural*. You're an awe-some photographer. Not to mention a pretty fucking stellar tomato-sauce hunter. And you just quoted *Heathers*."

He lets out a throaty laugh. "Yeah. If you're into the whole pop-culture-addicted-superdork thing"—he points to him-self with his thumbs and gives me a cheesy smile—"I'm your guy."

I elbow him in the ribs. "Shut up! I'm serious."

He runs his fingers down my arm. "Well, thank you. I think you're pretty cool, too. You've read the Firestone books even more times than I have. You kick ass at Six Degrees of Kevin Bacon. You watched all the *Paranormal Activity* movies with me even though they gave you nightmares. And when I try to flirt with you, it takes approximately 1.2 seconds for your cheeks to turn pink."

I feel my cheeks heat up, and he laughs. "See? Just 1.2 seconds."

Embarrassed, I change the subject. "Shh! I think Dean is about to do something awesome."

"Dean is always about to do something awesome."

"Exactly."

A smile spreads across my face, and I lean back against him

to watch the TV. He rests his chin on the top of my head, and I fall asleep in his arms, feeling safe with him, with us.

The next morning, I walk up the steps to the back of the stage, adjusting my trench coat self-consciously. I pause to tug my jeans up a little and make sure my cosplay is on point. As I do, I hear two voices from the other side of the stage, somewhere in the shadows behind the curtain.

"That girl who forgot to stand on the star is here," one whispers. She must think I can't hear her.

"Oh, yeah, I was so embarrassed for her," a second voice replies.

I pull my phone out of my pocket and pretend I can't hear them.

"She won't win," the first voice whispers. "She's not good enough to be queen."

"What do you mean? Her trench coat is, like, straight out of canon."

"Yeah, but look at her. She's not Queen Firestone. She's Queen *Fat*stone."

My heart stops. I stand as still as a statue.

The other girl gasps, unamused. "That's mean. I can't believe you said that."

I hear footsteps and see the second girl walking away, out of the shadows. I really want to get closer and see the first girl's face, tell her that she's a cruel person who needs to wake up. But I don't. I know I could never get the words out. I run back down the stairs and into the nearest bathroom. Locking myself in a cubicle, I pull out my phone again, open up the Tumblr app, and start typing.

QUEENOFFIRESTONE:
To the girl who just called me Queen Fatstone . . .

You said I won't win this contest because I'm not good enough.

I know I wouldn't be able to say any of this to your face. The words would get stuck. So I'm writing it here.

Maybe you or someone out there will see this and think twice before you make an offhand comment about a body that belongs to someone else.

Fat. Chubby. Curvy. Overweight. Plus-size. Whatever you want to call it.

Those words don't have to be insults.

I'm not offended by the word "fat," even though you said it like it was the worst thing ever.

I don't care what some random person thinks about my body.

I like my body.

But it's not the most interesting part of me.

If you judge me based on the way I'm shaped, then
you miss out on how awesome I am.

And I am awesome.

I love wearing my Queen Firestone cosplay.

I feel strong in it.

I feel powerful.

I feel beautiful.

Your fleeting superficial judgment won't change that.

My body is healthy.

My heart is beating.

My lungs are strong.

And right now my blood is boiling.

I guess it's not so much what you said that makes me
angry; it's that you thought it was okay to make
comments about my body at all.

It pisses me off that the world thinks my body is my most important quality.

And that everything else about me is somehow secondary, or measured against my appearance like some sort of gauge for worthiness.

Fuck that shit.

To the girl who hid in the shadows and tried to body-shame me, I'm sorry you thought that was a good use of your time and energy.

I hope you find happiness within yourself.

You deserve that.

We all do.

And if you do find that happiness, I hope no one ever tries to take it away from you.

No one deserves that.

I want to write more, but I hear someone walk into the bathroom. I sit quietly as she enters the stall next to me and promptly bursts into tears. I quickly hit POST and close the app before opening the door. The crying turns into shallow, choking breaths.

She's hyperventilating. She's panicking. I hesitate, standing near her door and wondering if I should say something.

"Um," I sputter. "Are . . . are you okay?"

"Taylor?" she whimpers.

"Brianna?"

I hear a click followed by a creak, and the door opens. Brianna is standing there in her Queen Firestone cosplay, her eyes red and cheeks wet from tears. She steps out with open arms and wraps them around me, resting her head on my shoulder and crying so hard her whole body shakes. At first I'm surprised that she feels comfortable enough to openly weep in my arms—we hardly know each other.

Then I put my arms around her and ask, "What happened?"

My first thought goes to the mean girl backstage, and I hope she didn't say anything hurtful to Brianna.

"That's the thing," she says. "Nothing happened. I just started to feel . . . really . . . nervous. And then . . . I . . . couldn't . . . breathe."

I nod. "Have you ever had a panic attack before?"

"Never."

"Okay. I think that might be what this is."

She pulls her head and shoulders back, her eyes wide with surprise. "What? Really?"

"Maybe."

Her expression changes from one of surprise to sheer horror, and she begins to wail. "Oh no!"

She rests her head on my shoulder again, and I rub her back like my mum always does when I'm panicking.

"It's nothing to be ashamed of," I say. "I've had plenty of panic attacks. I'll help you through it."

For some reason, I'm strangely calm. I reach an arm out and hold the cubicle door open. "Here, sit down."

She sits down on the toilet seat, sucking in loud, halting breaths between the tears. I tear off a chunk of toilet paper and hand it to her. I wait, knowing that all I can do is just be here for her. After a few minutes, her breathing starts to slow down.

"I don't think I can go out there," she whispers. "I can't do it. I'm going to drop out of the contest."

I crouch down in front of her and look her in the eyes. "It's totally up to you. But let's not make any decisions yet. Right now, the contest doesn't matter. It doesn't even exist, okay?"

"Okay."

I give her a slight smile. "When I start to panic, I do this counting thing that seems to help. You wanna try it?"

She nods, and her honey-blond fringe bobs up and down over her red, puffy eyes.

"Okay, we're gonna focus on breathing. Try not to think, just concentrate on breathing. Take a deep breath in through your nose, and I'll count."

She lifts her chest, sucking in air through her nose, and I start. "One . . . two . . . three . . . four . . . five. And breathe out slowly through your mouth."

She does, and I count to five again. We repeat this a few more times until her tears have stopped and her breathing has relaxed. Brianna like this, so vulnerable and fragile, seems so different from the girl I met the day before. Yesterday, Brianna had a few nerves, but overall she was confident, cheery, outgoing. Hell, she *strutted* along the stage, twirled, and took a bow. And now she's sitting on a toilet, having a panic attack, and crying to a virtual stranger. I find it hard to reconcile these two different sides of the same girl, and I wonder if my idea of what it looks like to be confident has been wrong this whole time. Or maybe it's not confidence that I need to rethink, but people.

Maybe it's not just me.

Maybe everyone is just as on edge as I am.

Maybe they just know how to hide it better—not just from others, but from themselves.

"How do you feel?" I ask, placing a hand on her knee.

She nods. "Better. A bit tired, but better."

"Do you need anything? Maybe some water?"

"No, I think I'm fine." She takes in another deep breath. "I'm fine."

"Do you want to talk about it?"

She bites the nail of her index finger and nods uncertainly. "I just really want to win this, you know? Skyler is my life. But I'm really scared about answering those trivia questions . . . out there in front of all those people." She shivers. "When I was a kid, I used to have a stutter. It was only small, but it was enough for the other kids to tease me about it." Her eyes open wider, like she's scared. "I thought I was over it. I thought it didn't really have an effect on me." Tears fill her eyes again. "But I guess it did."

I rub her knee. I want to comfort her, to say something that will make all her pain go away, but I can't think of the right words. I wonder if I should tell her about all the times I was bullied at school. Maybe it will help her feel less alone. Or maybe it will sound like I'm just trying to make this about me.

I decide to stay quiet.

"I'm so sorry for dumping this on you," she says, sniffing.

I shake my head. "Dude, it's fine. I know exactly how you're feeling right now. I'm terrified of going out there, too. In fact, yesterday, when you first came up to me backstage, I was about to leave."

She frowns. "You were?"

"Yep. But then you said you were nervous, too, and that we could be nervous together. That really helped me, Brianna. I would have left and never known if I could have made it through."

She smiles. "Well, I'm glad you stayed."

"Me too."

She chews lightly on her bottom lip, contemplating something. "I think I'm ready to go back out there now," she says with a nervous smile.

I stand up and hold out a hand for her. "You've got this, Brianna. Besides, we can be nervous wrecks together, right?"

She laughs. "You got it." Her arms wrap around me again, and I squeeze her close. "Thanks, Taylor. You're my hero."

That feels nice to hear. I don't think I've ever been someone's hero before. When we go back out into the contest hall, the seats are filled, and the contestants are walking onto the stage. We run up the stairs, take our numbers, and join them just as the lights turn on.

A girl with shiny black hair and a SupaCon T-shirt walks out to the front of the stage, holding a microphone. "Hey, everyone!

Welcome to the second and final round of the Queen Firestone SupaFan Contest!"

The crowd goes wild with applause, and I spot Jamie sitting front row center, cheering for me. I grin at him and feel my heart pounding so fast I think it might explode out of my chest and all over the stage.

I look at Brianna, and she looks back at me, smiling.

"We've got this," she says.

CHAPTER 24

CHARLIE

I WAKE UP WITH ALYSSA WRAPPED AROUND ME, HER LIPS softly grazing my back as the sun peeks in behind the curtains. If there was one word to describe this moment, it would be softness. Cuddled together under the marshmallowy soft blankets, our heads sharing one cloudlike pillow.

I've always been nonstop. Ever since I was a kid, I hated standing still, sitting still, waiting still. I'm high energy, constantly on the go, moving from one place to another and chasing the next exciting moment. But right now, for the first time in my life, all I want is to be still. I wish this was a video game that I could pause, and just live right here forever.

I never thought that this would happen to me, that I would find a part of me that craves stillness, that appreciates quiet, that lives in the now without thinking about the next.

What is happening here? What is this magic?

I roll over to face her. Her eyes are closed; our noses are almost touching.

I lie still, watching her breathe like it's the most miraculous thing I've ever seen.

This girl.

This girl who talks about art and science and technology like they're her lovers.

This girl who is kind, confident, smart, and openhearted.

Last night.

Last night, which was fun, free, and full of expression and ecstasy. I felt vulnerable, yet safe. Exposed, yet in control.

This moment.

This moment, which is entirely ours and no one else's. This, right here between the silky sheets, our legs intertwined, is sacred.

In the very public lives we live, full of illusions and drama and movement, this is private, uncomplicated, and still.

This is real.

Joy rises from somewhere deep inside me and shows itself as a giddy smile. All I want to do is jump up and down on the bed and laugh and scream and dance because I'm just so happy. But I can't tear my eyes away from her, so I just lie here with her, smiling like an idiot while she sleeps. And soon, my lashes fall and I drift back to sleep by her side.

Some time later, I'm woken up by the sound of "Shake It Off," T-Swift filling the room with her killer tune.

Alyssa leans out of bed and turns the music off, then rolls over with a groan. "Sorry," she says with a yawn. "That's my alarm."

"You like Taylor Swift?"

She raises an eyebrow. "Doesn't everyone?"

"Yes. Yes they do."

She sits up on her elbow and gives me a crooked grin. "Good morning."

I notice she has the cutest little dimple on her cheek, and I sit up slightly to kiss it. My lips move from her cheek to her mouth, kissing her softly. There's that word again: *softly*. Soft and sweet and beautiful. That's what this is.

I fall back onto the pillow, stretching my arms above my head. "Good morning."

She cuddles up to me, resting her head on my breast. Her eyes flutter up to mine, looking up at me, dark brown and speck-led gold. "You want some breakfast in bed? I can order room service."

I nod. "That sounds perfect."

She reaches for the phone on the bedside table and orders us coffee, eggs Florentine, and pancakes. Then she resumes her position on my chest, sliding an arm over my stomach.

I draw hearts on her shoulder with my finger. "What are you doing tonight?"

"SupaCon After-Party," she says. "You're going to that, too, yeah?"

"I was going to, but I couldn't get tickets for Tay and Jamie. I don't have enough clout for that yet, apparently. I wouldn't feel right going without them, so we'll probably have our own little party in the hotel room."

"Aww, that's nice of you." She lifts her chin up and kisses my neck, sending a shiver down my spine. "I gotta go to the after-party. But would it be okay if I swing by your room after?"

"Um, *yes*. Definitely. You have to meet my BFFs."

"Cool. You think they'll like me?"

I laugh. "They already like you. In fact, you're Tay's second favorite YouTuber, after me, of course."

She chuckles. "What are you doing today?"

"Tay is in the final round of the Queen Firestone SupaFan Contest, so I'm gonna go cheer her on and watch her win. What about you?"

"I've got press to do, mostly. But I wish I could just stay right here all day."

I moan in agreement. "Me too."

It's midmorning before I manage to drag myself away from her and go back to the con for Tay's final round. I borrow one of Alyssa's baseball caps and tuck my hair under it because I don't feel like being recognized today.

I arrive at the contest and stand in the doorway, watching from the back.

My phone buzzes.

Alyssa: Miss you already xo

I grin to myself and reply: Miss you. So much xo.

Even though I didn't get much sleep last night, I feel energized.

Awake.

Alive.

The contestants file onto the stage, with Tay following cautiously at the back. I smile at her even though I know she can't see me. I chew on my bottom lip. She seems nervous, which isn't a surprise, but I can see her anxiety forming like a fog around her whole body, and that worries me.

I push through the crowd to get closer, hoping that seeing me here might help boost her confidence. I am unable to get any closer than about halfway to the stage. But I'm close enough to see that her cheeks, neck, and ears are hot pink. Her feet are shuffling back and forth subtly, her knuckles kneading against her palms, her eyes glued to the space in front of her, concentrating on it like she's trying to figure it out.

"You can do this, Tay," I whisper.

A tall girl with black hair steps into the middle of the stage, holding a microphone so close to her mouth that I'm sure it must be touching her lips. "Hey, everyone! Welcome to the second and final round of the Queen Firestone SupaFan Contest!"

She starts waving her hands to encourage the audience to cheer, and they clap and shout excitedly. "Congratulations, contestants, on making it to the final round! The winner of the Firestone SupaFan Contest will be dining with Skyler Atkins herself tonight, then be her guest at the überexclusive SupaCon After-Party, and will even be attending the premiere of the next Firestone movie in LA!" The host starts walking down the stage, talking to the contestants. "Here are the rules, so listen carefully. Each of you will be asked a random trivia question based on the Firestone books and movies. You will each have ten seconds to give your answer. If you answer incorrectly, you need to leave the stage immediately. The last person standing is the lucky winner and will be crowned the ultimate Queen Firestone SupaFan!"

I start searching the crowd for Jamie. I don't see him, but I know he's here somewhere. He wouldn't miss Tay's shining moment for anything. The first question is asked, directed at the first of the ten contestants. Tay is number five, and she uses the time to take a few deep breaths.

Once it starts, it all happens very quickly. Contestants two and three both give wrong answers and are immediately out, leaving the stage as the audience claps for them. When it's Tay's turn, she has a big, toothy smile plastered on her face, even though her eyes are wide with fear. I've seen her smile like that before, whenever we had to do a presentation or debate at school.

The host asks her question. "What year was the first Firestone book published?"

"In 2004." Tay's answer is quiet but quick, and when the host tells her it's correct she relaxes a little.

Before it's her turn again, another two contestants have left the stage. The girl beside Taylor reaches out and takes her hand, and I immediately love her. She must be Brianna, the girl Tay told me about. She smiles at Tay as the host asks her question.

"What is Queen Firestone's first name?"

Brianna jumps a little when she realizes she knows the answer. "Agatha!"

Tay claps for her new friend and then stands very still to hear her own question.

"In which chapter of book one does Agatha Firestone learn that she's the one true queen?"

"Chapter eighteen."

"Correct."

My phone rings; it's Mandy. I cancel the call and switch my phone to silent.

The questions become increasingly hard, and I get more nervous by the second, so much that I can hardly breathe, but Tay is rocking it. For one fleeting moment, she even stands in superhero pose after answering a question correctly. Soon it's only Taylor and Brianna left on the stage.

"This is it," the host says. "Whoever gives the next incorrect answer is out, and the contestant standing is the winner." She continues to remind everyone of the grand prize, and I wish she would stop. She's only making Tay shake with nerves. "This is it, girls. One of you will be sharing dinner with Skyler tonight. One of you will be living the dream. Who will it be?"

"Jeez," I whisper to myself. "No pressure there."

The guy standing next to me laughs at my sarcastic remark. I glance at him and see a spark of recognition in his eyes, so I pull my cap lower to hide my face.

I'm so immersed in the drama unfolding on the stage that I ignore my phone buzzing in my pocket. But on the fifth call in a row, I pull it out. All the missed calls are from Mandy, plus a voice mail and three texts demanding I call her back. Something must be seriously wrong. I head toward the back of the room so I can make the call.

"Hey, Mandy," I say. "What's up?"

"I am so sorry, Charlie."

I glance at Tay up on the stage, still focused on making sure she's okay. "Sorry for what?"

"Wait . . . you haven't heard?"

"Heard what?"

"Where are you right now?"

"At Tay's contest. Why? What's wrong?"

Mandy lets out a shaky sigh. "Remember before you went into the zombie maze? When you asked me to go to your room and upload the collab video? I . . . I must have uploaded the wrong one."

My heart skips a beat. "Mandy, be specific. What video did you upload?"

There's a long pause before she answers, and when she does her voice is quiet. "I didn't watch it before I uploaded. I uploaded the wrong file. I thought it was the edited footage, and I didn't know about the end. With the kiss. So I uploaded it. I thought it was the right video, I swear. I'm so sorry. The moment I realized, I deleted it. But it's too late. Twitter is blowing up, and bloggers are already talking about it. . . . It's even a gif."

My heart beats faster, louder, harder.

"Fuck."

So much for privacy. I break out into a cold sweat.

This is exactly how it happened before, with Reese.

Everything was fine, and then photos were leaked, turning my world upside down in an instant.

"You there?"

"Yes." My voice cracks.

"I'm in the green room," Mandy says. "Reese is here. We need to talk."

I let out a frustrated sigh. "Fine. I'll be there soon. I need to be here for Tay first."

I'm already annoyed in anticipation of the media spreading gossip and the Chase shippers lashing out. But mostly, I'm sad.

I'm sad because I feel like, in a small way, what Alyssa and I have isn't ours anymore. I hate to say it, but it feels polluted somehow. I feel the pressure and opinions of others already seeping in. But I shake it off, knowing my focus right now needs to be on supporting Taylor.

CHAPTER 25

TAYLOR

"IN BOOK THREE, WHAT DOES QUEEN FIRESTONE'S SISTER GIVE to her on her eighteenth birthday?"

I can feel the host looking at me, waiting for my answer. I can feel the audience looking at me. Countless eyes on me, waiting, watching, judging.

I keep my gaze on the floor and open my mouth, but no words come out. I'm burning up, trembling, and definitely not breathing. I know the answer.

Don't I?

I do. I should. I know everything about Queen Firestone.

So why can't I answer the question?

How much time do I have? It feels like I've been frozen in place for hours. Is it obvious that my palms are sweating? More important, is it obvious that I don't know the answer? They must think I'm an idiot. They'll be laughing at me soon.

Shh. Stop it, Taylor. Just think of the answer.

What was the question again? Shit. Am I allowed to ask them to repeat it?

"I'm sorry," the host says. "You've run out of time, which means Brianna is the winner!"

The crowd erupts, and I implode.

No.

I'm a hardcore Queen Firestone fangirl. I can't lose this.

But I have. I lost.

The host's voice booms through my shock. "Congratulations, Brianna! You are Queen Firestone's biggest fan!"

I clap, happy for my friend, but I can't believe I lost. I make myself smile and step forward to give Brianna a big bear hug.

"Congratulations!" I say as confidently as I can, then I walk hazily offstage. I don't know whether I'm meant to stay or go, but I suddenly feel like I'm being suffocated by the crowd, the noise, the lights, all of it.

I run down the stairs and hurry through the crowd, keeping my gaze on the ground while I try to breathe. My bottom lip quivers, and my eyes blur from tears, making me walk even faster until I'm out of the hall. I run out of the venue, down the block, and don't stop until I reach the hotel lobby. Someone grabs my hand, and I spin around to see Charlie, her eyes filled with worry.

"Tay." She doesn't say anything else. She doesn't need to. I hold my arms out, and she wraps me in a hug, holding me tight. I squeeze my eyes shut, trying to block out the rest of the world.

"Do you need anything?" she whispers. "Water? Food? Jamie?"

I laugh, but it's forced. "I just want to go upstairs and lie down. Maybe watch a movie. But *not* a Firestone movie."

She holds me at arm's length and frowns. "Don't let this ruin the Firestone series for you, Tay. It's too important to you. It's part of who you are. You may not have won the competition, but you're still a true Firestone fangirl. No one else can tell you what you're a true fan of. That's part of the beauty of fandom, right?"

I sniff back more tears and nod. Her phone starts ringing, and she pulls it out of her pocket and cancels it. A second later, it buzzes with a text.

"What is it?" I ask when I see the concern on her face.

"Mandy," she says. I suddenly get the feeling that something isn't right, that Charlie isn't telling me everything.

"Charlie, what's going on?"

She looks away and groans. "It's out."

I pinch my brows together. "What's out?"

"Mandy accidentally uploaded the unedited collab I made with Alyssa. The one where we kiss." She cringes and slaps a hand over her eyes. "A video of me and Alyssa making out has gone viral. Mandy is in damage-control mode." She drops her hand from her face and sees me staring at her with my mouth hanging open.

"Holy fuck," I say. "That's . . . kind of huge. You need to go."

She hesitates, watching me carefully. "No, they can wait. Let's go upstairs."

She takes a step forward, but I stop her, shaking my head. "No. You can't hide from this anymore. You need to go. Talk to Mandy, then find Alyssa." A pained look washes over her face, and I grab her hands and smile. "This doesn't have to be a bad thing, Charlie. It doesn't need to be damage controlled. This can be good. It's out there now, so you can stop worrying about what others want you to do and just focus on what *you* want to do."

She opens her mouth to protest, but I start backing toward the elevator. "Go."

She looks me in the eye. "Love you, Tay."

"Love you back."

I step into the elevator with a group of teen girls chatting excitedly about a panel they just saw. I turn to see Jamie running straight past Charlie and toward me, making it into the elevator just as the doors close. In my haste to flee the scene, I forgot that he was in the audience. A rush of guilt washes over me, joining the already rampant anxiety, humiliation, and failure that are fighting hard to break me. Jamie sidesteps over, glancing at me. I avoid his gaze; I can't stand to see the worry in his eyes. I'm cracking. I can feel it.

It always starts in my heart, the cracks rapidly cutting through me internally, spreading like vines climbing up a tree, until I'm torn apart. It's an implosion, unseen by anyone around me.

One of the girls sees me. "Oh my God! That is the coolest cosplay ever!"

All her friends turn to look at me, admiring my costume.

I force out my kindest smile. "Thanks." My voice is quiet, strained by the lump in my throat. She opens her mouth to say something else, but I'm saved by the ding of the elevator at their floor.

They walk out in a flurry of chatter and the doors close, leaving Jamie and me alone.

Jamie turns to me. "Are you—"

The elevator bounces unexpectedly, and I gasp.

The lights flicker for a few seconds before shutting off completely, and we come to an abrupt stop in between the tenth and eleventh floors of the hotel.

"Shit," Jamie says.

Jamie starts pushing random buttons again and again, trying to get the elevator to move. The emergency lights kick in, glowing an offensive orange, but it's still so dark I can barely see my hands in front of my face. Even though I'm stuck in a dark metal box hanging nearly eleven stories high by wire cables, I still feel safer in here than I did fifteen minutes ago, standing on that stage. I let out an exhale and slide to the floor, tucking my legs up against my stomach and resting my head against the wall.

I hear a click as Jamie picks up the emergency phone. "Hello? . . . Yeah, we're stuck in here. . . . Okay . . . Okay . . . thanks."

He steps back and sighs. "It's some tech problem. She said we should start moving again in a few minutes."

"Cool."

"Where are you?"

"Down here."

"Did you fall?"

"No. I just can't stand anymore."

He's quiet for a moment. I see his silhouette, his hands pushing through his hair. "Do you mean that literally or figuratively?"

I smile a tired smile. "Both."

He sinks down next to me and stretches his long legs out in front of him, resting one leg on top of the other. "You're not claustrophobic, are you?"

I shake my head. "Nope. Are you?"

"I wasn't until about thirty seconds ago."

"We'll be fine. I'm sure Keanu Reeves and Jeff Daniels will be along any second to rescue us."

He laughs, but it sounds a little forced, nervous even. We sit quietly for a minute, and I hear the sound of him breathing. It's oddly calming. I close my eyes and listen to it like it's music.

"You were the clear winner," he says suddenly.

"No, I wasn't," I say, fighting down the lump in my throat. "I messed up. I didn't answer the question."

"But you *knew* the answer. You just got tongue-tied. It's understandable."

I drop my face into my hands. "I didn't get tongue-tied. I forgot the answer. I lost. And now I'm never gonna meet Skyler. And I'll have to . . ."

"You'll have to what?"

"Promise you won't laugh?"

He traces his finger over his chest. "Cross my heart."

I roll my eyes at myself for what I'm about to say. I know it's not going to make any sense. "I'll have to go to uni without meeting her."

"Wait," he says, clearly confused. "What does going to university have to do with Skyler Atkins?"

"I know it sounds stupid, but I thought if I could just meet her, if I could be in her line of sight, talk to her . . . it would give me the confidence to go to uni next year. To leave home and move to LA."

Saying it out loud hurts more than I expect, and I can't hold back the tears anymore.

"Tay, are you crying?"

My breath catches in my throat, answering his question.

"Oh, Tay." He tries to put his arm around me, but I shake it off.

"Please don't," I mumble. "I don't want to be touched right now."

"Shit, sorry," he says as he pulls his arm away. "I think I understand. Skyler is your mushroom, like in Super Mario. Meeting her is your power-up, turning you into Super Taylor. Then you can zoom off to LA and college and clock it. Right?"

I laugh through the tears. "Exactly. It's like meeting her is validating somehow. If I have the guts to meet the person I admire most in the whole universe, then I have what it takes to face the horror of uni."

"Horror? Uni will be a blast!"

I scoff. "Maybe for you, Mr. Extrovert. But for me, it's going to be hard. It's a whole new set of daily social hoops I'll have to jump through. New places, new people, new rules. Just getting to class every day is enough to make me implode emotionally. And Charlie will be filming; you'll have your own classes to go to. I'll be totally alone, in uncharted territory without a fucking map." I sniff back a new round of tears and sigh. "Do you get me?"

"I'm trying to."

I think for a moment, trying to think of a way to explain how I'm feeling. "Do you remember that scene in *Indiana Jones and the Last Crusade*, when he's solving the word puzzle and any wrong tile he steps on crumbles underneath him?"

"Of course. It's a classic."

"That's how I feel. Like the ground is giving way beneath me. *All. The. Time.* Nothing is ever stable. Any minute, the earth could collapse beneath me, and I'll fall into a chasm. But unlike Indy, I don't know the answer to the puzzle. I don't even know the question."

"Jesus, Tay," he says. "Have you always felt like this?"

"Pretty much. It's more intense lately, with exams and graduation and LA and uni coming up. Everything is changing." I wipe away more tears. "Jamie, I'm really scared."

"Why haven't you ever told me any of this before?"

I shrug. "I don't like focusing on stuff that makes me anxious. And I don't want to annoy people with my problems. Especially when, to most people, these things aren't even considered problems. And"—I pause, squeezing my eyes shut—"I don't want you to think less of me."

"Taylor," he says with a sigh. "First of all, I'm your best friend—more than that now. I'm supposed to be there for you when you have problems. That's what friends do. Second, nothing could ever make me think less of you."

Disobedient tears run down my cheeks, and I swipe at them

in frustration. "But don't I sound so pitiful? Thinking meeting Skyler is the solution to all my problems?"

I can just barely see him shaking his head in the shadows. "No. It's not pathetic at all. The Queen Firestone books and movies helped you get through stuff. And unlike everything we're going through, Queen Firestone won't ever change."

"Exactly," I say, turning toward him in the darkness. "And it's even more than that. Those books and movies have taught me so much about myself. Queen Firestone faces all her worst fears and transforms from this scared little girl into a powerful woman who rules her queendom. It gives me hope that I can be powerful, too."

"I get it."

I look up at him. "You do?"

"I do." He takes in a deep breath and rubs the back of his neck with his hand. "I've never told anyone this, but when I first moved to Melbourne, I hated it. I didn't know anyone. Back in Seattle, I was very close to my family. My abuelo lived a block away, and I'd go there every day after school. My cousins all lived nearby, and so did most of my friends. When I got to Melbourne, it was just me and my parents, and I was pissed at them for making me leave Seattle. I felt very isolated, and I hadn't worked up the courage to make friends yet. So I dove into movies and comics and books. They helped me cope with all the change. And then, when I saw you reading the Firestone books at school, it gave me the opportunity to talk to you."

I hear a smile in his voice, and it makes me smile, too. I take his hand and lift it over my head, putting his arm around me and scooting closer to him.

He kisses me on the forehead. "I have no doubt in my mind that you will clock uni. And we'll clock LA together."

"But I'll have to meet new people and do things I've never done before and leave my comfort zone." I lean into him, resting my forehead in the crook of his neck.

"Tay, you've just done all that right here at SupaCon. Meet new people? Check. Done things you've never done before? Check. Leave comfort zone? Check." He breathes out a laugh. "I mean, you just stood on a stage in front of hundreds of people. And look, here you are, still standing." He pauses. "Well, sitting. But you did it. Everything you're afraid of about uni, you've already done."

"Holy crap! I did do all that, didn't I?"

I met new people, and I didn't die. I stood on a stage and didn't run away even though I really, really wanted to. I even embarrassed myself, and everyone laughed at me, and the ground didn't open up and swallow me whole. All the things I'm most afraid of have happened here at SupaCon, and I'm fine.

In fact, I'm pretty great.

If I can do all that, then maybe uni is something I can do, too.

I snuggle closer to him and exhale. "I'm really glad you moved to Melbourne. I'm glad you talked to me that day at school."

He nods. "Me too. And I'm glad you told me all this. I want to be the person you feel safe enough to share your mess with."

"You are."

"But I'm sorry you didn't win."

I push out a tired sigh. "Same. My mind just went blank. I guess I got flustered being up there in front of everyone. And I was distracted. Some mean girl said something shitty backstage. Then Brianna started panicking, and I talked her down. I didn't have time to mentally prepare for going out on that stage. It totally threw me."

"What mean girl? What happened?" His voice is serious, angry.

"I overheard her talking about me. She called me Queen Fatstone. Like the size of my cosplay outfit is more important than my passion for the fandom. It made me so mad; I couldn't think straight." I huff out a short breath. "I don't understand it. Don't people know that when they say stuff, it affects others? Don't they ever just stop and think, 'Hey, if I said this, how would it make that person feel?'"

And then I burst into tears again. Angry tears that burn like acid.

He pulls me in closer. "Don't listen to what anyone says about you. Some people try to bring others down to make themselves feel superior. You know what I do when I'm angry at the world for being full of shallow, insensitive assholes?"

"What?"

He swallows. I feel his Adam's apple rise and fall. "I think of you."

I stop crying. I don't even breathe. "Huh?"

"I think of you," he says again, this time more resolute. "Because you're kind, hilarious, smart, gorgeous, and the most awesome person I've ever met. If there can be someone like you in the world, then it can't be such a bad place after all."

My heart expands so wide it could hold the whole elevator.

I lift my head so that I can feel his breath on my lips. His breathing falters, and I feel his heart beating hard. He leans in. He's being cautious, giving me time to back away if I want to. But I don't want to. Not even a little bit. Because Jamie is my best friend, the one who always seems to know what I'm thinking. The one who gives me space when I need it but is always there when I need him. He's the one I can sit in the darkness with, hovering eleven stories up in a metal box, and still feel like I wouldn't want to be anywhere else, with anyone else. He's the one I can share my mess with. He's the one I can share my weird with. He's the one.

He pushes his lips to mine, and I push back, kissing him gently. And then not so gently. His lips are smooth, and when he opens his mouth, mine instinctively does the same. I smile, and he smiles, too, but breaks our kiss.

"You know," he says hesitantly, "if this—if you and me—is too much for you right now, we can take it slow. As slow as you need. We don't have to kiss or even hold hands if you don't want to."

I answer him by crushing my lips to his.

He breaks away again. "But what about the ground crumbling and *Indiana Jones and the Last Crusade?*"

"Well, if coming to SupaCon has taught me anything, it's that new experiences are always scary, but they aren't always bad. Maybe this isn't the part where Indy steps on crumbling tiles. Maybe this is the part where he takes the leap of faith and finds the Holy Grail."

I can hardly see his face, but somehow I know he's smiling. "I love it when you reference classic movies to explain life."

His lips brush mine, and the temperature in the elevator spikes about ten degrees. A sigh escapes my lips, and he responds by sliding his arm down my back and pulling me in by the waist. He runs his other hand through my hair, sending sparks down my spine. A rush of courage overcomes me, and I sweep my tongue over his. He sucks in a sharp breath and pushes his chest against mine, pulling me so close that I'm almost on top of him. We're sitting awkwardly, with his back against the wall and both of us twisting to face each other, so I decide to make a move to get more comfortable.

Keeping my lips firmly planted on his, I rest my hands on his shoulders and lift myself onto his lap.

It's a move that surprises him, and he gasps into my mouth. Then his gasp quickly turns into a moan, and then his hands are on my hips, bringing me closer to him. My forwardness surprises both of us. In all the times I'd entertained the idea of fooling around with Jamie, I was sure I'd be cautious—like I am in every other part of my life. But I don't need to hesitate with him. I don't second-guess myself.

There aren't any rules with Jamie, no social conventions or expectations to live up to. All I need to do is be who I already am. I'm free to be as cautious or as daring as I want to be.

And right now, I choose daring.

We're kissing so fervently now that my whole body is on fire, and I'm sure my glasses must be steaming up. Something flashes, and for a moment I think I'm seeing sparks, but then I realize the lights are flickering back on. We freeze like deer in headlights, our mouths pulling apart and eyes snapping up to the ceiling.

"Really?" Jamie shouts at the fluorescent bulb. "Now?"

I bite my lip to suppress a giggle. We wait for a second, and the elevator roars back to life. It starts moving, and I jump up so fast I almost lose my balance. Jamie climbs to his feet, and we stand on either side of the elevator as the doors open. By the time we compose ourselves, we're back on the ground floor, the lobby still as busy and loud as before.

A family of four step inside, and Jamie and I play it cool, all the while swapping smiles and stolen glances. The doors close, and we rise up. It's as though the elevator hadn't been stuck at all. In a weird way, it's like fate had intervened, pausing time to bring Jamie and me closer and force us to truly open up to each other. The elevator stops with a ding, and the doors open. The family step out, Jamie presses the button for our floor, and the doors close.

We're alone again.

He steps toward me so fast that I move back into the wall, where he crushes his mouth to mine.

He pulls back just far enough that I can see his face, and runs the back of his fingers down my cheek. "Do you want to order room service and watch movies with me tonight?" he asks with a crooked smile.

I look up into his eyes. "Hells yes."

CHAPTER 26

CHARLIE

WHEN I WALK INTO THE GREEN ROOM, ALL EYES ARE ON ME. A SupaCon staff member hurries up to me. "Mandy asked me to tell you she's in there." She points to a door and I open it, seeing Mandy by the window, talking quietly on her phone.

Reese is on the couch, scrolling through his phone.

"I left a very shaken-up Tay to be here, so this better be good," I growl.

"You're trending," he says, looking up at me. "Number one worldwide."

I sigh and fall into a chair across from him.

"Awesome," I say, my voice thick with sarcasm.

I look over at Mandy when she ends the call. "I'm guessing that was the studio?"

She nods and tightens her loose bun. "Yes. They made a bad

joke about how it would have been a great marketing tactic had you been making out with Reese in the video, but other than that, they didn't say much. To them, any publicity is good publicity, and this has got everyone talking about you and, by association, the movie. Mostly they wanted to know why they weren't informed of this before."

I cross my arms. "There isn't any 'before.' This is new. And it's also none of their business." I lean my head on the back of the chair. "Why am I even here? I haven't done anything wrong."

Mandy leans over and gives me a hug. "Honestly, Charlie. If I had known . . . I'm just so, *so* sorry."

I pat her on the back. "It's okay. It was an accident. I should have renamed the edited video or saved it in a different folder. Believe me, the next time I'm on my laptop, I'm trashing the mess of clips and files so nothing like this ever happens again. It's no one's fault. And it's really not that big a deal."

Reese scoffs. "Do you have any idea how this makes me look to the fans?"

I glare at him. "How the hell does this affect you in any way whatsoever?"

"The fans, Charlie." He says it with such condescension that I want to punch him in the jaw. "They love Chase."

"Not all of them. And I definitely don't."

He leans forward, resting his arms on his knees. "You can't just dump this bomb on them. They're heartbroken."

I sit up straight. "First of all, *I* didn't dump anything on them. If it were up to me, this would stay private for as long as possible.

Certainly longer than a day. Second, the Chase ship hit the proverbial iceberg over six months ago. This isn't a surprise."

Mandy nods. "You're right, Charlie. You are. But with all the press you and Reese have been doing together here, I think some wires got crossed. The fandom went into overdrive with speculation that you were back together."

I groan. "I don't know how. I must have said we're not together a thousand times by now."

Reese gives me a smug look. "It's the photos and the interviews. We've been seen together. That's enough to get the Chase ship sailing again. The poor kids got their hopes up. And you've just crushed 'em."

I clench my jaw and stare at him. "I bet this is what the studio wanted all along. We're just props they positioned in front of the cameras to sell tickets. None of this would have happened if you had just stayed away like you were supposed to."

He rolls his eyes. "Right, *I'm* the bad guy here."

"Well, you're not the good guy," I say. "That's for sure."

"Guys," Mandy says, sitting on a chair next to me, "there's no need to argue. Like you said, this isn't a big deal."

I turn to her. "What's the general vibe of the fandom right now?"

"It's a little divided," she says, nodding. "Most people are excited. They're shipping you and Alyssa hard. Others are—"

"Shattered," Reese interrupts. "Pissed. Betrayed."

I roll my eyes at him. I know my fans. Ninety-nine percent of them are wonderful, amazing people. But that one percent can say some mean things. I worry about the tweets that must be filling Alyssa's reply feed and her YouTube comments section right now.

Mandy purses her lips and puts a hand on my shoulder. "They'll get over it. And like I said, most people are excited. I've seen the social media posts to prove it. They're happy for you, and they love Alyssa to bits."

Reese lets out an arrogant laugh. "And the rest just want to tear her to bits."

I squeeze my eyes shut and groan. "That's just great. Nothing like a little bit of cyberbullying to start our relationship."

"Charlie," Mandy says. "You're focusing too much on the negatives here." She glares at Reese. "And you're not helping. Everything is completely fine."

I throw my hands up in exasperation. "So what's going on? Why are we even having this discussion?"

Mandy's phone buzzes, and she cancels it. "I just wanted to make sure we were all on the same page. And see if there was any damage control we needed to do. Do you want to make a statement about your new romance?"

I shake my head. "No." I don't say that there might not be a relationship after Alyssa finds out about all this.

"Hey," Reese says. "Why are you so bitchy today?"

I narrow my eyes at him. "I'm 'bitchy' because I really like Alyssa, and I doubt she'll like me much longer if she's getting harassed by keyboard warriors just because she's *not* you."

"If I were her," he says, raising an eyebrow, "I'd be more pissed about the fact that you want to keep your relationship so top secret. For someone who's supposedly out of the closet, you sure are trying hard to stay in it."

I stand up. "This has nothing to do with closets and everything to do with how messed up I was after what you did. I wanted to keep it secret because my love life isn't public property."

"It is now." He smiles that smug smile, and I can't be in the same room with him anymore.

"I'm leaving. I need to go see Alyssa."

"Tell her I say hi," Reese says with a sleazy wink.

I turn to Mandy. "Mandy, can you please call the studio back and tell them I won't be doing any more press with Reese Ryan? Ever. I won't take no for an answer on this."

She smiles and nods while Reese stares up at me, speechless.

I look down at him. "We're done here."

Mandy stands up and gives me a hug. "Don't worry. Everything is fine. I'm happy for you. You deserve someone good like her."

Out of the corner of my eye, I see Reese's jaw drop.

"Thanks. I'll see you later."

I leave and walk through the green room, feeling like a storm cloud is hanging over my head.

"Charlie!" I turn to see Mandy coming out of the room and hurrying toward me. She pulls an envelope out of her handbag and gives it to me. "I almost forgot. I know this doesn't make up for posting your make-out session all over the Internet, but I hope it's a start."

"Mandy, I told you—"

"Just open it."

I take the envelope and look inside, finding three VIP passes to the SupaCon After-Party. My head snaps up. "What? How?"

"I hustled," she says. "Now you and Taylor and Jamie can go and celebrate in style."

I throw my arms around her. "Thank you so much, Mandy. I promise, all is forgiven. It's okay, okay?"

She nods, then pushes me away. "Go find your girl."

I slide the envelope in my pocket and leave. I pull out my phone and scroll through the hundreds of Tumblr posts and tweets about me. There are a few cruel ones, and they hurt. There needs to be an app that pops up on screens when a nasty tweet is about to be sent that says, "Are you sure you want to say that? It's mean." But until that happens, I have the trusty BLOCK button. Thankfully, the majority of posts are positive, supportive, and supersweet.

I only hope Alyssa thinks I'm worth all this mess.

"The video of us kissing got online," I say before I'm even in Alyssa's door.

She raises an eyebrow at me as I enter and swings the door closed. "Hello to you, too."

"Sorry." I sit on the couch and pull my knees up to my chin, hugging myself. "I'm just freaking out a little."

Alyssa sits next to me and tucks a strand of pink hair back behind my ear. "Talk to me."

I throw my head back and groan. "It's all over the Internet. Twitter, Facebook, Tumblr, gossip blogs. We're trending everywhere."

"I know. I've seen it. So?"

I look at her, surprised by how calm she is. "Well, it's not exactly the most private of relationships now."

She gives me a half smile. "It was never going to be completely private."

"I know," I say. "But I thought we'd at least have this weekend, you know? I thought we'd have SupaCon. I just . . . I hoped I wouldn't have to go through all this again."

She leans back against the arm of the couch, hurt. "Hey. This isn't the same situation. At all."

I reach out and take her hand. "I didn't mean it like that. It's just, some of the fans, they feel betrayed. They love Chase. And I guess seeing Reese and me together this weekend got them excited, and now with this out in the open, some of them are pissed."

She lets go of my hand and crosses her arms over her chest. "They're pissed? Why?"

I shake my head. "It's nothing to do with you. It's just because you're not Reese. Parts of the fandom only want to see me with him, and now that they know it'll never happen, the backlash has started."

She shrugs. "They'll get over it." A smile grows on her lips. "Besides, I think not being Reese is kind of a pro."

I let out a short laugh, nodding.

"It's not just that," I say, sucking in a deep breath. "This just makes me nervous. After the public scrutiny I went through, it took me so long to put myself back together."

I feel a tear escape my lashes, and I wipe it away with my

thumb. "I felt like it was my fault. That I just wasn't good enough. I spent months trying to figure out why he chose someone else over me, trying to figure what I did wrong, why I was wrong. I'd stare at the mirror every morning and search for the part of me that was so unloveable that he felt the need to cheat. And for weeks, I didn't tell anyone I felt that way, because I was so ashamed that I was falling apart over a guy. If it wasn't for Taylor and Jamie, I don't think I would have come out of that nightmare."

Alyssa and I stare at each other, both of us quietly crying now.

"Listen," she says. "There's nothing to be ashamed of. Falling in love is risky. I know you enough to know that when you do something, you do it with your whole heart. So getting it stomped on like that . . . you didn't deserve it. And it's okay that you fell apart. Everyone does sometimes."

I take in a shaky breath. "I guess, with millions of eyes on us now, it's just scary. I don't want to go through that again."

She looks at me with a frown. "So, you wanna end this before it even starts? Is that what's happening?"

I wipe my cheeks and shake my head. "No. I don't. I *really* don't. But if you don't want all this craziness, I need to know now. I don't want to bring you into this mess. I'm stuck with Chase, at least for a while longer. But you don't have to be."

She looks at me with heavy-lidded eyes. "That's the thing. I know I don't *have* to be. I *want* to be. I like you, Charlie. I learned a long time ago that what other people think about me is their problem, not mine. I can handle it." She slides closer to me and puts her hand on my knee. "All I want to know is, can you?"

I cock my head to the side. "Huh?"

She drops her gaze, straightens her shoulders, then looks at me again. "I get that you've been burned. I do. You don't want the opinions of others to dictate your life. Neither do I. But I've been burned, too. I've been the girl who has to be kept secret, and it was the most painful thing I've ever experienced. I don't want to hide from the world. And I especially won't allow myself to be hidden by someone else. No matter how much I like you, if you want to hide me for any reason, I'm out. I hate that I have to say this, Charlie, but I'm not Reese Ryan. I'm not gonna play games with you. If you still can't separate your history with him from a future with me, then maybe you're not ready for this. But you need to tell me. You need to tell me if you're in or you're out."

Tears sting my eyes. "I'm in."

She narrows her eyes at me. "You sure?"

I nod, but the fear must be evident on my face because she shakes her head.

She puts a hand on mine, then lets go and stands up. "I think we need to hit pause on this. You've got some things to figure out. Maybe you should go. I'll see you tonight."

I leave the room, but her words stay with me, lingering in my mind and cutting into my heart. *I won't allow myself to be hidden. . . . Separate your history with him from a future with me. . . .*

The words go round and round in my head as I wait for the elevator.

CHAPTER 27

TAYLOR

JAMIE AND I ARE LYING ON THE BED, A HALF-EATEN CHEESE pizza next to us and *The Breakfast Club* playing on the television.

"Who's your favorite Breakfast Clubber?" he asks.

I don't even need to think about my answer. "Allison. The basket case. What about you?"

"Isn't it obvious?" He smirks. "Bender. The badass."

I laugh. "Actually, he's the criminal. Besides, isn't the whole big life lesson they learn in detention that everyone has their baggage and that they're all more similar than they are different?"

Charlie walks into the room. She sees us lying on the bed together and covers her eyes with her hand. "Oh God! Am I interrupting something? We're gonna need a system from now on. Especially if we're all going to be living together next year."

"Charlie!" I say. Jamie and I laugh at her animated reaction. "Relax. We're just watching a movie."

She peeks between her fingers. "Oh, okay." Her eyes are red from crying, and I sit up with a start.

"Charlie? What happened with Alyssa?"

She sits solemnly on the bed and bursts into tears. "I think I screwed up."

Jamie and I shuffle to the edge of the bed and sit on either side of her, hugging her tight. We listen as she tells us everything: the video, Mandy, Reese, and her tough talk with Alyssa.

She rubs a hand over her face and groans. "This weekend just hasn't gone how I wanted it to. I had so much I wanted to prove to everyone, and I feel like it's all just one big mess now. And once again, it's all on display."

I shake my head. "You don't need to prove anything to anyone. I know the last six months have shaken your confidence, but you need to wake up. Your perception of yourself is being warped by everyone else's opinions. That's relatively normal for most people, but it's not normal for *you*." I take in a deep breath, hoping my words are helping her. "Ever since I met you, you've been self-assured and independent. You always had such a spark. It dimmed a little last year, but it's coming back. Brighter than ever."

She presses her lips into a line, and her eyes lose focus, like she's looking past me into some distant memory. "You think so?"

"I *know* so. You didn't get this far because of anyone else but yourself. You started from nothing, built your channel, landed that movie, all without Reese. People don't love you because you dated some movie star. They love you because you are unapologetically yourself. Stop putting all this pressure on yourself to step out from his shadow. You've never been in anyone's shadow. You are your own light source." I squeeze her hand to cement my message.

Jamie nods. "Tay's right, and I think Alyssa is, too. If you want to be with her, you gotta stop expecting it to end in flames like it did with Reese."

I rest my head on her shoulder, and she breathes in a shaky breath. "I can't believe it," she says. "I've spent all SupaCon trying to show others that he didn't break me, but that still makes everything about *him*, doesn't it? I need to stop trying so hard. Hating Reese so much has only been hurting me. And trying to change the public's perception of me has done nothing but exhaust me. I've been giving my power away to everyone. I know Alyssa is right. And I know I want to find out if what we have is *something*, but it's"—she whispers the next word—"scary."

I lift my head up and look at her, unsure at first if I heard her correctly. Maybe it's naive of me, but it never occurred to me before that Charlie could ever be afraid of anything.

I smile at her and say, "Well, as an expert in being scared, I can tell you you're not alone in feeling that way. But if this weekend has proven anything to me, it's that fear doesn't always mean stop." I stifle a giggle. "Did that sound super cheesy? I feel like it was covered in cheese."

Jamie and Charlie laugh, and the mood in the room lightens. Charlie slides an arm around my waist and pulls me closer.

"Thanks, Tay," she says. She looks at the half-eaten pizza on the bed and grins. "Speaking of cheese . . ." She picks up a piece, takes a bite, and chews happily, then jumps up and reaches for something in her pocket. "I almost forgot!"

She makes a *zoom* sound and holds up three sparkly pieces of paper.

"What's that?" I ask.

"These," she says, staring at them with hungry eyes, "are three VIP passes to—wait for it—the SupaCon After-Party!"

Jamie and I stand up so fast we get whiplash. "What?"

She grins like the Cheshire cat and nods rapidly. "Yep! Mandy scored these for me as an apology. I guess this is a positive to come out of my make-out video going viral. So, my two best friends in the whole wide, awesome world, we are going to rock out with the who's who of SupaCon tonight!"

I leap up onto the bed, covering my mouth with my hands. "Do you know what that means?" I squeak. "Skyler will be there! I'll get to meet Skyler!"

Charlie steps onto the bed and Jamie stands up to join us, and we commence freaking out.

We jump up and down, sending pieces of pizza bouncing all over the place, but we don't care about the mess we're making. Messes aren't so bad, so long as you have people to share them with.

We go down to the con for one last round of exploring before it closes, then at five p.m. we get back to our room and start getting ready. Jamie throws on a new tee and watches *Breaking Bad* while Charlie and I take over the bathroom. I sit on the edge of the bathtub while Charlie gently strokes eyeliner over her eyelids.

"So, are you ever going to tell me about your date last night or are you going to keep me waiting forever?"

She smiles. "I thought you'd never ask. Tay, she's so amazing. I've never met anyone like her. She took me to the SupaCon arcade so we could have some privacy and nerd out as much as we like. Then we ate pizza and drank Coke out of champagne glasses. It was like the perfect blend of romantic and fun."

She lights up when she talks about Alyssa, and I smile at how sweet it all is. "I figured it must have been a good date when you didn't come back last night."

Her shoulders lift all the way up to her ears as she blushes and swoons.

I laugh. "That good, huh?"

"Mhmm. Even the memories of it are pure bliss."

"Wow." I suck in a breath. "Not gonna lie. I'm kinda jealous."

She breathes out a laugh. "Well, unless I fix this with Alyssa, there won't be anything to be jealous of—wait, so . . . you and Jamie didn't?"

I shake my head, feeling the nerves run rampant in my stomach. "No way. I think we could have, but I was too nervous. I'm not sure I'm ready for that yet. I'm still getting used to being able to kiss him."

She nods like she knows exactly what I mean. "The nerves are normal. And there's no rush. You gotta do what feels right for you."

Sex has always been a much bigger deal for me than it ever has been for Charlie. She's just so comfortable with her sexuality and her body. "I kind of envy how easily you can open yourself up to someone like that."

She lets out a loud laugh. "No pun intended." I blush and she laughs again. "I wouldn't exactly say it's easy. I was nervous with Alyssa at first, you know."

"You were?"

"Of course! It wasn't just my first time with her; it was my first time with a girl. I was trembling with nerves. But we took it slow, and she asked more than once if I was okay. I knew that if I wanted to stop, I could, and she would understand. I felt safe. I wouldn't have done it if I didn't."

I nod, chewing on my bottom lip. "Do you regret having sex with Reese?"

She thinks for a moment. "No. It felt right at the time. I wanted to do it. You know me—I don't have regrets. Why? Do you think you would regret sleeping with Jamie?"

"If I did it before I'm ready, yes. Physically, I'm totally ready." I feel awkward saying that and train my eyes on the tiled floor while I talk. "But mentally, I still need some time to prepare for it."

"And you're entitled to take all the time you need. Remember that."

"I will."

She glides the feathery brush over her lid once more and steps back to see her handiwork. "I should do more makeup tutorials for my channel."

"That would be awesome." I push my glasses up on my nose, admiring her beauty. The black eyeliner looks flawless, flicking up at the outer corners to give her that cool cat-eye effect.

I stand up and study my reflection. I've got a few pimples on my chin that I'd rather cover up if I'm going to meet Skyler, but I don't like the way makeup feels on my skin—and Charlie's concealer is too dark for my pale complexion anyway.

"You look gorgeous," Charlie says, looking at me with knowing eyes.

I give her a sheepish smile. "Thanks. So do you."

She flicks her hair back theatrically and sighs. "I know." She laughs and puts an arm around me. "Thanks, Tay. Love you." She kisses me on the cheek.

"Love you back."

I open up my hair product and dip my fingers in, pulling my short hair up and pushing it back to create a quiff. Standing side by side at the bathroom mirror, we both look vastly different. She's glamming it up in a flame-red Iron Man minidress, complete with a glowing arc reactor graphic. She slides red lipstick over her lips and smacks them together.

I still want to feel like myself when I meet Skyler, so I'm wearing jeans, one of my new Queen Firestone T-shirts, and my turquoise Converse sneakers with rainbow laces. I decide to wear my trench coat, too, in case I can get Skyler to sign it.

I put an arm around Charlie's waist and grin at our reflections. "We look awesome."

She smiles and nudges my hip with hers. "Duh." She studies me for a moment, and I avoid her gaze, feeling self-conscious. "Thank you," she says. "For always encouraging me. I'm sorry I couldn't stay and be there for you when you needed me today."

I shrug. "I was fine. You know I don't like talking about that stuff anyway."

"I'm proud of you," she says softly. "If you can get up on stage in all your awesome fangirl glory and be exactly who you are, then so can I. I know I can figure things out with Alyssa. I just need to show her that I'm in, for real." She thinks for a minute, then a giddy smile spreads across her face. "I have an idea."

We strut into the party like we're Derek Zoolander.

"There's Alyssa!" I say to Mandy, and she rushes over to the DJ to set Charlie's plan in motion. Soon, she gives me and Jamie a thumbs-up. A second later, the many televisions on the walls go dark. Then, in the blink of an eye, Charlie's face appears on the screens.

Silence fills the room and all eyes turn to the televisions. Charlie takes in a shaky breath, and so do I. Even though I know how this video goes—I was in our hotel room when she filmed it only an hour earlier—I'm filled with nerves. She smiles, then starts her heartfelt speech.

"So, obviously by now you all know what happened. In case you're one of the few who missed it: a private moment between me and someone I care about was accidentally uploaded to my channel. It's trending. The gif is everywhere. News sites are writing articles about it. I guess we broke the Internet. I know people all over the world are talking about it."

She lets out a sigh. "Here's the thing: people are going to talk about me, no matter what I do. People are going to spew their judgments and opinions on what I wear, who I'm with, what I say, all of it. And for a while, that was all I cared about. Now? Not so much. I have some really good friends in my life." She pauses and glances off camera, at me and Jamie in the hotel room. "And they set me straight about what really matters. And someone I know recently said something that I can't get out of my mind: she told me she didn't want to spend her life hiding out of fear of others' opinions. Actually, there's a lot of things about her that I can't get out of my mind."

She smiles the sweetest smile before she continues. "Anyway, I refuse to spend my life so consumed by hate and anger and worry about what others think that I miss out on being happy." Her eyes glisten with tears, and she tries to hide it by flicking her hair back. "So, seeing as I'm already the talk of the online world today, I figured, why stop there? So here I am. Yes, I'm on camera in front of three million, nine hundred and fifty-two thousand people, but I'm only talking to one: you hit pause so I could figure myself out. Well, this is me, all figured out. You don't wanna play games. The only games I wanna play with you are video games. I'm in. I'm *so* in. If you wanna hit play, I'll be waiting with a roll of quarters." She holds up the roll and grins, then the screens go black. The party erupts in cheers, but the only person I'm looking at is Alyssa.

She's standing in the center of the room, still staring at the televisions. But she's smiling the biggest, brightest smile I've ever seen. And then she turns and runs out the door as her friends cheer her on.

I fist-pump the air and squeal. "Yes!"

The music starts blaring and the party rages on.

I hear someone calling my name and turn around to see Brianna walking toward me, arms outstretched. "I'm so happy to see you!" she says as she hugs me. "Are you okay? I couldn't find you after the contest."

"I'm great!" I say. "What are you doing here?"

"Um, I kind of won the contest, remember?" She smiles.

"Oh my God! How could I forget?" I hug her again. "Congrats again!"

"Thanks," she says. She seems relieved to see that I'm happy for her. "There's someone I want you to meet."

Brianna turns around and waves to someone I can't see behind all the partygoers. When I do see her, at first I can't believe my eyes. It's like a dream. She seems to glide over to me in slow motion, her long red hair flowing over her shoulders, her bright blue dress swaying. She stands before me, her eyes looking into mine, and smiles. "Hey! You must be Taylor!" She extends a hand out to me. "I'm Skyler Atkins."

My mouth hangs open, my heart stops beating, and I don't even blink for fear that it will make her disappear. It takes more than a few beats for my brain to catch up to the moment.

"Hi?" I say, but it comes out more like a question than a greeting. I notice her hand is still out, and I take it, shaking it a little too enthusiastically.

She gives me the sweetest, warmest smile. "It's so funny; Brianna was just telling me about you, and now here you are!"

I laugh and throw my hands up into the air. "Here I am!"

Brianna giggles. "I was literally just telling her how you saved me from dropping out of the whole contest."

I smile and nod because I can't remember how to do anything

else. Skyler Atkins is standing right in front of me. Looking at me. Smiling at me. Talking to me.

"Brianna told me how you helped her," Skyler says, leaning in so I can hear her over the music. "I think it's so great to see women supporting women, and for you to help Brianna—even though you hardly knew each other and were competing against each other—it's inspiring."

I snort and gesture to her. "You're the inspiring one! Queen Firestone has honestly helped shape who I am. The world you created has pulled me through some of the hardest moments of my life."

"Oh, that's so sweet of you to say!" She grins. "It means so much to hear that. Thank you so much." She's blushing.

Skyler Atkins is blushing. And I am the cause of her blush. I'm trying so hard to be calm, but I can feel myself fangirling into oblivion.

Skyler lowers an eyebrow. "Are you from Australia?"

I nod. "Yes!"

She puts a hand on my arm excitedly. "I knew it! I could tell from your accent. I love Australia; it's such a beautiful country."

"Thank you," I say, as though I'm solely responsible for my country's aesthetic qualities.

She takes a sip of her wine. "Actually, I'll be there in December for the next Firestone premiere. Why don't you come?"

My jaw hits the floor, and my tongue rolls out like a red carpet. "Seriously?"

She nods. "Seriously. Come! Bring your friend." She gestures behind me, and I suddenly remember that Jamie exists. I glance behind me and see him wide-eyed and smiling at Skyler, just as starstruck as I am.

"Oh my God!" I say, pulling him forward to stand with me. "I'm so sorry; I should have introduced you all." I point to him. "This is Jamie, my . . ." I trail off, because we haven't had that conversation yet. The one where we decide we are boyfriend and girlfriend.

Jamie gives me a crooked smile, then reaches out a hand to Skyler. "I'm her boyfriend."

I squeeze my mouth shut to suppress a squeal. My heart flutters when I hear him say the word *boyfriend*. I love the way it sounds.

"Hi," Skyler says as she shakes his hand. "Great to meet you!"

He just smiles and nods, and I feel much better about my own awkwardness in the presence of the queen herself. Skyler is so down to earth and kind that I almost forget how much of a superstar she is.

I spot Josie talking to some people on the other side of the room, and run over to her. "Josie!"

She hugs me when she sees me. "Taylor! I didn't know you'd be here. Having fun?"

I grin so wide my cheeks hurt. "Fuck yes. Look!" I gesture to Skyler with my thumb, and watch with glee as Josie's jaw drops. "I just met her. She's even more awesome than I'd dreamed about."

"You *met* her?"

I beam with pride. "Yep! You wanna say hi?"

She looks hesitant for a moment, but then nods. I take her hand, and we hurry across the dance floor. I introduce her to Skyler, and within minutes, we're all talking and laughing like we've been friends for years.

Pharrell's "Happy" starts playing, and Skyler gasps. "I love this song!" She takes my hand and pulls me out onto the dance floor, and our friends follow. We dance and dance until my feet hurt, and then we dance some more. I lock eyes with Jamie and pull him in close by his T-shirt, kissing him hard on the mouth. He gives me a mischievous grin, takes my hand, and spins me around. Then he slides his arms around my waist, and we sway to the music together.

"I don't think it can get any better than this," he says in my ear.

I nod excitedly. "Agreed."

I give a sideways glance to Skyler, who is dancing awkwardly with her eyes closed and a big, goofy grin on her face.

I giggle and say to Jamie, "Look! She's just as weird as we are!"

He looks over at her and laughs. "I knew she would be. She's too awesome not to be weird."

I put on my best American accent. "We are the weirdos, mister."

He raises an eyebrow. *"The Craft."*

I stretch up on my tiptoes to whisper in his ear. "Can we just be weird together forever?"

Jamie's eyes run over me, and I feel a rush. He smiles. "Hells yes."

CHAPTER 28

CHARLIE

I WAIT NERVOUSLY IN THE MIDDLE OF THE DESERTED CONVEN-
tion floor, picking at the roll of quarters in my hands. The lights
on the arcade games flash all around me, but they seem far away.
All I can think about is what's happening upstairs. The SupaCon
After-Party is in full swing on the top floor, but I'm here. Alone.
Waiting.

The video must have played by now. I imagine Alyssa at
the party. I wonder if she smiled when she saw me appear on
the screen. I hope she's on her way to me.

The sound of a door creaking open echoes through the hall,
followed by rushed footsteps. My stomach leaps into my throat
and I hold my breath, not wanting to get my hopes up. She could
be coming to say yes or to break my heart. I won't know until I
see her face. The footsteps get closer and closer, and then I see her

round the corner. The moment our eyes meet, she stops running. I don't breathe. A flirtatious smile spreads across her face.

That's when I know she's with me.

This is happening.

She struts toward me fast, smiling wider with every step. When she reaches me, she raises an eyebrow and says, "Play."

Before I can reply, she takes my face in her hands and kisses me. My arms drop to my sides, and the quarters spill out of the torn paper roll and all over the floor at our feet. I let go of the empty wrapper and drape my arms around Alyssa's shoulders, melting into her.

A spark surges down my spine. I'm falling for this girl faster than the speed of light. It's scary—but it's the kind of scary that I want more of. So much more.

Alyssa pushes forward gently, and I move with her, my back pressing against *The Rising* arcade game. All I can hear is the sound of my rapid heartbeat as our lips meld together. I run a hand down her back and pull her in closer, wanting more of her.

I feel her smile against my lips. "Be my date to the after-party?"

I smile back. "I'm in."

My eyes are closed. The rhythmic pulse is vibrating out of the speakers and through my body, making my bones tremble. My heels collide with the dance floor time and time again. My hips sway. My head bops. My lips curl into a smile. The heat of all the bodies around me is palpable, making me sweat. I feel her close to me. Her hips sway with mine. Her hands on my shoulders, my back, my waist.

And when my eyes open, there she is.

Her eyes are closed. She's moving to the music like she's creating it one beat at a time. As if she senses my gaze on her, Alyssa opens her eyes. There's that smile. The smile that tells me everything she's thinking. Everything she's feeling. Everything she wants.

I move forward, closing the gap between us. Tracing my eyes down her body and back up again, falling on her lips. She lifts an eyebrow ever so slightly, daring me to do something about it. Not one to run from a challenge, I do. I wrap my arms around her neck and pull her in, crushing my mouth to hers. Blending my red lipstick with her plum shade.

Kissing her makes my heart explode.

So I don't stop, not even when the song does. I'm not even slightly concerned about who might see us. There are photographers here. TMZ. *Entertainment Now.* Randoms with camera phones, ready to tweet pics out to the fandoms. I can see the flashes through my closed eyelids. But I don't care.

The media, the Chase shippers, they can all say what they want about me. Let them blog about how I should be with Reese. Let them tweet. Let them.

My true fans want me to be happy.

And one look at me right now, in this moment, will tell them I am. I won't let the opinions of others get in the way of my happiness again. We break our kiss and I feel fingers wrap around my own and tug on my hand, and turn to see Tay pulling me off the dance floor with a bright smile. I follow, because she's my best friend and I know that wherever she's leading me, it will be great.

She points to the other side of the party. "Look!"

I giggle. "Yes! We have to. We just have to."

We run over to a photo booth and jump inside, throwing on an array of wigs and oversize sunglasses and bow ties. We take more than twenty photos together, laughing and hugging and having the best time of our lives. Soon, Jamie, Alyssa, and Tay's new friends Brianna and Josie join us. Even Skyler Atkins gets in on the fun, squeezing in with us. We are a mess of giggles and grins.

While we're waiting for the photos to print, Tay gives me a hug. "Thank you for bringing me here. SupaCon has literally changed my life."

I squeeze her tight. "You are so welcome, TayTay. Thanks for coming."

We hear a click as the photos fall into the hatch, and immediately burst into laughter as we go through them.

"We look like the biggest weirdos alive," I say.

Tay smiles proudly. "We *are* the biggest weirdos alive."

Jamie slides his arms around her from behind, looking over her shoulder as we flip through the photos. Alyssa has her arm around me. Skyler, Josie, and Brianna are giggling at how ridiculous we all look in the pictures.

Taylor's eyes glisten. "No matter what happens, we'll always have these photos. When Charlie is walking red carpets in LA, when Jamie's photographs are hanging on gallery walls, when my stories grace the shelves or the screen—we'll always have this." She squeezes Jamie's arm. "And we'll know that right now, in this moment, we were happy. We are happy."

The party lasts long into the night. As the sun comes up, Alyssa and I are standing on the balcony, admiring the orange sky.

I lean my elbows on the glass railing and exhale. "If I could pick any weekend to live over and over again, *Groundhog Day* style, it would be this one."

Alyssa pushes a strand of hair behind my ear affectionately. "Me too."

I look over my shoulder and see Jamie and Taylor, both asleep on one of the couches, huddled in each other's arms. A proud grin spreads across my face.

Alyssa follows my gaze. "They're pretty cute together."

"The cutest."

She raises an eyebrow. "I don't know about that."

She puts an arm around my shoulder and kisses my temple. "I can't believe I'm standing here with you."

I let out a loud laugh. "Um, no. I can't believe I'm standing here with *you*."

Alyssa gives me a crooked smile, showing me that one adorable dimple. "I've kinda had this big crush on you for, like, two years." She threads her fingers between my own. "Ever since that video you did for your parents' twentieth wedding anniversary. You were telling the story of how they met at college in Beijing and moved to Australia. And how your mom is a rebel and a science teacher and your dad is an account manager with a heart of gold. Your eyes got all dewy from tears. It was so sweet."

"Oh my God, I forgot about that!"

"Well, I remember. I can tell your family is really important to you."

"They are. It's going to be hard to leave them next year."

She tilts her head to the side. "Where are you going?"

"Here. Well, to LA. It's really the best place for me, career-wise. I've been thinking about it for a while. Jamie and Tay are coming with me. It's going to rock."

She smirks and dips her chin. "You know . . . *I* live in LA."

"That information has been pretty clear to me for a while, actually."

She chuckles. "So, maybe we could hang out. I can show you around. Help you settle in."

"That would be awesome."

"When do you plan to move?"

"Not till next year. Maybe January. I want to graduate first and spend the summer with my family."

"Cool." She licks her lips and watches me carefully as she says her next words. "I've been thinking; it's been too long since I took a vacation. Maybe I'll spend a week or two in Australia soon. Maybe Melbourne."

I grin. "You know . . . *I* live in Melbourne."

"Yes, that information has been pretty clear to me for a while."

"The weather there right now is pretty crappy, though. It's the middle of winter."

She lowers an eyebrow at me and smirks. "I'm not going there for the weather."

She moves her mouth to my shoulder, her lips fluttering over my skin like butterfly wings. I marvel at what my life is right now. The spectacular sunrise, the blissfully tired feeling I have, and this girl by my side. I started SupaCon obsessed with changing the way everyone sees me, but now I know I'll never be able to control what other people think.

It's not my job to convince others of who I am. My only job is to *be* who I am. All I can do is find what makes me happy, and live it.

"You know, I'm really liking this," I say. "Everything's so much easier when I'm not filled with paranoia about what other people think."

"See?" she says. "It's a pretty Zen way to live. And smart—because come on, when you look at the big picture, does it really matter what anyone thinks or says about you?" She points up at the sky, the stars fading as the sun takes over. "I mean, way up there, about five thousand light-years away, is a magnificent wonder of the universe called the Unicorn's Rose. NASA shared some gorgeous telescopic images of it a couple years ago. It's a mess of pinks and blues and stars and swirls."

Her eyes turn from whimsical to contemplative. "Whenever I get too involved in little things like gossip or rumors or life in general, I look up and think of that Unicorn's Rose. No matter what happens, it's a constant beauty that will always be shining down on us. There's something about knowing it's up there, being all quietly miraculous, that always makes me feel better. It reminds me of what's important, and what most definitely *isn't*."

I stare at her, in awe. "You're kind of a Unicorn's Rose yourself."

She shakes her head. "Nuh-uh. I'm not quiet about how miraculous I am."

I smile. "Good, because I'm not quiet about how miraculous I am, either."

CHAPTER 29

TAYLOR

QUEENOFFIRESTONE:

I'm wired with this need to always know what to expect.

Sometimes, this need serves me well.

Other times, it makes things harder.

A week ago, I thought this needed to be fixed.

I thought I needed to be fixed.

But now I see differently.

I don't need to be fixed.

Because I am not broken.

Many unexpected things happened to me at SupaCon.

I laughed. I cried. I fell in love.

My worst fears came true.

And so did my wildest dreams.

Before SupaCon, I thought I was just . . .

Afraid.

Weird.

Awkward.

And I was right.

I am all these things.

And that's okay.

I am all these things.

But I am also . . .

Brave.

Heroic.

Royal.

I'm not saying I'll never be afraid again.

I'm afraid right now. I haven't beaten that.

Maybe I never will.

Maybe I don't need to.

I'm not saying I'll never have bad days.

Days when anxiety will knock me down.

I will have those days. That's real life.

And sometimes real life sucks hard.

As long as I have my family, my friends, and my fandom . . .

I'll be okay.

No matter how messy life gets.

Because I have a league of superheroes by my side.

Some I've known for years.

Others I've just met.

Even more who I'll never meet.

I'm surrounded by superheroes.

And that means I must be one, too.

And everyone knows that

No matter what darkness they face,

Heroes are destined to win.

#IAmTheOneTrueQueen #FamilyFandomAndFriends
#TheEnd

ACKNOWLEDGMENTS

I will never be able to fully express how thankful I am to everyone who helped make this book come to life, but here goes. . . .

Firstly, thank you to everyone at Swoon Reads for making my dream of seeing my book on the shelf a reality. In particular, thanks to Jean Feiwel, Lauren Scobell, Anna Poon, Starr Baer, Rich Deas, Kim Waymer, Jo Kirby, Kelsey Marrujo, Emily Settle, Holly West, Teresa Ferraiolo, Janea Brachfeld, Madison Forsander, Kelly McGauley, and Emily Petrick.

Thank you to Liz Dresner for the stunning design. I feel so lucky to have a cover that's so absolutely gorgeous I still can't stop drooling over it.

Huge thanks to my amazing editor, Christine Barcellona, for your never-ending support, wisdom, and enthusiasm, and for loving these characters as much as I do. And of course, I send rainbows of gratitude to all the awesome people who read, voted for, and reviewed *Queens of Geek* on Swoon Reads.

I am eternally grateful to the beta readers who took the time to read *Queens of Geek* and offer thoughtful feedback: Katherine Locke, LeKesha Lewis, Lucy Mawson, and Tara Doyle. Your insights and encouragement helped me more than you know.

Special thanks to everyone at Wattpad HQ. I'm so proud to be a part of the Wattpad Stars family, and I'm so grateful for the continued support and opportunities you've sent my way.

To all the Wattpadders out there, thank you, thank you, thank you. When I posted my first story to Wattpad in 2012, I had no idea it would lead to this. But it's safe to say I wouldn't be here without you. Your excitement over the imaginary worlds I write about gave me the courage to pursue writing as a career. I wish I could hug each and every one of you.

A couple of years ago, I went to my first con, and it changed my life. I've never felt more at home than when I'm surrounded by cosplayers, geeks, and fandom fun. So to all the fangirls, fanboys, and fankids out there who let their geek flags fly and make our community fun and welcoming for all, thank you. You rock!

To my family, for thinking I'm awesome all these years, even when I was a total pain in the butt. And in particular, to my brother, Rob, for speaking in movie quotes with me since we were kids, long before it was cool.

Lastly, to Mike. I'm not exaggerating when I say that if it wasn't for you, I'd be a starved insomniac who never got off the computer. Thanks for reminding me to eat and sleep when I'm hyper focusing on writing a story for weeks and weeks. And thanks for being the Jamie to my Taylor—and for always making sure there's tomato sauce at the table.

FEELING BOOKISH?

Turn the page for some

Swoonworthy EXTRAS

A Coffee Date

between author Jen Wilde and editor Christine Barcellona

"Getting to Know You"

CB: What was your favorite book when you were a kid?

JW: I had a few that I really loved: the Goosebumps books by R. L. Stine, the Adrian Mole series by Sue Townsend, and *Girl, Interrupted* by Susanna Kaysen.

CB: What are your favorite books now?

JW: It's so hard to choose! Usually, though, my favorite book is whichever one I'm currently reading.

CB: Who is your OTP, your favorite fictional couple?

JW: Piper and Leo, from *Charmed.*

CB: Do you have any hobbies?

JW: Is binge-watching TV shows a hobby? I do that a lot. I also love going to the movies, reading and writing (of course!), drawing, and traveling as much as I can. Oh, and cosplaying at cons!

CB: If you were a superhero, what would your superpower be?

JW: Flying! Or maybe teleportation. Any power that would allow me to travel to any part of the world whenever I wanted to.

CB: What are some of your favorite fandoms?

JW: I think the *Supernatural* fandom is definitely my fave. It's like one big, global family, and the amazing causes, cons, and movements that have sprung from it make me so proud to be a part of it. Seeing the creators and cast get so involved in the SPN family is the best. I'm also a devoted member of *The Walking Dead* and *Back to the Future* fandoms, but really, I'm a supporter of all fandoms. Fandoms bring people together to have fun and get excited about something they love—it doesn't get any better than that!

"The Writing Life"

CB: You were a Wattpad author before you were a Swoon Reads author, so you've been tapped into the online writing world for a while. How have the Internet and online writing communities changed the way you write?

JW: Honestly, I would never have started writing if it wasn't for Wattpad. Before I joined Wattpad in 2012, I'd never really written fiction before. But once I started, I fell in love with it. Having a community of readers supporting me, reading each chapter and wanting more, made me think seriously about making a career out of writing. I'm so grateful for the Wattpad family and all the support and encouragement they've given me.

CB: What sparked your imagination for this book?

JW: I'm a huge fangirl and love going to cons, so that was a huge part of why I wanted to write it. I knew it would be incredibly fun to write (and hopefully even more fun to read!) a story set entirely at a con. I was also angry. I was angry with the constant sexism, racism, ableism, homophobia, and general bigotry I'd witnessed both in my life and online. As an autistic, bisexual girl with anxiety, I was angry that people like me were either represented in media as burdens or the butt of a joke, and that's if we're represented at all. I was angry that society wants to put me in a box or stereotype me and my friends. And I'm still angry about all that. Just like Taylor, I have trouble verbally expressing my emotions, so I deal with it the best way I know how: writing. I put all that anger into action and wrote characters who deal with all those issues and represent the realities of the world we live in, while still falling in love, achieving their dreams, and being awesome. At the end of the day, I wrote the book I wanted to read, the book that would have saved me when I was a teenager and felt like I was broken, and I hope readers who've always felt ignored or misrepresented see themselves in these pages.

CB: What type of research did you for this book?
JW: My research for this story started long before I wrote the first word and hasn't stopped since. As someone who understands how life-changing and affirming it can be to see yourself represented as a whole person in a positive way (and conversely how damaging it can be to see yourself portrayed poorly), I knew I had to do whatever I could to get these characters right. I spend countless hours reading books and websites like We Need Diverse Books, Disability in Kidlit, DiversifYA, Everyday Feminism, The Mary Sue, and the Swoon Reads blog. I follow chats and discussions on social media about #ownvoices, intersectional feminism, YA news, and the issues to be aware of as a white writer writing people of color. I've learned a lot from watching intersectional feminist YouTubers, educating myself on important social justice issues, listening to others, and doing my best to check my privilege, but I know I'll still make mistakes along the way. One of the most important and helpful things I did was have many beta readers, and then listen to their suggestions on how to improve both the story and characters.

CB: When did you realize you wanted to be a writer?
JW: I'd always admired writers and thought it would be such an amazing job, but I never thought I'd be any good at it, so I didn't try. When I

started writing my first story on Wattpad, it was just meant to be a fun hobby, something creative to do because I was burned out from running my business. But I quickly realized that writing was something I wanted to do full time, and now that I am, I feel like the luckiest person in the world.

CB: Do you have any writing rituals?

JW: I need a few things around me when I write: a fresh cup of coffee, a bottle of water, and my stack of story notes. I normally use the SelfControl app to block social media, and most of the time I write at my treadmill desk.

CB: Do you ever get writer's block? How do you get back on track?

JW: For me, whenever I feel stuck on a story or a scene, I find it's more than likely because I'm not excited about it. And if I'm not excited to write it, then it probably won't be too fun to read, either. To fix that, I brainstorm ways to make the scene more interesting and exciting. If I can't find any, then I either work on a different scene that I *am* excited about and come back to it later, or I scrap it completely.

CB: What's the best writing advice you've ever heard?

JW: When writing: torture your characters. Ask yourself, "What's the worst thing that could happen to this character right now?" and then do it. Write twists, turns, close calls, failures, successes. Put your characters through hell, and see how they get themselves out of it.

After you finish your book: write the next book. Being prolific not only makes me a better writer, it keeps me in the creative zone and means I get so much more done. I usually need a break between books to recharge and let ideas percolate, but I try not to wait too long before I get to work on the next story.

CB: What advice would you give aspiring authors?

JW: Don't wait for permission to write your story. You don't need permission; you don't need to have a certain amount of readers or followers; you don't need to be an expert; you don't even need to know where your story will go. Just start, whether you think you're ready or not. Choose the idea that excites you the most, then just sit down and start writing. You'll learn along the way.

"The Swoon Reads Experience"

CB: How did you first learn about Swoon Reads?

JW: One of my Wattpad friends sent me the link, and the moment I clicked over to the site, I knew I had to submit a story.

CB: What made you decide to post your manuscript?

JW: I'd already posted another manuscript, but with no success. After following the Swoon Reads blog and reading Holly's post about Comic-Con and all the amazing posts about diversity in media, it helped me find the courage to write a story I'd wanted to write for so long: a story about an autistic girl and a bisexual girl. I wrote it in a month and submitted it just in time to make the next Swoon Reads deadline.

CB: What was your experience like on the site before you were chosen?

JW: It was a roller coaster of emotions. As I mentioned, I originally submitted a manuscript that wasn't selected, so for those few months I was constantly checking the site to see who had read and commented on it. I'm not a very patient person, so the waiting was driving me crazy. Once I accepted that my first manuscript didn't make the cut, I got straight to work on the next one. This time, I promised myself I wouldn't obsess over it, so I submitted it and tried to focus on other stories. The day after submissions closed, I got an e-mail from Swoon HQ, and the next morning I was on the phone to New York, getting the good news and hoping Christine and Lauren couldn't hear my teeth chattering from nerves, ha ha!

CB: Once you were chosen, who was the first person you told and how did you celebrate?

JW: When I first saw the e-mail, I kept it to myself for about five minutes, ha ha! I told my husband, and we spent the next twenty-four hours being cautiously optimistic. He was actually sitting next to me while I took the call because I was so anxious. As timing would have it, that day I had lunch with my BFF and dinner with my whole family for my brother's birthday, and I couldn't say anything to anyone. I've never been great at keeping secrets, so I'm pretty proud that I managed to stay quiet about it. But I still managed to celebrate: I bought myself a cool brown satchel bag that I always imagined "real" writers would have.

"The Swoon Index"

CB: On the site we have something called the Swoon Index, where readers can share the amount of Heat, Laughter, Tears, and Thrills in each manuscript. Can you tell me something (or someone!) that always turns up the heat?

JW: Sam Winchester. I know Dean is the more popular choice, and I get it, but I'm definitely a Sam girl. Unless, of course, we're talking about Dean from *Gilmore Girls*. ;)

CB: What always makes you laugh?

JW: My husband makes me laugh every single day. He is the biggest dork and just as geeky as I am. Plus he scares easily. Spiders, bugs, loud noises, shadows he sees from the corner of his eye, he's just very jumpy. Like screaming at the top of his lungs, jumping out of his chair, dropping anything he might be holding kind of scared. I once saw an open packet of crackers fly through the air when he got scared—and he was only watching *Elf* at the time. It was the scene with the jack-in-the-box. I'm cracking up just thinking about it.

CB: Makes you cry?
JW: Anything to do with an animal being hurt or mistreated.

CB: Sets your heart pumping?
JW: Horror movies. Or watching the news, which is kinda the same thing.

CB: And finally, tell us all what makes you swoon!
JW: My husband. He's my best friend, the Jamie to my Taylor. We've been together for ten years, and he still makes me swoon and laugh and feel like the luckiest person in the world. He's the one who listens to me ramble on about my fictional worlds, and feeds me when I'm in hyperfocus mode, writing for hours on end. Without him, I would be a starved insomniac who never gets off the computer. And on one of our first dates, we watched *Supernatural* (which was still in season one at the time). We've watched it together ever since. To me, it doesn't get more swoonworthy than that!

Two nerdy best friends navigate high school,
drama club, *Star Trek* fandom, and being gay
in this debut novel from Swoon Reads.

Why focus on your own problems when your
friend's love life is so much easier to fix?

Meg
&
Linus

HANNA NOWINSKI

Keep reading for a sneak peek.

Linus

MEG IS ALREADY SITTING IN our usual back corner of the cafeteria by the time I manage to get my own lunch.

I walk over to her, drop into the seat opposite hers. It's weird that it's just us this year; usually Sophia was always here with us. Her absence feels strange to me now, not only because I'm used to having her around but also because I'm not sure I should mention that I miss her. I don't want to upset Meg.

When I sit down, she looks up from the book she has propped open against a pile of other books and frowns at me, hand pushing at an errant lock of red hair that has escaped from her ponytail. "You're late!"

I shrug. "Sorry. Had to stop by my locker."

It's not exactly the entire truth. Well, I did have to go by my locker to get rid of my disgustingly heavy physics book. But I would have been here faster if I hadn't spent an extra few minutes pretending to sort through some papers while I was really very secretly watching Danny talking to someone a few lockers down. He is just so cute when he talks, waving his hands around wildly when he gets excited about something.

"I'm sorry," she says, and sighs. "I didn't mean to be rude or anything. I guess I just have separation anxiety after—you know."

I smile and try to look as reassuring as I can manage. "You know I wouldn't leave you without a heartfelt text message consisting of at least one hundred characters and a really vague emoticon."

She puts a hand over her heart. "Stop it, you're too good to me! You're going to make me cry!"

"Maybe I would even slip a note in your locker."

"As long as you didn't write me a poem."

"Not even if it's a really moving one about the power of friendship and the optimistically idealistic message that no matter where we are in the world, we'll always totally be besties for life, exclamation point, smiley face, less-than-three?"

She laughs. "Especially not if it's anything like that."

I sigh deeply and shake my head at her. "Your strange aversion to poetry is really baffling. What happened to you as a kid that makes you reject beautiful, emotional word imagery?"

She rolls her eyes at me and kicks me under the table. "Shut your face and eat your lunch before it gets cold."

"I'll actually have to open my face for that, though," I point out.

"Besides, I am not categorically against poetry per se," she tells me. "I just like it better when it's set to music."

I nod. "That's what we call a 'song' among experts."

"Smarty-pants."

"I'm just trying to help!"

"By the way," she says, "have you given any thought to your extracurriculars for this year? Because I thought we could maybe sign up for something together."

"I like that idea." I take a sip of my soda and consider all the clubs at this school, and then I catch a glimpse of familiar spiky black hair a few tables over, right in the middle of the usual drama club crowd, and I can't control the way my face heats up. It just makes me wish I was a little less fair-skinned so that not everyone could see me blush all the time. "I was thinking of maybe trying something new this year," I blurt out before I can stop myself.

Meg squints at me and I know she can see the way my face has turned red. I'm just hoping she'll let it go.

"New?" she asks. "Like what, for example? Drama club?"

I pretend to think about it, even though that was exactly what I was going to suggest. She must have seen me glancing over at the drama club lunch table just now. I nod slowly so that I won't seem too excited about this. "Yeah, why not? That could be interesting."

She stares at me for a bit and I try to keep my face as blank as possible so that she won't guess at my true motivation. Which she can't, because she doesn't know about Danny. Well, she knows there's a guy. She even knows where he works because I can't help it, he's so cute, I couldn't keep it all inside all summer, I had to mention him to her eventually. Repeatedly. But . . . it's not like it matters. Nothing's going to happen with him anyway.

I know I should tell her I want to join drama club because of him. I feel weird not telling her. But I do know that I have set my sights way too high with this, so . . . I guess it's going to stay my little secret.

Of course, just at that moment I hear him laughing over at his table with the people I assume are his new friends, and my eyes have already darted in his direction before I can stop myself. Have I mentioned yet that he has a really cute smile? Because he has. It's the kind of smile you don't want to miss seeing, because it's like Lembas bread—one tiny morsel of it can sustain you for quite a while.

I quickly look back at my lunch tray as soon as I realize what I've been doing, but it's too late—Meg has already turned her head to see what captured my attention and when she looks back at me, there's this little gleam in her eyes that rarely means anything good.

To make matters worse, I can feel myself blushing quite furiously.

"I see," she says, sounding very smug about it.

"No you don't," I try, but she just smirks widely.

"He's cute."

"I really hadn't noticed."

The way she is able to raise one eyebrow almost to her hairline has always been slightly frightening to me, and it's even worse when that look is directed at me.

"Meg—" I start, but she interrupts me.

"Can it. Is this the coffee shop guy? He's joining drama club, and you know it, don't you? He's sitting with them. And I saw him signing the sign-up sheet this morning. Your secret plot has been revealed."

"There is no secret," I assure her. "Please, just let it go? Maybe joining this particular club isn't such a great idea after all."

"No, we should totally join the drama club," she says. "Trying new things is good. And it would give you the perfect excuse to talk to him."

That makes me laugh. "Like he'd be interested in talking to me."

She frowns at me. "What's that supposed to mean?"

I shrug. "I'm kind of chubby and a bit boring and he is, like, really good-looking and probably has a million friends—"

"Okay, what does his number of friends have to do with anything?" she asks, confused. "And he's a drama geek; they're not exactly popular, either, are they? Plus, he's the new kid. How could he already be popular? He's definitely not popular yet! He'll be happy to make new friends!"

"He's more popular than we are. Plus, those drama club kids are actually pretty cool. Aren't they?"

"Sophia was in drama club," Meg reminds me. "And she still dated me. For two years."

"All right, but—"

"Also, you're cute as a button," she continues. "He'd be lucky to have you!"

"I'm not—"

"And since when are you boring? When have you ever been boring?"

"My idea of a perfect Friday night is rewatching *Firefly* and then reading until I fall asleep on the couch."

"So?"

"I own not only a pair of *Star Trek* pajamas but also Batman pajamas."

"Which are both awesome."

"The Batman pajamas have a cape attached to them."

"Even more awesome!"

"I actually like going to class."

She groans and throws both hands up in frustration. "Because you actually like most things! You're one of the most passionate and intelligent people I have ever met in my life—how is that a bad thing?"

I stare sullenly at my pasta that's slowly getting cold and scowl just to prove her wrong, even if all the nice things she is saying about me just make me want to get up and hug her. "Meg, can you honestly see someone like him even looking at someone like me? If he even likes guys, which I doubt he does!"

Check out more books chosen for publication by readers like you.

JEN WILDE

is a writer, geek, and fangirl with a penchant for coffee, books, and pugs. She writes YA stories about zombies (*As They Rise*), witches (*Echo of the Witch*), and fangirls (*Queens of Geek*). Her debut series, The Eva Series, reached over three million reads online and became an Amazon bestseller. When she's not writing, Jen loves binge-watching her favorite shows on Netflix, eating pizza, traveling to faraway places, and going to conventions in Marty McFly cosplay. Jen lives in a sunny beachside town in Australia with her husband and their cheeky pug, Heisenberg.